TRUE LORE

A NOVEL

SIOBHAN MOORE

This is a work of fiction. Names, characters, places, and incidents either are the product of the author's imagination or are used fictitiously. Any resemblance to actual persons, living or dead, events, or locales is entirely coincidental.

Copyright © 2023 by Siobhan Moore

All rights reserved.

No portion of this book may be reproduced in any form without written permission from the publisher or author, except as permitted by U.S. copyright law.

Cover design by Sanja Vulicevic

❀ Created with Vellum

For Kyle—
Who believed in me from our second date

A WORD OF CAUTION

Dear reader, I want to make you aware of some content in *True Lore* that could potentially be triggering, namely: suicidal ideation and attempts, murder, violence, attempted rape/discussion of rape, and child death.

PART I

When the magician first begins her journey, her mind will fight against the deconstruction of the confines of her chosen status quo.

The writings of Seamus Dannan

1

Naturally occurring symmetrical rings of mushrooms, also known as 'fairy rings,' were commonly associated in folklore with evil. In reality, they are simply evidence of the existence of magic inherent in nature.

Seamus Dannan, *Lore: The True History of the Celts*

Saoirse Dannan's life was a ticking clock, every second counting down to complete and annihilating change, and she didn't know it.

She sat in her cubicle, idly chewing the end of her pen. A phrase from a high school anatomy class a decade ago asserted its relevance into her mind: "The digestion process of food begins inside your mouth with your own saliva." She put the pen down.

"Mr. Williams," she interrupted the man speaking through her headset, "it says you were 40 days late with your payment in April of last year because your grandmother died, and then again in January of this year for the same reason. How many grandmothers do you have?"

"I have four, you smug bitch, this is my step-grandmother."

Stifling a yawn, Saoirse typed *step-grandmother funeral* into her notes. "Regardless, it's not okay to pay late. I need you to make your payment now."

"Do you have cum in your ear? I said I don't have it."

Saoirse's eyes widened. That was a new one. "Sir, it says here your car payment isn't due until the 15th. I'm assuming you haven't paid it yet. You need to make your mortgage payment with that money and let your car payment be late. It's not okay to delay paying your mortgage."

"But I need my car."

"Oh, are you going to live in it?" Saoirse retorted.

"I bet your husband can't stand you," Mr. Williams hissed. The line went dead.

"That would probably be true if I had one," Saoirse muttered to herself. She lazily noted the conversation (omitting the more colorful parts) and went to the next call in her queue.

Before she could dial, an email popped up on her screen. She groaned.

"What is it?" asked Betsy, her cubicle mate. Twenty years Saoirse's senior, Betsy had taken the collections job after retiring from the police force to spend more time with her kids. Her raspy, menacing voice scared most people into giving her their routing and account numbers on the spot.

"Dalton," Saoirse said. "Wants me to come to meeting room three."

Betsy rolled her eyes, which were ice-blue, rimmed in thick eyeliner, and accompanied by thin, penciled-in eyebrows. "It's his 'career opportunities' pep talk bullshit. He's been calling everyone on the team in."

"I guess I'd better get it over with."

"Wanna take a break after? I need a smoke," Betsy replied with that tense, sour glare she got whenever she was overdue for a cigarette break.

"Yeah, see you out there." Saoirse brought a notepad and the chewed-up pen with her to show good faith. Then she began the winding journey through cubicles to the meeting room.

All around her she saw exhausted faces speaking in stern tones into their headsets. To offset the inherent misery of a collections center, the company had conceived to boost morale by making the surrounding atmosphere as cheerful as possible. Irritating posters spouting quotes about work ethic and teamwork adorned the walls, which were painted in bright primary colors and made Saoirse feel like she worked in a preschool. Even the thin carpet she walked on was covered with geometric shapes in brightly clashing colors. The entire call center floor consisted of open cubicles, something the CEO said would foster a more "collaborative work environment." It certainly made it easier for everyone to mutter jokes to each other at his expense.

Dalton, her manager, smiled at her from the table in the small, sterile meeting room. "Close the door, S."

Saoirse's name was pronounced "Sur-sha" but she was used to being called a variety of other things (including nothing as the person trying to address her froze in a perplexed silence). However, Dalton had never even bothered to attempt it, immediately announcing that "S" was his pet name for her when he became her manager four years ago.

He continued to grin at her as she closed the door and

took the chair opposite him. Saoirse shivered, partly due to the sub-zero temperature of the room, but mostly because of Dalton.

His long face was extended by his enormous smile, which showed all of his massive teeth and pushed up his shiny, pink cheeks. With his neatly parted hair and flat, cold eyes, Dalton looked unnervingly like a ventriloquist dummy.

"So, S, how are the calls going today?"

"Great," she replied, forcing a smile of her own.

"Hear any new zingers?" He couldn't have been more than a few years older than she, yet he insisted on using terminology belonging to men over fifty. It must be some management tactic he learned from YouTube: *Be as fatherly as possible to gain the respect of your subordinates...*

Saoirse would rather die than repeat the vulgarity of her most recent call to Dalton. "Not yet, but the day is young."

He winked at her and she wondered if he had listened in on her call. His eyes lingered on her chest. She brought hair over her shoulders to cover it. Perv.

"Well, S, it's that time of year. I'm sure you've seen all the positions posted from different departments. Ready to finally go for some upward mobility?"

She knew his motivations for pestering her to seek a promotion was two-fold. While outwardly, the company claimed to have a *culture of growth*, Dalton thought striving for a promotion might make her work harder. The other reason was that Saoirse had received four years of obligatory merit-based raises and the company didn't want to keep paying her this much for an entry-level collections job.

"Honestly, Dalton, nothing really interests me. I like where I'm at."

His eyes grew steelier as his smile widened. He looked capable of swallowing her head whole.

"I know you're used to collections, but as a mortgage lender we have much more to offer such a bright young woman." His cold eyes roamed over her hair and she pushed it back over her shoulders. "In confidence, the department head of Loan Originations has you on his radar. He wants me to encourage you to apply for his open position. What do you think?"

Saoirse frowned. "How did I get on his radar?"

Dalton shrugged. "You're clever, good at communicating. That's what they look for over there."

Her face grew warm in a not entirely unpleasant way. She was flattered against her will. They thought she was clever. And it was a desirable department; it paid a far higher salary than she got here. Maybe even higher than Dalton's, she thought with satisfaction.

The feeling faded as fast as it had come. She knew what would happen if she tried for something she really wanted. It was the same thing that always happened before.

"Sorry, I don't think that's a fit for me."

It radiated off of him; Dalton hated not getting what he wanted. It was why she always declined going out for drinks after work with the team. Under no circumstances would she be caught in a dark parking lot with him.

She had to get him off her back. "You know, it has been a long time since I've checked out the other departments. Maybe I could shadow someone in Foreclosures."

"Loss Mitigation," he corrected her with the company's new, more helpful-sounding term.

"Yes, Loss Mitigation."

"Well, excellent," he said, his giant teeth shining like his cheeks. "I'll make an appointment with Candace for you to observe one of her top Loss Mitigation representatives."

Having appeased him, Saoirse endured a few more minutes of small talk before she was finally able to join Betsy on her smoke break.

"He's such a fuckwad." Betsy breathed out a cloud of smoke.

The two women stood at the edge of the property, their backs turned firmly away from the looming office building. They faced a large, unruly green space that was supposed to help with pollution but was likely either city-mandated or a tax break for the company. The gentle September wind was chilly but welcome. Saoirse gazed out over the tall grasses and shimmering tree leaves. She had her weekly hike with her family tomorrow and breathed easier simply thinking about it.

"You know, he hasn't tried to have one of those meetings with me in years?" Betsy said as she stretched, her cigarette hanging out of the side of her mouth.

"He's scared of you."

"Damn right," Betsy said. "I'd eat that little shit alive. He's probably one of those guys who lives alone with cats and smears food on himself so they'll lick him. I bet he can't wait to go home and get licked by his cats."

"You're gonna make me puke."

"Hey, I ever tell you about that cat lady in Houston?"

Saoirse grinned at her friend. Betsy's thin mouth was in a perpetual straight line, except for when she talked about two subjects: her young sons or her time as a police officer. Even though she'd heard the Houston cat lady story several times, Saoirse shook her head.

Betsy blew a few smoke circles first to build up the suspense. "So, my partner and I get a call for a wellness check by the neighbor of an old woman whose mansion had some terrible smell coming off it. We figured the woman had died and been rotting for a while, but when we pull up, we're blasted by this stench like a lion's den—nothing like a dead body." She took another long drag. "Lady comes to the door in a headdress, I shit you not, and is trying not to let us in but we tell her to move aside. The second we're in the foyer, we see dozens of cats scatter like roaches. We moved from room to room and it's just cats and piles of cat shit everywhere, the bottom layers of shit turned white from time. The local animal services agency estimated there were at least a thousand cats in that house."

"You're kidding me," Saoirse giggled.

"So that's probably the life Dalton's headed for—hey, what the fuck is that?" Betsy asked suddenly, pointing to their right.

Saoirse didn't know how she had missed it. A few yards away, in the yellowing grass, laid a large circle of mushrooms.

"Fairy ring," Saoirse whispered.

"What?"

But she could hardly hear Betsy now. She approached slowly, both wanting to run and at the same time drawn to the phenomenon as if by a magnet.

The mushrooms blossomed like fat, white flowers in a symmetrically perfect ring. Her mind drifted back years and years into the past. *Dozens of them on the sprawling lawns of the beautiful estate, at the base of the giant oak tree in the woods beyond...*

A sense of foreboding, of things not talked about and memories put away, closed in on her. Standing in the middle of a circle of mushrooms. A wind violent enough to peel skin. Rain stinging and slashing her face. The eerie melody of a song she'd forced herself to forget.

And blood.

"What did you say?" Betsy asked sharply.

Saoirse started, her mind springing back to the present. "A fairy ring. It's what my grandparents called them." She took a deep breath, willing herself to calm down. "They were all over their property. I used to go there as a kid."

"Used to?"

Saoirse stood up, the desire to put distance between herself and the circle of mushrooms overpowering now. "Yeah, I haven't been there in like twenty years or something."

"They die?"

Saoirse swallowed. "No. I mean, not that I know of."

Betsy peered at her with her sharp, blue eyes, still a cop at heart. Saoirse glanced away and checked her phone.

"Better get back to work."

The next day, the family hike was cut short by not one of her twin younger siblings falling in a freezing creek, but both of them. Saoirse now found herself in her parents' kitchen enduring a tense silence.

She was helping Janey—the more thoughtful and deliberate of the twins—cut bananas and strawberries for her dad's famous liege waffles. Patrick, the spastic one, sprinted around the house pretending to be a racecar. The twins' moods, once they'd been bathed and dried, had much improved from their screaming in the car. Even though they'd given her a splitting headache, she couldn't help gazing fondly at them, their newly-washed hair all a fluff.

Saoirse had made her debut into the world when her parents were freshman in college. The twins were a startling surprise twenty years later. If she was honest with herself, she came here every weekend for them.

"I don't understand why you wouldn't go for it, that's all," her dad said.

Saoirse said *"Dad,"* right as her mother said *"Cillian"* in the same exasperated way. The three—parents and adult child—wanted to smile at each other at this. But the personal motives of each prevented a moment of humor from softening the tension.

"You know we've done a lot for you to be able to pursue —to live your life," her dad continued.

And here's the guilt.

Saoirse didn't understand why she'd felt compelled to confess to her dad about the promotion offer. She knew exactly what would happen. It was a conversation they'd had in a cyclical manner since she'd dropped out of college years ago.

Enter Mom.

"Get off her back, she isn't ready," her mother scolded. "If she's happy where she is, then let her be. She's doing fine."

She's doing fine. This line gripped Saoirse with an even fiercer irritation than her dad's guilt trip. A burden to one parent. Incapable to the other.

It fit. Her dad, a noted motivational speaker with a rather impressive TikTok following, peddling self-development and inspiration. How did it reflect on him that his adult daughter was impervious to his motivation?

As for her mom, the constant bailing out had gone from welcome to intolerable.

You're not ready, you're doing fine, you've been through a lot, it's not your fault, it's amazing you made it this far given what happened.

And what exactly had happened, Mom? For neither of her parents would tell her. It was the incident that meant she hadn't seen her grandparents or cousins or aunts and uncles since she was six. It was why the fairy ring had shaken her so much yesterday, a reminder of that sinister *something*.

"You coddle her," her dad dared utter.

At the sight of her mom bristling, Saoirse gathered the twins.

"Guys, go play in the backyard, I'll be right out," she said softly, ushering them out the backdoor. She closed the door after them just in time.

"I *coddle* her? You *push* her. Is this how you treat your clients?"

Fair point, Saoirse thought. If only her mother stopped there.

"Sweetie," her mom said with bright eyes. "Don't let anyone tell you that you're not doing great. You have an apartment, a solid job..."

Saoirse looked at her in mock expectation. "That's it?"

"I mean... who says you need to *accomplish* all these *things* or get serious about dating..."

Something burning deep down in her roared at her mother's words. She glanced through the back window, trying to detach. Patrick was hanging upside-down like a fruit bat from a trapeze swing bar attached to their playset. Janey amused herself on the swing next to him, her soft blonde hair flying back from her grinning face.

"Take your time," her mom plowed on, "there's no rush—"

"Kate, you are selling our daughter short," her dad

snapped, finally facing his wife. "She is talented, intelligent, she has so much potential. She limits herself—"

"She limits *herself*? Don't you remember what *happened* to her?"

Her dad's eyes, blue like her own, darted to her and back again.

"On that topic," Saoirse said casually, feeling anything but casual, "I saw a fairy ring yesterday. It was right outside my office."

Her parents' faces blanched. She'd never done this before. As a kid, she'd enjoyed the secrecy of her unknown trauma and the babying and overprotection it had afforded her. But now in her twenties, she was just pissed off. And she was done not knowing.

"Did you guys forget I was here? You've been talking about me like I'm not." She kept her voice calm, gearing up.

"Saoirse..." her dad said.

There was a story, the one her father told in all of his speeches: how he had been raised wealthy and pampered by his overbearing parents, living a life of extravagance and luxury. *Generational wealth,* he had called it. And how he had made the *brave* decision one day to cut it all off, to make his own way, to live his own life. Funny how this decision had occurred when she was six, right after the night they had ripped her from the estate and never brought her back again.

"I remember them," she continued, ready to make her final blow. "I remember seeing them all the time at Nana and Granda's house."

Her mother closed her eyes like she was being forced to listen to something depraved.

"What, you don't remember them?" she asked. "Has it been too long?"

"Stop," her dad barked.

"Stop what, Dad? I thought you didn't want to coddle me or sell me short. Am I not capable of knowing what the hell happened to me?"

Her father opened his mouth to reply, his face red with anger, when something behind him made her gasp. Her body froze with terror.

A man stood in the foyer. The front door was open behind him. He wore a gray delivery driver outfit, a black balaclava ski mask, and sunglasses. He started down the hall toward them.

Saoirse's parents whipped around.

"Hey, what do you think you're doing?" her dad demanded.

The man didn't speak. He pulled something black from his pocket. A long, deadly blade flicked out.

He reached Saoirse's mom first and punched the knife into her chest.

Saoirse screamed.

Her dad lunged toward them as her mom staggered back against the counter. The man slashed her mother's throat. Blood sprayed as the knife swung in an arch from her mom to her dad. Her mother's body had barely fallen to the ground. Her father's body joined hers with a thud. The man knelt and stabbed the knife repeatedly into their fallen bodies. Then he stood, and stared at Saoirse.

She couldn't move. The man advanced on her.

And then walked past her.

She spun around.

No.

He opened the back door.

"No!"

Patrick and Janey stood still in the grass, gazing in confusion at the man.

Saoirse grabbed the knife she'd been using to cut fruit and sprang after him. She was wild with one need, one goal.

The children were frozen, staring up at him.

Saoirse screamed as she brought the knife down on his back. The man roared and twisted toward her, lashing out with his blade.

But then, something happened.

A burst of energy surrounded her like an electric charge. It made the hairs on her arms stand on end. A hum filled her ears. His knife was rushing toward her gut.

The crackling energy detonated.

Saoirse flew backwards onto her back. The wind was knocked out of her; she gasped for breath. She scrambled to her feet...

It was too late.

They were so small, they couldn't fight, couldn't run...

The grass ran red...

A sound came out of her, inhuman with anguish.

That sound was the last thing she remembered for a while.

2

While many writings of Celtic history and myth exist, most are based on conjecture or manipulated by the political or religious motives at the time of their writing. The true knowledge was protected through oral tradition, passed down from one generation to the next.

Seamus Dannan, *Lore: The True History of the Celts*

Saoirse knew she was in a hospital. She could feel the tug of an IV attached to her wrist, could hear the steady hum of the forced-air warming blanket on top of her body. Those times of wakefulness, flat and groggy, were mere moments until she slid easily back into a dreamless sleep.

Sometimes when conscious, she picked up information from nurses: they were keeping her comfortable, helping her cope. They would start to wean her soon.

After some time, she stayed awake longer, more lucid

though still flat. She was thankful for this. She remembered what happened. She didn't want to talk about it.

Unfortunately, this wasn't an option for long.

"Dear, the police need to speak with you now that you're awake," a female doctor with a kind voice said.

"Okay," she said, staring at the white grid ceiling.

Two uniformed officers came into her periphery. She kept them fuzzy in the corner of her eye.

One of them expressed condolences and reassured her that between footage from her parents' doorbell camera and the testimony of neighbors, she was not a suspect in her family's murders.

"Can you tell us from your perspective what happened?" the officer asked.

"He came in and stabbed my mom and dad and then—" She stopped talking. She sensed their discomfort and hesitation and did not care.

"How did you escape?" the other one asked, his voice less kind than his partner's.

"I didn't."

"Did he try to harm you as well?"

"Not—not at first."

"What do you mean?" the officer said.

"He skipped me. I don't know why."

The officer with the harsher tone made a sound of disbelief. "Then what happened?"

"He went outside."

The cops hesitated. Then,

"There was blood on your knife that didn't match the rest of your family's. You tried to stop him?"

She nodded, thinking of the freak electrical burst that had thrown her backward. She'd never heard of anything like it, but instead of curiosity she felt hatred for it. If it hadn't happened...

"How did you defend yourself?"

"I didn't. He... ignored me." She tried to find shapes in the pockmarks of the ceiling.

"Can you describe him?"

"Medium height. Not particularly muscular. Wearing a gray delivery driver outfit and black mask and sunglasses."

"How tall exactly?"

"No idea."

"Did you recognize anything else about him?"

"No."

"Did you speak to him?"

"No."

The severe officer, who had completely taken over the interview, said, "Okay, so he entered through the front door, stabbed your mother first and then your father. Then he went past you—without trying to hurt you—into the backyard where your younger siblings were playing."

Saoirse blinked slowly at the ceiling.

"You tried to stop him—how?"

She clenched her jaw. The ceiling was starting to blur, too.

"I stabbed him in the back."

"And instead of trying to hurt you, he carried on with your siblings?"

When she didn't respond, the doctor spoke, kindly but firmly.

"I think that's enough for today."

Before leaving, the nicer cop spoke in a low voice.

"Your home is no longer a crime scene. You can return whenever you're ready."

Once they left, she closed her eyes, ready for oblivion to take her back, when the doctor spoke again.

"We're going to start tapering what we've given you so that you can be discharged soon."

"What they'd given her" was some kind of cocktail of sedatives and depressants, she assumed.

"You're lucky to be alive," the doctor added.

Saoirse opened her eyes. She rolled her head slowly to face the doctor and stared at her, not looking away until the woman left.

The drugs faded over the next day. Presumably because she didn't start thrashing and screaming, the doctor asked if she could call anyone to take her home.

She thought of one person.

A nurse wheeled her to the hospital entrance and helped her into Betsy's strong-smelling car. Saoirse sat in silence, clutching a pharmacy bag of pills. Betsy, to her credit, didn't say much besides asking if she wanted to go back to her apartment.

"No," Saoirse replied, and gave her the address to her parents' house. They rode the rest of the way in silence, Saoirse nodding off a few times.

When they arrived, Betsy said gruffly, "You got relatives meeting you here?"

Saoirse shook her head. Her mom didn't have anyone, had grown up in the foster system with no siblings. And her dad... he hadn't spoken to anyone on his side in almost two decades. She doubted she could even find their numbers.

"Want me to stay?"

"No, I just need to get some sleep."

Betsy grabbed her in a crushing hug. Saoirse stayed limp until she was allowed to drift out of the car and through the front door.

Trying not to look anywhere but straight ahead, she plodded through her childhood home. She walked up the stairs to the bedrooms. When Saoirse had first moved out of the house, her parents turned her room into a home gym. Then there was Patrick's room, Janey's room, and her parents' master bedroom. She chose the last, the least of all evils.

The master bedroom was bright and sunny, the white bed made, the curtains flung open. Saoirse shut these. Her hands shook while she fumbled to open the stapled prescription bag and took out the rattling pill bottle. She read the label. *Clonazepam*. One should be plenty, the doctor had said at discharge. Saoirse dry-swallowed two, stripped off her clothes, and crawled into the bed.

She held on, buried deep in the bedcovers, willing herself not to think. Finally, apathy warmed her from the inside-out, followed soon by sleep.

At some point, voices woke her. When the bedroom door opened, she cracked an eye to see one of the elderly neighbors poking her head in, her pile of gray, cottony hair illuminated by the light in the hallway.

"Are you hungry, dear?"

Saoirse shook her head, which felt like it was floating, and closed her eyes.

Sometime later, the aroma of stale cigarette smoke, so familiar, filled her nose. Saoirse opened her eyes at once.

Betsy sat next to her on the bed, holding the bottle of Clonazepam. "These are great, can I have one?"

"What are you doing here?" Saoirse asked, her tongue thick and sluggish. Sunshine peeked through a tiny gap in the curtains; was it the next morning?

"Did you think I was gonna dump you here and not check in on you?"

Betsy nudged her aside and heaved herself onto the bed next to her. She handed Saoirse a to-go cup of coffee.

"Thanks." She sat up a little and took a sip, then grimaced. "Black?"

"Is the coffee not to the princess's liking?"

Saoirse almost smiled. She took another mouthful, letting the bitter, hot drink scorch her throat.

"Dalton tried to come in, by the way. I caught him when I got here. Told him to fuck off."

"Thank you," Saoirse said fervently.

The two women lay, gazing at nothing for several minutes, not saying a word.

"So, what's the plan now?"

Saoirse glanced at Betsy. "The plan?"

Her friend stared back at her, her blue eyes piercing within their ring of black eyeliner, her skin rough and leathered by decades of smoking. "Your family died. You should have, but you survived. It fucking sucks, but you have to make a choice. What are you going to do now?"

Maybe this was why she always liked Betsy so much. While her parents had treated her like a Faberge egg, Betsy's bluntness made her think the ex-cop thought she was tough. Strong.

She wasn't.

Saoirse jerked her head toward the pill bottle Betsy had placed back on the nightstand. "Those."

"*Those* are going to run out eventually."

Saoirse covered her eyes with her arm, knowing she couldn't voice how she really felt to Betsy. "I don't know. I haven't thought that far."

Betsy opened her mouth to say something more when a sharp knock rapped against the door.

"Miss Dannan? Are you ready?" an authoritative male

voice spoke.

"*I'll tell you when she's fucking ready!*" Betsy erupted, making Saoirse jump. She turned back to Saoirse. "I forgot to tell you, I was supposed to come in here and get you to come out and talk to these guys."

Saoirse raised her eyebrows.

"One's a lawyer. He said he takes care of your family's estate."

"What estate? All we have is this house."

"Not your parents'. Your grandparents'."

Saoirse frowned. "Why would my grandparents' estate lawyer be here?"

"You didn't know?"

"Know what—oh," she said, stunned. Her grandparents were dead, too?

"The other one's a detective, I guess you met him in the hospital," Betsy said.

Saoirse gaped at her. "They said I wasn't a suspect."

"Don't worry, I'll be with you." Betsy motioned to a suitcase in the corner. "Your roommate dropped off all your clothes. I'll let you get dressed."

Alone again, Saoirse had a moment of fretting over what to wear to talk to a lawyer and a detective. Then she realized her life couldn't get any worse, even if she was falsely accused of murder, and decided on an old, oversized t-shirt and sweatpants.

As she made her way through the house, she clenched her jaw and kept her gaze straight ahead. Someone had picked up the kids' toys (two of everything, as is custom with twins) in the living room and opened all the curtains. Sunlight poured through the house and it looked bright and lived in, even though it wasn't being lived in at all.

The kitchen was clean, like the mess of blood had never

been there. It was full of flowers and cards and packages of food. Beyond, in the breakfast nook, near the sliding door to the backyard, sat two men. Betsy stood sentinel nearby.

Saoirse froze, averting her eyes from the windows that showed the yard beyond.

"For fuck's sake, switch places," Betsy snapped.

The men rose at once and shuffled around the table so she could take the seat with her back to the windows.

The man on the left was older, rotund in his suit, with a ring of white fluff around his otherwise bald head and glasses perched upon his nose. He regarded her eagerly across the table, half-standing with his hand extended.

"Hello, my dear. My, you are lovely as ever," he exclaimed.

Saoirse allowed him to wring her limp hand. "Do we know each other?"

"We've met; it's been quite a long time. Mel Fife, I'm Melinda and Seamus's estate attorney. Say," he said, waving a hand around the kitchen, "you don't need help managing your parents' affairs, do—"

The detective, whom Saoirse hadn't looked at properly in the hospital, cleared his throat and Mel stopped, sitting back down. The detective was younger, though not young, and while he wasn't wearing a suit, his neatly pressed shirt and pants were even more formal somehow. He looked bored, his lightly lined face impassive.

Saoirse gazed at the table she and her family had eaten dinner at her whole life. Her dad, who was always fiddling with one project or another, had made it himself in their garage.

An ache, unbidden and torturous, spread through her. Patrick had been comforted by familiar foods, requesting his meals from a short list of options (chicken nuggets, pepperoni pizza, macaroni and cheese) and rarely relenting to try anything new. Janey had loved food with a passion and would try anything her parents made with gusto. She'd been that way since she was old enough to hold a strip of steak in her chubby hand and suck all the juice from it.

Betsy sat, pushing a slice of toast on a plate toward her, which Saoirse ignored.

"Just fucking eat it," Betsy said.

Saoirse took a small bite.

"Well, you're probably wondering why I came all this way." Her grandparents' estate manager glanced at the stone-faced man sitting to his right. "And why Detective Kirby is here."

Saoirse glanced down at a spot next to her folded hands where Patrick had carved his name with a fork, much to their parents' annoyance. She moved to cover the image of his name from her sight and forced herself to swallow the dry, flavorless toast.

"So my grandparents are gone too?" she said, forcing her voice to remain steady.

Mel cleared his throat but it was Detective Kirby who spoke.

"To say the least."

"Excuse me?" Betsy snapped, eyes darting between the two men.

"I..." Mel rubbed a spot between his eyebrows and glanced at the detective. "You want to explain?"

"Happy to," Kirby said drily, and Saoirse wondered if the man had ever been happy in his entire life. "Miss Dannan, can you confirm that the following people are your relatives?" He drew a sheet of paper from a folder on the table next to him. "Seamus and Melinda Dannan, your grandparents. Your aunt Aednit Howard—" This he pronounced

Adnit instead of the correct *Ey-nit*—"and her husband Michael. Your uncle Mendel and his wife Kayla."

"What's with the names?" Betsy whispered.

Mel, having heard her, brightened. "Ah, Seamus was a celebrated Celtic historian and Melinda's life work was science, so their children's names were an homage to their respective passions."

"So, our names are all either unpronounceable or after dead scientists," Saoirse murmured to her friend.

Betsy grunted. "Can't decide which is worse."

"Anyway," Detective Kirby said, "Miss Dannan, are these names correct? These are your relatives?"

"You're missing my cousins but that's the majority of them," Saoirse replied.

"They're dead."

She choked on her own breath. "What? How?"

"Murder. Same M.O. as the killer of your family. All happened in the days leading up to your family's deaths."

Disbelief froze her in place. The unbearable feelings Saoirse had battled to keep stifled under numbness and apathy clawed for release at his words.

They were dead. All dead.

She pressed her hand harder over Patrick's carved name.

"Same M.O., same perp?" Betsy asked.

Kirby hesitated. "We have reason to believe so."

Betsy stared at Saoirse, who stared back.

"Miss Dannan, do you know who would want your family dead? Were you aware of any family business, or political—"

Saoirse laughed without mirth. "Uh, no. My dad was a motivational speaker. He hadn't talked to his parents or siblings in decades."

"So, no family business—"

"No. Like he said—" she motioned to Mel, having forgotten his name. "My grandfather was a historian and my grandmother was a scientist... I guess they had money but my dad always said they'd inherited it. I don't know what sort of business it came from."

"So, you're not aware of any enemies your grandparents or other relatives had?"

"No."

Kirby's mouth formed a tight, thin line. "Why didn't the killer kill you, too?"

Betsy moved slightly and Saoirse knew her friend was curious about this as well. She was about to explain what happened when the man tried to stab her when she stopped. It sounded unbelievable.

"I told you. He skipped me. I don't know why."

"And then went on to slaughter your two younger siblings."

"Hey," Betsy growled.

Saoirse closed her eyes. It was coming closer, crawling from the depths of her: the need she'd felt from the moment she saw the bodies of the children and the red grass beneath them...

Betsy took her hand and gripped it tightly.

Mel waved his hands apologetically at the two women. "This isn't how I would have wanted to tell this—"

"And yet you asked me to tell her instead of doing it yourself," Detective Kirby retorted.

"I thought in your profession you might have a smidge more finesse—"

Betsy laughed hoarsely. "Clearly *finesse* isn't the detective's forte." She glared at Kirby. "You've got a shitty way of telling someone their entire family has died—"

"Well—" Mel interrupted. "Not her *entire* family."

Saoirse's gazed snapped to him.

"As you noted, Detective Kirby omitted the names of your three cousins." He glanced down at his own papers. "Hawking. His twin sister Linnaeus. And your cousin Eoghan." He said this last name as *Eegan*.

"It's pronounced 'Owen,'" she said automatically, frowning. These were the cousins she had known as a child. They had spent countless hours together at the estate, playing hide n' seek in the dozen or so bedrooms of the manor. She remembered sprinting across the lawns and into the forest, where they'd fought imaginary goblins and elves with swords made out of sticks... "They're alive?"

"They are indeed," Mel said, "and undoubtedly enduring the same rounds of questioning as you are."

She tried to be relieved at their survival but it had been so long since she'd seen them, they may as well have been strangers. The darkness inside her continued to pool.

"While no longer active crime scenes," Kirby said, "this house and the estate may still need to be accessed from time to time as our investigation continues. We'll notify you."

The estate.

"They left it to you," Mel said. "To the four of you. Split equal ways, you've inherited your grandparents' entire fortune, including the aforementioned residence."

Kirby turned to the lawyer and said sharply, "This was specified in the will?"

"It was."

"These four were specifically named as heirs?" Kirby demanded.

"Yes."

"Not their own adult children? Not Miss Dannan's younger siblings?"

Mel opened his mouth and closed it, looking confused. "No."

"And how would Seamus had known to name these four in his will as heirs? Why not name all the surviving grandchildren, even if he didn't want his estate to pass to his own children?"

Mel appeared unable to speak. Betsy glanced at Saoirse.

"When was this will revised?"

"T-two weeks ago," Mel stuttered.

Kirby turned his piercing gaze to Saoirse. "How would your grandfather know to name you and your surviving cousins two weeks before everyone else in the family dies?"

"I don't know. I don't understand any of this."

The benzos had worn off, and she was acutely aware of everything now. The jagged, hideous curtains over the breakfast nook window that her mother had made in a misguided attempt at being a more accomplished homemaker. Janey's spot at the end of the table with bits of omelet stuck to the surface—her favorite breakfast food. An endearing yet terrifying picture of the family Patrick had drawn at kindergarten hanging on the wall. The glaringly clean spots on the Pergo wood flooring where blood had been scrubbed out. The suffocating, gargantuan bouquets of flowers brought to this house as condolences because they were all *gone*—

"All right," Betsy said, standing up. "Detective Kirby, I think it's time for you to go. If Saoirse thinks of anything else to help you in your investigation, she'll let you know. Mr. Fife, it's best if you leave as well."

Kirby looked less than pleased at being ordered to leave. But he obliged, handing Saoirse his card and gifting her with another intimidating stare before he stalked out of the house.

Mel fumbled with his things, appearing bewildered and none too relieved at the meeting's abrupt end.

"Here," he said, thrusting a large folder into her hands. "This contains the details of the transfer of ownership of both residence and assets. Read them over when you have a chance. And—" He tugged something from the front of the folder and placed it on top. A sealed envelope with her name written in a sloping cursive. "Seamus gave me this during the will revising a couple of weeks ago. He told me not to give it to you until—until you became an heir." He looked haunted.

After Mel left, Betsy glanced at her, chewing her thin lip. "That was a lot."

Saoirse nodded, staring again at the spotless kitchen floor. The panic, the darkness, the need was rising rapidly now, threatening to choke her, to drown her.

"Pretty fucking suspicious circumstances. Can't blame Kirby for investigating, even if he is a dick," Betsy said. "You're sure your family isn't mafia or something?"

"No," Saoirse said, muffled thoughts racing through her mind. It was screwed up, all of it, and the mystery of it didn't make her any less alone. Her head and heart and body were about to break in two. The only people she cared about in this whole world were here one moment, gone the next, in the blink of an eye or the snap of her fingers. Or the swift motion of a knife.

Betsy heaved a big sigh. "I gotta get back to my boys. You gonna be okay for a while? I'll come back tomorrow morning to check on you before I head to work."

"Yeah, fine. I'm just going to sleep," Saoirse mumbled.

"Well, make sure you eat something. Looks like you've got a full buffet in your fridge."

Saoirse gave a weak attempt at a smile. Before she knew

what was happening, Betsy had pulled her into another smothering hug, the cigarette smell overwhelming her. Then her friend kissed her quickly on top of her head and left, the smell of her lingering like a ghost.

Alone in the house, Saoirse lifted her eyes to the backyard through the sliding glass door. The lawn was clean, too, but here she thought she saw a shadow of what was once there, depressions of the tiny bodies in the grass.

It was a sick compulsion, destructive and vile, to make herself look at it. But she needed to. She needed the pain, the loss of hope, the crushing torment and the terror that she would never be happy again. She needed it all to help her do what she had decided the moment she found out that almost everyone else had been murdered, too.

Under her father's side of the bed sat a small safe. Her parents had told her the code in case she ever needed it. Their anniversary.

Saoirse opened the safe, and pulled out the gun.

3

The possibilities of magic have been long speculated, but only one who has encountered true magic can attest to its reality.

Seamus Dannan, *Lore: The True History of the Celts*

Saoirse shook as she knelt on the bedroom floor. *Women are four times as likely to threaten suicide*, she had learned in an intro to psychology course during her brief sojourn in college. *But men are four times as likely to go through with it.*

She wouldn't be like the other three-fourths of her sex. No half-assing it.

Her family was gone, and so was she. It was already over —the future she could have had. Maybe she would have actually tried for a promotion. Maybe she would have told Dalton to go fuck himself and gone back to college. Or perhaps eventually she would have figured out, as her father always called it, her "purpose."

She hesitated for the smallest fraction of a moment.

No. There could be no turning back now. Because those futures were impossible. All that lie ahead of her now was pain.

Saoirse forced herself to take a last look around her parents' bedroom. All her life, she had found them here at night reading books in the soft lamplight. She'd thought this was how everyone's parents went to bed. They were always happy to put their books down and chat with her. She remembered lying here at their feet, comfortable and safe.

Racking the slide to load the chamber took all of her waning strength. The gun was heavy as she raised it to her head.

That same weird sensation she'd had in the backyard hit her.

The electric feeling right before the killer killed the children thrummed around her. She was confused, taken aback by it, wondering how and why it was back. She lowered the gun and cried out through clenched teeth.

Patrick's huge, warm brown eyes shining with the pride of some new feat accomplished.

Janey snuggling into her, tiny arms around her neck.

The energy hummed in time with Saoirse's heartbeat.

Now.

She put the gun to her right temple and pulled the trigger.

The trigger compressed. She heard the click. But no bullet came.

Panting, hands shaking, she released the magazine as her father had taught her and saw the row of bullets there and clipped the magazine back in. She checked the chamber again.

Saoirse placed the cold metal of the gun inside her mouth, angling it upward toward her brain, and pulled.

Once again, though the trigger was compressed, nothing came out of the gun.

With a bellow of frustration, she held the gun in front of her and fired. This time, a bullet blasted out of it, the sound deafening, the kick of the gun throwing her backward as the wood of her parents' dresser exploded.

"Okay," she panted, her ears ringing. "Okay." She loaded the chamber again and put the gun back in her mouth.

The gun did not fire.

Eyes wide, she took it out of her mouth and pointed it at the dresser in front of her again. Another thunderous blast, another bullet went through the wood.

"What the hell—"

Coughing in the dust, she went back and forth, over and over, pointing the gun at her own face where it may as well have been a toy, and then anywhere else in the room, where bullets demolished everything in their paths.

She ran out of ammunition.

Quaking, Saoirse stalked into the bathroom. She didn't know what was going on with the gun. But she forced herself not to think about it. She needed to get this done.

Admittedly, she would never have chosen to do it *this* way. Avoiding her own reflection, she fumbled with the razor her dad used to shave his face until she was able to take out the blade.

Saoirse stared at the razor next to her wrist, frowning. Should she get in the bath? Didn't people usually take baths when they did this in movies? And how was she supposed to slash it? Dimly she remembered some argument she heard about the right way. Was it horizontally or vertically?

"Fuck it, just do it."

The hum filled the air. She gripped the blade as hard as she could in her quaking hand.

And brought it down against her wrist.

It slipped; slipped around her wrist without making contact, and hit the laminate countertop. Eyes narrowed, she tried again, and again the blade slid away, as if the blade and her skin were the opposite ends of two magnets.

"No." She slammed her left arm down on the counter, her wrist exposed, and with all the strength she could muster, forced the blade down.

It met an invisible barrier. The humming was louder, as loud as it was when the man tried to stab her.

Slowly, Saoirse raised her gaze to her reflection in the mirror. Her eyes were disturbed, sunken in her gaunt, bloodless face. Her cracked, papery lips were parted in shock.

She dropped the razorblade, opened the medicine cabinet, and found her mother's favorite prescription sleeping pills and a bottle of Dramamine. Then she went back to the bedroom and grabbed her own bottle of benzodiazepines. All three of these she brought to the kitchen.

Though they weren't big drinkers, her parents always kept some tequila in a high cabinet for celebrating their anniversary.

The tequila burned like artificial sweeteners mixed with fire, but it made swallowing the fifty-odd pills much easier.

Saoirse sat on the Pergo floor, breathing deep and slow, until the urge to vomit passed, thanks to the Dramamine. Then she leaned her head against the cabinet behind her, and waited.

The light faded from the windows. The kitchen became so dark that she could no longer make out Patrick and Janey's soccer schedule stuck to the fridge, the magnet from their family trip to Yellowstone, nor the dry erase calendar where Saoirse's mom had detailed their hiking plans for the month. Her father's favorite quote was stuck amongst all this, which, although she had memorized it, she had never understood:

If you want to understand the secrets of the universe, think in terms of energy, frequency, and vibration.

Nikola Tesla

Soon, she was cloaked in darkness.

There was no heaviness to her body or her mind, not even the unconcerned calm of the clonazepam.

Saoirse was wholly and vividly alive.

She got to her feet, her mind working, her grief taking a backseat.

The gun wouldn't fire at her. The razor blade wouldn't touch her. And she had enough tranquilizers and alcohol inside her to kill a small elephant, yet she didn't feel a thing.

The air continued to hum around her.

And the killer. Skipping her after murdering her parents like he had known that he could have no effect on her. The energy blasting her away from him, out of harm's way.

It was impossible, sick, and unfair. It couldn't be true...

Saoirse wracked her brain. She thought of two more things she could try, and she really, really didn't want to attempt either of them.

Acting before she could change her mind, Saoirse grabbed a key from the hook on the kitchen wall and went to the garage.

Ever since she was little, her father's most prized possession was his Mitsubishi Lancaster Evolution. He tinkered with it and modified it and would take her for joy rides almost every evening after dinner. The black car didn't look like much but made her yelp in delight when he revved the engine on empty roads, the sheer power of it pinning her to her seat, her stomach leaping with the g-forces. She remembered how mad her mom would get when he would take it out during the twins' naps, whose rooms were right above the garage. The kids would awaken, screaming in their cribs, from the vibrations the car caused. Her father had taught Saoirse to drive it when she was sixteen, something very impressive to the boys at school.

Streetlamps illuminated her path as she raced out of the neighborhood, the engine rumbling with power. Once she merged on the freeway, which was empty on this weeknight, she shifted gears and hit the accelerator hard.

Her back pinned to the seat, Saoirse unclipped her seatbelt as she hit ninety miles per hour. Reflective signs lit up by her headlights flashed faster and faster as she topped one hundred. One-ten. One-twenty. She had never gone this fast in her life, doubted even her father had. The car roared and shook, and she roared with it as she gripped the steering wheel and kept pushing. One-thirty. One-forty.

Saoirse shut her eyes tight and jerked the wheel.

It did not move.

She pulled harder.

The steering wheel was locked in place.

She let go of it entirely. The car stayed on course. She grabbed the handle of the door and tried to fling it open.

The door wouldn't budge.

Panting, her body and the air around her both thrumming with that same frantic energy, Saoirse took control of the wheel again.

Time for Plan B.

"This is so fucked up," she muttered to herself an hour later as she parked at the same trailhead she and her family had hiked only a few days ago. After locating a flashlight in the trunk, she began.

Saoirse was underfed, dehydrated, and not in great shape before all this, but pure adrenaline kept her going as she marched up the rocky path. The forest was eerie in the night; several times she caught sight of glowing eyes in the beam of her flashlight. Black bears lived in this area, she knew. For the first time in her life she wasn't afraid of them.

Any other time she would have welcomed this invincibility, but now she only hoped she was wrong. The rumble of a waterfall grew louder and louder as she hiked.

It looked ghostly in the glow of her flashlight. She paused here, letting the mist spray her face. Her mind wandered to excruciating places.

Patrick and Janey giggling as they slipped up the rocky trails. Hoisting Janey onto her shoulders while Patrick whined, wanting to be picked up too, before being swept up in the strong arms of her father. The time Janey slipped in an icy creek and they had to spread her tiny naked body on a rock in the sun to stop her hypothermia. Patrick routinely climbing up trees he couldn't climb down.

She swallowed. Time to move on.

The minutes passed rapidly as she climbed higher and higher until the trees cleared and the vastness of the sky opened up to her. She walked to the edge, the cold glow of the moon overhead, lights twinkling both above and below as she gazed out over her city.

Saoirse hated heights most of all. She couldn't count the number of nightmares she'd had of falling to her death, awakening drenched in sweat. She had never come so close to the edge of this lookout, no matter how much her parents begged her to come see.

Now, she would see. Now, she had a worse fear than falling to contend with.

Slowly, she backed up to where the clearing began and breathed in the clear mountain air. The trees appeared to bend toward her and a fierce, icy wind whipped around her body like it was trying to hold her in place.

Saoirse took another deep breath and broke into a run.

Her feet pounded the dirt, her hair flew out behind her as the wind rushed against her, the hum in the air now a howl. She flung her arms wide as she jumped at the edge of the cliff, leaping into oblivion.

The crackling, sizzling, wildly vibrating force of energy that had been with her in the kitchen, that had hummed around her when she tried to use the gun and the blade and the pills and the speeding car, wrapped around her airborne body and slammed her back onto the ground.

She laid on her back, panting, and she could almost see it glimmering above her. Then it was gone and she was alone.

Saoirse sat up, her body limp and aching, all adrenaline drained from her. This was it, and she didn't care at all why. She was in hell. No matter what she did, she couldn't harm herself.

No matter what she did, she could not die.

4

The Tuatha dé Danann were an ancient people who worshipped the goddess Danu. Warriors capable of great magic, they are most known for the defeat and imprisonment of Carmun.

Seamus Dannan, *Lore: The True History of the Celts*

Saoirse's first thought when she woke up and peeled her parched lips and eyelids apart was that this was the longest she had ever persevered without giving up. *Dad would be proud*, she mused.

Her second thought was about the thirst.

While the hunger had gone away by the third day, the thirst was relentless. It gnawed at her mind and body every waking moment. Torturous as it was, she was glad to have the distraction. What she could absolutely do without, though, was the incessant buzzing and crackling of electricity. The mysterious energy was working as hard to keep her alive as she was trying to die.

Betsy still came by every day to yell at her. Her friend assumed Saoirse ate and drank enough, because she wasn't dead yet, but said she could tell it wasn't much. Betsy had no idea that not one drop of water or scrap of food had passed her lips in a week. The visits were getting shorter and shorter, Betsy more and more agitated with every day that passed, but still she came.

Today, she was surlier than usual.

"I've been ignoring him like you asked me to, but he's a persistent sonofabitch. You need to talk to him."

Saoirse groaned. She let her phone die days ago to avoid this exact thing. "About what?" she croaked, her throat desiccated.

"He only says it's important. I never should have given him my number," Betsy said, holding out her phone. "Take it."

Saoirse took the phone and, weak as she was, immediately dropped it.

Betsy's mouth was an extra thin line. "If you don't start taking care of yourself, I'm calling the police and they can cart you off to the mental hospital, because you're not fucking dying on my watch."

"Don't worry, I won't," Saoirse said, knowing a moment of guilt as she caught Betsy's icy gaze. She picked the phone back up and tapped the number on the list of dozens of missed calls. He really was persistent.

It rang once.

"Betsy!" Mel exclaimed. "Finally—"

"Mel, it's me. What do you want?"

"Soriss, I've been trying to reach you for a week. I trust you're doing well? Good, good. My dear, I've arranged a meeting with your surviving cousins to discuss the future of the estate and its assets at your grandparents'—well, *your*—jointly owned mansion, in two days. We will need you there to make some essential decisions. First and foremost..."

Saoirse closed her eyes, which were so dry that they stung whenever she kept them open for too long. Mel's voice became an unintelligible drone.

Surviving cousins. His wording made her think. Could they be as immune to death as she was? If not, why wouldn't the killer have murdered them, too?

"I don't know, Mel. I'll think about it."

"But—"

"Don't bother Betsy anymore, please. I'll charge my phone." She hung up.

"Thank you," Betsy said grumpily. "What did he want?"

"I guess my cousins are getting together at my grandparents' place." She chewed her papery lip.

"You want to go?" Betsy asked.

Saoirse studied her friend. Multiple times, she had considered telling Betsy the truth about her failed suicide attempts. She even thought of showing her proof that she couldn't harm herself. But she feared Betsy would care less about the peculiarity of it and more about getting Saoirse help for her mental state. The last thing she wanted was to be committed.

"I don't know," Saoirse replied. "Seems like a lot of effort."

Betsy flared her nostrils. "You need to *do* something. Lying around in a catatonic state isn't helping you. I don't blame you for not coming back to work and since you're a millionaire now, you don't have to. But go see your family. It might be good—they lost their people, too."

"Yeah, but I don't *know* them," Saoirse said, not meeting Betsy's gaze. "I haven't seen them since we were kids and I was so young I don't even remember them."

"Blood is blood," Betsy said. "When you're family, you're automatically obligated to each other, whether you like it or not."

Saoirse shifted under the covers as she considered this.

"Well, if you do decide to go," Betsy said as she got up to leave, "take a shower first. You smell like shit."

Saoirse stayed in bed, gazing up at the ceiling. How far away was the estate? Four, five hours? Going recklessly fast through the country in the Evo didn't sound too terrible.

She grabbed the stack of papers Mel had left her, intending to look up the estate's address, when the sealed envelope with her name on it fell out.

"Oh, yeah," she murmured. In her rush to kill herself, she had forgotten about it. With unease, she ripped the envelope open and slid the letter out. The writing was hurried, barely legible. It was dated two weeks before the accident.

Dear Saoirse,

I am sure your grief is more than you can bear. Our hearts ache for you and for Hawking and Linnaeus and Eoghan. We wish we could be there to help all of you. But know that we have done everything possible to protect you, and of that protection you can be sure.

I know you have many questions. I prom-

> ise, the answers you need are in the estate. They won't be easy to find, a precaution we were forced to take, but with each other's help, you will find them.
>
> P.S. If you do find yourselves in danger, remember the song.
>
> Love,
> Granda + Nana

Saoirse read the letter over and over. Finally, she crushed it in her fist and hurled it across the room.

"*Motherfucker,*" she screamed, tearing her raw throat.

Protection. They did this. They knew her family would die—that was why they changed the will. And somehow, they protected her with this infuriating *buzzing*, keeping her alive and in misery. For what? Why do this to her? Why doom her to a living hell?

Why not protect her family, too? At least Patrick and Janey? What kind of monsters would let two little children die?

Angry tears would have come to her eyes if she wasn't completely dried out.

She didn't care why Granda needed to take *precautions*. Fuck him for not giving an explanation in the letter. For making this so hard.

Saoirse set her jaw, her chest heaving. She would go. She would go to the estate, meet the cousins whose faces she barely remembered. And she would find out if these answers included the only one she cared about: how to die.

It took the next two days for Saoirse to figure out how to keep food and water down. Guzzling cold water in great gulps had only resulted in her vomiting it up. It was like recovering from the stomach flu but worse—small sips, waiting a while, then sipping a bit more. She had to ease back into food as well, her stomach shrunken and her appetite nonexistent. After regaining enough strength, she finally took a shower. It took three washes to get all the grease out of her hair.

Re-entering the bedroom afterward and getting a whiff of what she had been living like for weeks almost made her vomit again. Betsy was right; she really had smelled like shit.

At least the maddening forcefield or whatever the hell it was had left.

The next morning, Saoirse set out early so she could make it to the estate by lunch, when Mel said everyone else was arriving. She'd thrown an assortment of random clothes and toiletries into a duffel bag. At the last moment, she loaded the gun with more ammunition and tossed it in. When she did figure out how to die, it would still be her preferred method.

On the drive, she called Betsy.

"I'm going," she said loudly over the car's rumble.

"You'll miss the funeral," Betsy grunted.

The funeral. She hadn't thought of that. The image of the children's white faces in tiny caskets...

"I know."

"Well, good for you," her friend replied in a tone that was bright, even for Betsy. "You shower?"

Saoirse smiled a little. "Yes."

"I'm proud of you. You're tough. You're going to make it through this."

Guilt surged through her again. She knew Betsy had been a great cop, had sharp instincts and excellent judgment, but she had Saoirse all wrong.

"Thanks," was all she could say.

"And let me know what you find out," her friend said. "This whole situation is fishy."

You have no idea, Saoirse thought.

The five-hour drive to the estate was uneventful, although she did, at one point, violently jerk the wheel whilst going over a tall bridge. Instead of catching the mysterious energy force by surprise, it managed to slow the car significantly, as if threatening to make it stop working altogether.

Saoirse sighed and turned on the last music her father had been listening to. The Beastie Boys.

"Wow, you were a geek, Dad," she said, tears filling her eyes. She turned off the radio and rode the rest of the way in silence.

As the road took her out of the wide, sprawling country and into dense trees, familiarity settled over her like a shroud.

Autumn was taking its time to reach these woods: the trees were still bright green and mossy. She rolled down the windows and took the car into a lower gear so she could hear the wind rush through the forest, shrill sounds of birds and other things echoing.

Almost out of nowhere, a call box appeared at the start of a narrow drive. A tall fence extended from the gates, which were open wide to admit her car. She'd never known these details as a child, but after reading through the information Mel had given her, she learned that the estate took in over 400 acres of land. It was comprised mostly of forest, but also contained a decently sized lake, which she faintly remembered. She wondered if Mel knew how her family had acquired such wealth.

The mossy forest flanked her on either side as she sped up the long drive until quite suddenly, it parted to reveal a stunning stone mansion. The steep, pitched roofs and ornate round balconies gave it sort of a gothic look, but the multicolored stone and turquoise windows added warmth.

Saoirse laughed in spite of her nerves. Although she knew the mansion was large (36,000 square feet), it looked so much smaller than she remembered. She supposed this made sense. She was, after all, nineteen years older than the last time she saw it.

A wide driveway spread out before the front entrance. Three cars were parked there: a shiny black Mercedes sedan, probably belonging to Mel, a sensible Toyota Camry, and a monstrous truck wrapped in yellow and blue that gleamed garishly in the sunlight.

She pulled in behind the truck. The license plate said WINNR.

"Gross," she muttered.

She stood in the sun with her duffel bag over her shoulder, taking in the mansion and its lavish landscaping, which was overgrown but still beautiful. This place had been so magical to her. Until it wasn't.

Saoirse took a deep breath and stepped through the dark wood doors.

"Whoa," she breathed. Was it the scent of earth and old books and warm spices that caught her so off guard? Or the sight of the foyer with the grand staircase she had sprinted up so many times to explore the rooms above?

A small chirrup made her jump.

"*Kian?*" An enormous, handsome black cat stared at her with lamp-like yellow eyes from a doorway beside the stairs. Granda's cat, who'd been around since she was little. She recognized the shock of white fur on his chest. "You must be ancient."

The cat blinked slowly, as if irritated.

"Sarose? Is that you?" Mel's voice called from the room behind the cat.

"It's pronounced *Sur-sha*," a male voice corrected him.

"Thanks, Eggan."

"*Ow-en*," a female voice said.

"Well, in any case—"

Saoirse entered the sitting room. The details of the space barely registered—lots of ornateness and a rich feel—for she could only stare at the three who sat with Mel.

One of the men stood, smiling warmly at her. His face was pleasant and kind, though not handsome. He was medium height, with light brown hair and thin metal framed glasses. She remembered the glasses.

"Eoghan," she said.

He smiled wider. "Come sit."

She shuffled awkwardly, setting her duffel bag down before taking a plush armchair. Mel and Eoghan sat in armchairs across from her. Two others, who she presumed were Hawking and Linnaeus, sat at opposite ends of a couch.

Linnaeus's appearance was striking. She appeared to have copied her entire look from Amy Winehouse. Her black hair was teased up into a massive beehive and her blue eyes, like Saoirse's, were rimmed in thick, sweeping eyeliner. She wore a tank top in spite of the season, and her arms were covered in full tattoo sleeves (as well as a number of healed slashes on her wrists). Linnaeus didn't smile.

Hawking was his twin sister's opposite. The obvious owner of the foul truck, he lounged easily on his side of the couch. He was tall and well-muscled (which his tight shirt displayed) with a suspiciously perfect tan. His brown hair was carefully tousled, and his too-white teeth gleamed as he grinned and gave her a blithe up-nod, which she did not return.

Mel cleared his throat.

"Now that we are all here, these are devastating as well as unusual circumstances. I know you've all been in mourning, as well as dealing with questions from the police, so I appreciate your willingness to gather here while we discuss the estate as sensitively as possible."

Sounding anything but sensitive, Mel cheerfully fixed a pair of wire glasses onto his nose and plowed through an accounting of the estate's value, as well as the monetary assets held by the four of them, all of which were grotesque in amount.

"So, we're like, super rich," Hawking said.

"That is correct. Eoghan, as the oldest, you are the executor, which I have informed you of already and is, as you know, mostly a formality. You are each 25% owners of all assets and as such, any decisions made with shared property, such as this estate, must be made unanimously. On that topic, I already have several offers for the estate that exceed the valuation I just mentioned, so at this point we simply need to agree on some minute details in order to officially begin the bidding war."

"I'm sorry," Eoghan said politely, a hand held up. "I for one am not interested in selling. At least, not yet."

Hawking and Linnaeus murmured their agreement. They must have all received letters from Granda.

Mel's mouth fell open; he quickly recovered. "Typically, that is customary in such a situation; you aren't all going to live here together, although," he huffed a laugh, "you could probably pull it off without seeing much of each other, I mean, *three* kitchens—"

"I think we need to discuss this in private," Linnaeus said without Eoghan's politeness, her mound of black hair gleaming in the midday light.

Mel's eyebrows shot up. "But the upkeep alone, the property needs a staff, it needs care—"

Eoghan was already standing with a hand extended to help Mel out of his chair. "We'll call you when we're ready to make some decisions."

Mel spluttered all the way into the foyer and Saoirse wondered what sort of commission kickback he'd hoped to get out of this. Eoghan reappeared, smoothing the front of his nerdy khaki pants, into which he had tucked in a plaid button-down shirt. Kian slinked in behind him and trotted over to a patch of sunlight on the rug, where he settled himself in that particular way cats do that make them look like a loaf of bread.

Eoghan sat in the armchair and leaned forward.

"Well. Hi," he said, smiling. "We didn't really get to catch up with Mel here."

No one spoke. The silence was so painful that Saoirse had to look down, but Eoghan continued.

"Is this the first time everyone's been back here? Since..."

The air shifted at the mention of the last time they had all seen each other. They all nodded.

"Me too. Gosh, how long has it been? Twenty years?"

"Nineteen," Linnaeus spoke.

"Nineteen years," Eoghan said, sitting back in the armchair. "What has everyone been doing since? College? Work? Families?"

After a long pause, Hawking raised his hand casually. "Went to UPenn, joined up with Big Pharma after I graduated, top rep in my division. Although, I guess I can quit now, right?" he smirked.

Saoirse glanced around at the others. She didn't have a clue what he'd said.

"I'm also dating Davie Huntington," he added.

"Oh, you're—gay?" Eoghan asked politely.

"What? No. She's like, a super famous Instagram model? Here, check it out." He made to grab his phone.

"We're good," Linnaeus said loudly.

Saoirse suppressed a smile.

"Well, that's great," Eoghan said. "I'm happy for you, Hawking. I also went to school and I got my Masters in psychology. I've been working for about five years now."

"As a therapist?" Linnaeus blurted.

Eoghan nodded.

"What kind?"

Eoghan straightened his glasses. "I work in trauma counseling, as well as with patients with more acute diagnoses. Psychotic disorders, schizophrenia, multiple personalities."

Linnaeus raised her eyebrows at this. "You got a wife? Kids?"

"No, I haven't really found... Do you know anyone?" Eoghan chuckled self-deprecatingly.

Linnaeus didn't reply.

Clearly disconcerted by her, Eoghan turned to Saoirse. "What about you? What have you been up to since we were kids?"

This was her worst fear: being interrogated in the presence of two over-achieving family members. "Just work. Mortgage company," she mumbled.

Hawking became suddenly enthusiastic. "You're a loan originator? What state? I've got some investment properties my buddies and I are looking into and we need a good LO. What lender are you with?"

"I... it's mobile homes." Her face burned.

"Ah," Hawking replied and sat back.

"Okay," Eoghan said, "So, Linnaeus."

"Alright, stop," Linnaeus demanded. "Let's cut the bullshit and talk about why we're really here."

Thank you, Saoirse thought.

Eoghan put his hands up. "Of course, I only wanted to make everyone more comfortable before we got into—"

"Dude, we don't need you to be our therapist. Let's just get into it. Everyone was murdered except us," Linnaeus said. "Granda knew it would happen. He told us to come here to find answers. What do we do now?"

Even Hawking sat straighter at this, his bored facial expression gone.

"I mean..." Eoghan trailed off, rubbing his forehead. "I'm still trying to figure out how it's all possible. How he knew, and why..."

"Why we can't die," Saoirse said.

Everyone turned to stare at her.

"You mean why we *didn't*?" Hawking asked. "Why the killer didn't come after us, too?"

Saoirse shook her head and took a deep breath. "I was there. I was with them. The man that killed my family skipped me. I didn't understand why at first until I tried to stop him from..." Tears clawed at her throat. She swallowed, humiliated. "He almost stabbed me but then this force or something intervened."

Linnaeus peered at her.

"And then I experimented a bit... There's no way for me to die. From what Granda said in the letter, I assume that applies to all of us."

"Protection," Eoghan said.

"Like he did something to make us immortal?" Hawking asked, looking confused.

"I don't know if that means we can't age, that we'll *never* die, but..."

"We can't be killed," Linnaeus said. "She's right. I found out too."

"How?" Hawking asked.

"How do you think?" Linnaeus snapped.

Saoirse admired her for admitting it. She certainly hadn't.

"So what happens if you...?" Eoghan asked both of the women.

Saoirse and Linnaeus glanced at each other.

"Things just don't work," Linnaeus said.

Saoirse leaned over to grab her duffel bag. "Here. I can show you." She pulled out the gun and Eoghan stiffened. "It's okay," she said. She gazed around the room and decided against damaging any property. She stepped over Kian to the window he dozed underneath. He chuffed in annoyance.

"Okay," she said after opening the window. "Watch." She pointed the gun outside and shot it into the open air. The bang made everyone jump; Kian hissed and leapt across the room. Then, that crackling energy surging, she lifted the gun to her own head.

"Wait—" Hawking started.

She pulled the trigger. As expected, nothing happened.

"I've done this a dozen times. The gun will fire at everything but me. I can't cut myself with something sharp, can't overdose, can't fall off a cliff."

"Well, that was all pretty risky, wasn't it?" Hawking said.

"Are you fucking dumb?" Linnaeus said, and grabbed the gun from Saoirse. She aimed it at her brother and pulled the trigger.

"Hey," he shouted. "What the hell!"

"You're fine, idiot," Linnaeus grumbled as she tossed the gun onto the coffee table. "It may as well be an empty water gun for all it will do to you. Like Saoirse said, nothing can hurt us. Not even other people."

Saoirse raised an eyebrow at her.

"After I figured it out, I went to bad places, fucked with bad people. They couldn't touch me." Linnaeus grinned.

Saoirse had to admit, as a girl that would feel pretty good.

"What, like drug dealers and stuff?" Hawking stared at his sister, astonished.

"Calm down," she rolled her eyes.

"Do you feel that?" Eoghan said.

Saoirse knew he was referring to the electric charge that lingered in the air.

"Yeah," Linnaeus said. "It's always there."

"That's what's doing it. It's what's protecting us," Saoirse said.

"What is it?" Hawking asked.

She shrugged. "I guess that's part of what we're here to find out."

"And who the fucking killer is," Linnaeus said, her dark eyes narrowed. "Granda seemed to know a lot. Maybe he knew that, too."

There was a pause and then Linnaeus stood up.

"Well, he made it sound like there's hidden shit in here somewhere. Are we done wasting time chatting?" She looked around at everyone, challenging them.

"Yeah, I think we're done," Eoghan said.

"Good. Let's ransack the hell out of this place."

5

Two types of magic are currently at play: one made to create; the other, to destroy.

Seamus Dannan, *Lore: The True History of the Celts*

"This is so fucking weird," Linnaeus said, her beehive bobbing in front of Saoirse.

"I know what you mean," Saoirse replied. They ascended the grand staircase as a group, off for an adventure, like they had so many times when they were young.

But the walk down the hall to their grandparents' bedroom, the place they had decided was most logical to start looking, was gut-wrenching. Against the floral-patterned green wallpaper hung photographs of a young Melinda and Seamus with their kids. Saoirse forced her gaze away when she recognized the image of her father as a teenager, his blue eyes as piercing as his mother's, as Saoirse's. The others kept a quick pace as well.

While they had snuck around every room and corner of this place as children, the master suite wasn't familiar to Saoirse.

Like the rest of the house, the room was more warm than airy, with fine-looking dark wood, elegant and ornate. With a shudder, Saoirse wondered where in the house they had died.

Hawking went straight for the nightstands. Eoghan crouched down to sweep his hands under the bed. Linnaeus pulled out drawers of the wood dresser on the opposite side of the large room. With the sense of being in one of those escape rooms searching for clues, Saoirse took down framed pictures and looked behind them on the wall and in the paper covering the back of the frame. There was only one painful family picture in here and Saoirse left it facing away on the floor.

The rest were an odd assortment. A couple pictures were of simple images, like crude symbols. She picked up the first, a circular tree with its roots curving up to meet branches curving down. On the back was a scribbled title: *The Oak*. Another was of a triple spiral. This also had writing on the back that said *Triskelion: Forward Motion*. Had one of them drawn these? She took them and set them down on the cream bedspread. Hawking and Eoghan joined her.

"Nothing behind them," she said as she motioned to the pictures, noticing a light stain over one of the branches of the oak tree. She went back to the walls.

There were also newspaper clippings of a young Seamus. One of them read, *Professor Hits Gold with* Lore: The

True History of the Celts. Another said, *Award-Winning Book Grants Seamus Dannan Expert Status*. In both clippings, the photographs showed young Seamus grinning at the camera, looking quite collegiate. Though the photos were in black and white, Saoirse knew in color they would have shown Seamus's bright red hair, which had skipped her father (aside from his beard) and gone to her. There was no evidence that Seamus had published a single book since.

Hawking gave a loud snort.

"Whoa," he said as he held up a long pink item of a sensitive nature from Melinda's nightstand.

Saoirse's jaw dropped.

"You're disgusting," Linnaeus said. "Put that back."

"I bet Seamus has some Viagra in the bathroom," Hawking grinned as he dropped the vibrator back in the drawer.

"Well, that would be natural," Eoghan said as he continued groping under the massive bed. "I, for one, think it's a sign of a thriving marriage that they had an active intimate life. You know, they say the people with the most satisfying sex are older couples who have been together for decades—"

"You can stop now," Linnaeus interrupted.

Eoghan shrugged and moved on to the master closet.

After finishing with the bedroom and making thorough work of the closet and bathroom (in which they did indeed find a bottle of Viagra), the group moved on to the next likely place something important could be hidden: Seamus's study.

This was an exceptionally handsome room. It was circular, with fine wooden beams extended up the slope of the ceiling to meet in the middle where a large pendant light hung. Books lined the circular shelves, which were separated by a few built in desks. Opposite the doorway was a large fireplace with a single armchair and a plush rug.

Saoirse was hit with the breathtaking force of memory. They had cuddled on this rug, warmed by the fire as snow filled the tall windows, while Seamus had sat in that chair and entertained them with fairytales. She remembered running her small fingers over the soft fibers of the rug, tracing the patterns as the fire caused shadows to flicker around the room. Had her father and his siblings experienced the same thing when they were little? She was never allowed to ask.

They all hesitated on the threshold of the room, staring at the fireplace. Kian the cat now sat in the armchair, looking regal and unconcerned.

Linnaeus cleared her throat.

"Should we get to work?"

They divided and conquered once more. Saoirse moved to one of the built-in study areas, flipping on a lamp and opening the drawer of the desk. It was filled with junk: dried out pens, scraps of paper, random coins. After groping deep into the corners, she shut it and moved on to the next.

"Damn, our grandparents were horny," Hawking said, holding up a book entitled *The Passionate Marriage*.

Eoghan took the book from him. "Hawking, I get the sense that true intimacy is something you struggle with."

"What would you know about it? You're single."

Eoghan blushed.

"You probably only know theory. I bet you've never experienced the real thing," Hawking said as he bent over to select another book.

Eoghan clenched his fist, but he merely replaced the

book he had taken from Hawking and continued searching a different section of shelving.

"Men get together and just have to start measuring their dicks," Linnaeus muttered as she picked through the books stacked next to Saoirse.

Saoirse decided she liked Linnaeus; she reminded her of Betsy. "Maybe you should be the psychologist," she said quietly.

Linnaeus snorted. "Yeah, I might as well. You know all shrinks are crazy, right?" She glanced sideways at Eoghan, who appeared to be doing some sort of deep breathing exercise.

"He means well," Saoirse replied. "Your brother though... for twins, you two could not be more different."

Linnaeus put a hand on her heart. "That may be the best compliment I've ever gotten."

Saoirse smiled and swept her hand around the next desk drawer. She paused when she felt something cold and metallic and pulled it out.

She remembered this. It was a necklace she had played with as a child. A pendant made of a rather unimpressive gray stone, but framed with beautiful, intricate gold. Swift impressions of Melinda's warm, kind eyes, crinkled around the edges as she smiled and put the long chain around Saoirse's neck. Then she would pile on a feather boa, a small hat with a cloud of tulle, and one of her own silk robes. Saoirse would spin around in the mirror, giggling.

Glancing at Linnaeus, who was busy flipping through a book, Saoirse pulled the chain over her head and tucked the pendant into her shirt.

She wasn't sure why she'd done it—she supposed the necklace may be of value and she didn't want to start arguing with her cousins over possessions. All she knew was that it was something she'd loved as a child and she wanted it.

A low musical hum, a simple but eerie melody, made the hair on her arms stand on end.

She whipped her head toward the source of the sound right as Linnaeus and Eoghan did the same. It was Hawking, sitting cross-legged on the wood floor as he gazed through a book Saoirse recognized as Seamus's *Lore: The True History of the Celts*.

"Stop that," Linnaeus snapped.

Hawking glanced up, bewildered. "What?"

"The Song of Carmun, you were singing it."

His brow furrowed. "Sorry. I didn't even realize. He made us sing it so many damn times," he said, glancing at the rug in front of the fireplace.

Kian bristled from the armchair, startled by all the commotion.

Nausea roiled in Saoirse's stomach. She'd forgotten what it was called. She knew why the room had reminded him of the song—Seamus *had* made them memorize it, right here. And then they sang it, the last night she ever saw him...

Tra ghuthaan fasaah agas speraan rotea...

Shit, she thought. She didn't think she would remember the words, but Hawking humming the tune brought it back... why did Seamus tell them to *use the song* if in danger in his letter? What danger could possibly be posed to them, and why would the stupid song help?

She was about to ask this out loud, at the risk of upsetting everyone further, when Hawking spoke.

"Oh-ho!" He held up something gold in one hand and a false book box in his other.

"A key hidden in a fake book?" Linnaeus cocked her head.

"Could be significant," Eoghan said.

Saoirse stared at the key, her heart beating faster. Was it significant? Something that would help her find what she came for?

Linnaeus actually beamed at her brother. "Nice job. Now we just have to find out what it unlocks."

"Well," Hawking said, standing and stretching, his t-shirt coming up to reveal a ripple of meticulously shaved and tanned abs. He bent down and picked up Seamus's book and tucked it under one arm. "I say we take a break to celebrate. I'm starving."

Forty-five minutes later, they sat in the main kitchen, which was more modern than the rest of the house, stuffing themselves with delivered pizza. Hawking busied himself in the fridge, searching for beer.

"What are the other kitchens for?" Linnaeus wondered as she picked at a pepperoni.

"Uh, one is a caterer's kitchen, I'm not sure what the other is for," Eoghan answered absently as he texted on his phone.

"O'Douls, you've got to be kidding me." Hawing set a six-pack of green glass bottles on the wooden table. He glanced up at Eoghan. "Who are you texting? Your catfish girlfriend?"

"No, a client."

"One of the psycho ones?" Linnaeus asked.

"Dissociative identity disorder. Multiple personalities," he explained.

"Does that mean what it sounds like?"

"It does, actually," Eoghan said, putting his phone back in his pocket. "The affected will switch between different identities—like being possessed by different people. I observe him suddenly having an entirely different voice, mannerisms.... He often doesn't even remember his other identities or what they've said or done."

Saoirse and Linnaeus stared at him, mouths open.

"Anyway, people tend to stress when their therapist leaves town."

"Yeah, Davie was upset I had to leave, too," Hawking said as he sipped the non-alcoholic beer. "I was supposed to go with her to Baku for a shoot."

"Where?" Saoirse asked.

"It's the capital of Azerbaijan, right there on the Caspian Sea. It's incredible, you should go."

Saoirse, who had never even been to Mexico, had no idea what he was talking about.

Hawking's too-perfect teeth flashed as he grinned. "You can go anywhere now, Sursh. The whole world is yours."

Saoirse busied herself with a hearty swig of O'Douls, which tasted decent. She wished she could care about seeing the world. She wished she could enjoy this reunion with her cousins. But her ability to feel excitement or connection had died with her family.

They found a key. Whatever it unlocked may get her closer to her goal. She was eager to go back to searching, and was about to say so, when Linnaeus spoke.

"Where did Melinda work?"

"What do you mean?" Eoghan asked.

"She was this research scientist but all we've seen is Seamus's stuff. I haven't seen a book or journal or anything of hers."

Saoirse frowned. "Maybe she had a lab somewhere else."

"Maybe," Eoghan said.

"Alright," Hawking said, putting his bottle of O'Douls down. "This won't do. Linny, I'm sure you brought some... recreational substances." He mimed holding a joint.

"Don't call me that," she said, but she was smirking.

Eoghan looked uneasy.

"Come on, man," Hawking said, punching Eoghan in the shoulder so hard that he almost tipped over in his chair. "Live a *little*, for once. Even as a kid, you were uptight as hell."

Eoghan pursed his lips, then gave a small shrug.

"There we go," Hawking said, clapping his hands. "What say we enjoy the sunset in the solarium?"

Though irritated by this delay, Saoirse considered herself outnumbered. Minutes later, the group had settled themselves in the beautiful windowed room, lying on white lounge chairs and passing around a blunt. Eoghan exploded in a fit of coughing.

"Ah, I love a first-timer," Hawking said.

Kian mewled at them disapprovingly from the doorway.

"He must hate the smell," Saoirse observed. The weed kicked in. She suddenly couldn't remember why she was talking about the cat. Her thoughts drifted from each other, the last one she had gone so quickly that she couldn't even remember what she was thinking about. But she felt profoundly serene. She reached out a hand, wanting to touch the cat's soft fur.

"Come here, come on, Kian."

The cat stared at her, staying resolutely still and austere.

"Get the old grouch some catnip," Linnaeus said. The group erupted in giggles. Eoghan was hysterical, his face red and glasses askew. This made the group laugh harder and it was several moments before they calmed down.

Calm rested upon her like a blanket. It was better than the clonazepam, although she wasn't much a fan of the smell either. She had only smoked pot once before at a party in a rather disappointing experience.

"This is way better than that time," she announced to no one in particular. Her words came out slow and stupid.

"This is good shit, Linny," Hawking remarked, fiddling with a gorgeous fat blossom hanging over his chair.

"The flower?" Eoghan asked.

"The *weed*," Hawking said and Eoghan giggled and flopped back on his lounge chair.

"I stole it straight from the source," Linnaeus said. "His own personal supply."

Hawking sat up. "You don't mean—"

"I told you, once I figured out I couldn't die, I fucked with bad people. It felt amazing. They couldn't touch me," she said, stretching out luxuriously. "Didn't we bring snacks?"

"Snacks," Eoghan echoed longingly. "Ooh, go get the breadsticks."

Linnaeus drifted back into the house.

"Can you believe she did shit like that?" Hawking asked, staring back and forth between Saoirse and Eoghan. "She's always been crazy. Bat shit crazy." He paused. "She looks like a bat."

Eoghan howled at this. When Linnaeus returned, he clapped his hands over his mouth like a guilty child.

"What?"

"No. You'll be mad." He looked afraid. "I don't want her to hurt me."

"You're paranoid, it's normal," Hawking said.

"So, what's going on?" Linnaeus demanded.

"Hawking said you look like a bat," Eoghan burst out.

Saoirse looked at Linnaeus, wide-eyed, sharing Eoghan's anxiety about what her cousin would do.

"So, what," Linnaeus said, tossing Eoghan a breadstick. "He looks like Donald Trump."

Saoirse, Eoghan, and Linnaeus erupted in giggles again, tears streaming from Saoirse's eyes. Only Hawking remained silent, glaring at them.

They watched the sun set over the distant lake in silence until low lights inside the solarium came on. It was so comfortable, floating in this calm, idly chewing a breadstick. Not alone.

After an undetermined amount of time, her high faded a little. Her body was heavy and her mood felt lower, more somber. She closed her eyes, wondering how it would feel to sleep out here, when her eyes flew open.

She heard it again. The song.

"Sonofabitch, Hawk, stop," Linnaeus yelled.

"I'm sorry," he exclaimed. "I don't even notice I'm doing it."

"What did they do to us?" Saoirse asked suddenly. Her cousins turned to her. "I was so young, I barely remember. My parents wouldn't talk it about it."

"Ours wouldn't either," Linnaeus said.

"Yeah, but you guys were older. Do you remember?"

Linnaeus glanced at Hawking. "I remember."

"I do, too," he said, his eyes round. He stared at Eoghan. "You were the oldest."

"Of course, I remember," Eoghan said shakily.

"That's right," Linnaeus said, putting her tattooed arms around herself. "You had some kind of fit—"

"It was so scary," Saoirse breathed, the sudden image of

Eoghan writhing on the ground hitting her. "I remember that. But the rest... it's all fuzzy. Tell me. I deserve to know."

Eoghan glanced helplessly at Hawking and Linnaeus, far from his usual composed self. Hawking averted his eyes, but then Linnaeus spoke.

"We'll do it. We'll tell you what happened to us that night."

6

Creative magic is called Cruthu and destructive magic is called Scrios. In Scrios magic, there are four magically imbued artifacts called the Deantan.

Seamus Dannan, *Lore: The True History of the Celts*

The adults were laughing and drinking in the kitchen. The children were in bed, exhausted from a day of running around the expansive grounds, hunting for rabbits and chasing the irritable black cat. The storm hadn't begun yet, but the wind howling outside made them feel quite comfortable in their warm beds by contrast.

The door cracked open, light spilling in from the hallway.

"My dears," their grandmother whispered.

The children sat up at once, rubbing their eyes. The grandfather stood behind her, his dark figure framed in the doorway.

"Who's up for a late-night adventure?" their grandmother asked with a mischievous smile.

"Excellent!" the boy twin exclaimed. The grandmother put a finger to her lips.

"Let's keep quiet," she said. "It's our secret adventure."

The children crept after their grandparents in anticipation, taking the servants' stairs down to a door that led outside. Here, their grandparents helped them on with boots and coats.

"Are you ready?" the grandfather asked.

They nodded, their faces pale and eyes round with eagerness.

"Drink this first." His wrinkled hand trembled as he handed them each a small cup with what looked and smelled like the medicine their parents gave them whenever they were sick. "It's a magic potion," he added with a wink.

The children grinned at each other and drank.

"Pull up your hoods," the grandmother said. "It's going to rain."

The children followed their grandparents out the door and onto the lawn. The grandmother's long hair, streaked with blonde and gray, swirled and shimmered as the wind tossed it about. The grandfather held her hand and glanced back at the children with a smile.

Soon, they were far enough that the light from the house no longer illuminated the way. The grass became electric green whenever lightning struck from the dark, churning clouds overhead. The thunder made them jump and the wind whipped at the children, catching them off balance. The children giggled.

They crossed the edge of the meadow into the dark forest.

The grandparents grasped the children's hands and, in a chain, they wove through the trees. The wind no longer blew them about in here, sheltered as they were by the branches overhead. But the sound of it was like a roar. Occasionally, one of the children stumbled over a root or stray branch, but not even a scraped knee could detract from their anticipation.

Sneaking out into the night, away from their parents and into a storm, might have been an activity they were too young to enjoy at that time. But they knew their grandparents, loved and trusted them, and associated every visit to their labyrinthine house with magic and wonder. This night simply promised more of the same.

Soon, they reached what they knew to be their grandmother's favorite tree. She took them there often and studied it while the children climbed over the giant, gnarled, mossy branches. The trees around this one gave it wide berth, and a massive circle of mushrooms lie on the ground before it.

"Okay, my loves," the grandmother said, shouting over the wind that whipped at them in the open clearing. "Step inside the fairy ring. Take care not to tread on the mushrooms."

They did so eagerly. Once they stood inside, no longer traipsing through the forest, the children began to feel light-headed.

The grandparents glanced at each other, and the girl twin noted something off about the way they nodded gravely to one another. Then the grandfather stepped into the circle and pulled something out of his jacket, which he placed in the middle.

It was a gold cup. Tarnished and dented, it had an odd-looking handle: like a horn protruding and arcing upward. The oldest child found it ugly and it made him uncomfortable.

"You kids remember the Song of Carmun?" the grandfather asked over the deafening wind.

The girl twin rolled her eyes. "How could we forget? You make us sing it every night."

The grandfather chuckled. "For good reason. The Song of Carmun is a very special song. Tonight, we will use it to make magic."

The children looked up from the strange cup to their grandfather and grinned.

"Concentrate on the cup before you," he said as he stepped back out of the fairy ring. "And sing."

With more enthusiasm than they had ever sung the song before, the children raised their voices high over the wind.

Tra ghuthaan fasaah agas speraan rotea
Aann aan colteaan uaane agas braantan aard
Aair aisi iis aair adhar agas stada aann aan tiaam
Thas miir aair adh cuiir adh fuiiraach, thas miir
    aair adh cuiir guaa baas.

On the last word, lightning struck somewhere nearby in with a loud crack. The children laughed nervously as they glanced at each other. All of them were quite dizzy now.

"Good," the grandmother spoke as she and the grandfather entered the circle together. "The next part may seem strange—"

The boy twin snorted; stranger than singing to a cup?

"—but we want you to trust us that you are safe. We would never harm you. Do you trust us?"

The children nodded, unsteady on their feet. An odd warmth had settled over their bodies, making them relaxed and compliant. Of course, they trusted their grandparents.

The grandfather bent to pick up the cup by its crescent-shaped handle.

"Gloves off," the grandmother said. While the children did what she asked, she pulled a precision knife from her pocket and flicked out the blade.

"Hold out your hand," she said to the oldest child, whose eyes widened.

"I..."

"Trust me," his grandmother said, using her other hand to brush his cheek.

The boy swallowed and held out his hand.

The blade slashed quickly and expertly. The grandfather was there with the cup to catch the blood that spilled. The child did not register any pain. He simply stared as the stream of dark red dripped off his pale hand.

Around the circle they went, cutting and collecting. When finished, the grandfather swirled the cup, mixing the children's blood together. Then he held it out to the youngest.

"Drink," he said.

With trembling hands, she took the cup. It was warm, almost hot to the touch. She lifted it to her lips and drank the salty liquid.

"Good," he said with a tremulous smile, and moved to the twins, who drank as well.

When he reached the oldest child, he asked, "Why are we doing this?"

The grandfather's eyes were full of sadness.

"It's the only way to keep you safe."

The storm clouds broke and hard rain fell as the oldest child took the cup and drank.

At once, his eyes rolled back in his head and he fell to the ground, shuddering and jerking.

"No," the grandmother shouted, rushing to his side.

The other children cried as they stood helplessly with blood on their hands and lips. The wind and rain lashed against them. In the distance they thought they heard voices shouting their names but they could only stare at their cousin as he shook violently on the ground.

"Seamus, what's happening to him?"

The grandfather's face looked like death as he gaped at the boy.

"Is it a seizure?" she demanded, taking her husband's face in

her hands and forcing him to look at her. "How do we help him? Was this supposed to happen?"

"I—I don't know," he said. "Something went wrong."

"What have you done?" a woman's voice screamed.

The children turned to see their parents running toward them through the woods.

"How dare you do this?" the twins' father roared as he clutched his children to him.

"We had to," the grandmother cried, standing with her hands out. "We told you, we've been trying to convince you—"

"We told you no," the twins' mother shouted, tears streaming down her face. "We don't believe in this insanity."

"Eoghan," the oldest child's father shouted as he sprinted to his side. He was lying still now, staring up at the trees as rain drenched him. "What's wrong with him?"

"They're bleeding," the youngest child's father barked. "And what—" He picked up the cup and tipped it. Dark blood spilled onto the ground. "You—you—"

The other parents looked appalled.

The youngest's father grabbed the grandfather by the shirt.

"You will never touch my child again."

He shoved his own father away and scooped up the child and ran, her mother sobbing behind them.

They got in their car, and the child never saw the other children or the house again.

7

As Scrios is destructive magic, it only grants power to the wielder at a cost.

Seamus Dannan, *Lore: The True History of the Celts*

"Holy shit," Saoirse breathed, the effect of the weed gone now. She shivered inside the blanket she wrapped around her while her cousins talked, each filling in the gaps. As they spoke, her own memories sharpened and her mind was full of them now.

They looked as shaken as she felt.

"You've never talked about this before, have you?" Saoirse asked.

"No," Hawking said. "Never."

"We're such morons," Linnaeus said, putting her head in her hands. "Isn't it obvious what happened? *That* was the protection spell. We've been protected from death since that night."

Eoghan nodded vigorously, having come to the same conclusion.

"Spell?" Hawking said, his eyebrows raised. "We're really talking about magic here?"

"Yeah, dude, get on board," Linnaeus said. "There's magic."

"Why?" Saoirse wondered out loud. "What were they protecting us *from*?"

"The guy who killed everyone?" Eoghan offered.

"They knew our families would be attacked decades before it happened?"

"They said they did it to keep us safe," Linnaeus said. "Maybe they knew there was a threat."

They pondered this for a while. Something else occupied Saoirse.

"I grew up my whole life believing I was abused." She looked up at them, the horror of it settling upon her. "That I was broken by what they did to me. My parents wouldn't even talk about it. They were so upset…"

"Can you blame them?" Hawking said, his arms folded tight over his broad chest. "They drugged us, cut us, and made us drink each other's blood."

"Yeah, sounds pretty fucked up when you put it that way," Linnaeus said. "And what the hell happened to you?" She demanded, turning to Eoghan.

He shrugged, appearing just as baffled. "We never knew. My parents took me to a hospital that night but they couldn't find anything wrong with me and it never happened again."

Saoirse shuddered, seeing Eoghan's wide, staring eyes in her mind.

Eoghan cleared his throat. "It's clear now that the reason we were protected and the rest of our families weren't was because our parents didn't believe them. Like Linnaeus said, Seamus and Melinda must have known a threat was coming, but our parents wouldn't let them help them. Understandably," he added.

"Why did Seamus and Melinda die?" Linnaeus wondered. "If they knew how to perform this—ritual—why didn't they do it for themselves?"

Eoghan shrugged again.

"And my little brother and sister weren't born yet to be protected," Saoirse said, swallowing hard against the sudden, crushing pain.

"Damn," Hawking said, rubbing his forehead. "How old were they?"

"Five." She hung her head, squeezing her eyes shut. Her chest ached. If only her protection had extended to them... she would have done anything to protect them. She would give anything to get them back.

Saoirse didn't realize Linnaeus was kneeling before her until she felt her cousin's thin arms circle around her.

And without meaning to, Saoirse did what she hadn't done before, not even with Betsy. She let herself cry with another person—wracking, anguished sobs. The pain didn't feel the way it did when she was alone. She didn't sink deep into a hole of hopelessness, desperate for escape. She cried, and it hurt like hell, but when she stopped, the hurt was a tiny bit less.

When she pulled away from Linnaeus, her cousin gazed at her with dark eyes filled with tears of her own. They didn't speak. They didn't need to.

The group decided after that to get some rest and resume their search in the morning. Exhaustion made it difficult to heave her duffel bag up to one of the many spare bedrooms, her head pounding from crying and from all the revelations. She showered, more to get the stench of pot off of her than anything else. Once in the bed, which was smaller than the master bed but still grand with its detailed four-poster frame, sleep alluded her.

Who was she now? Not that it mattered, she told herself, but knowing that nothing bad had ever actually happened to her... it changed things. Admittedly, Seamus and Melinda's methods were shady—coaxing them out of the house in the middle of the night and drugging them so they would go along with the ritual. But when she thought about how death had come for her parents and Patrick and Janey with unstoppable force...

It's the only way to keep you safe.

Her grandparents weren't evil people. She didn't blame her parents for thinking so; it must have been terrifying for them. And all the coddling, the constant checking on her to make sure she was okay, treating her as though she was fragile, bailing her out of her own messes... their behavior made sense.

All she could be mad at now was her own behavior. The sports and clubs she'd signed up for and quit mid-season. Romantic relationships she'd begun only to back out before they got too serious. Losing all her scholarships in college because she'd laid in bed instead of attending classes. And worse. Much worse.

How many times had she used this "trauma" as an excuse for being a screwup? Who was she now that she knew that nothing in her was broken, that nothing inside her had ever really held her back?

"Doesn't matter," she mumbled through a yawn. She

noticed the bright yellow eyes of the cat staring back at her from the bedroom doorway.

"Come here, Kian," she called to him. He stayed put. "Suit yourself..." And she let her heavy eyes close.

Saoirse had the best night's sleep she'd gotten in a long time. The sunlight pouring through her bedroom window was beautiful and knowing she wasn't alone in the house was comforting. But the moment she acknowledged these things, her throat knotted up.

It was useless to feel happiness. The shadow of grief would always be there, on its heels, waiting to chase it away.

Becoming buddies with her cousins, finding out why her parents had treated her the way they had... it was all inconsequential.

Her family was still dead.

Whatever she and her cousins had gone through as kids, whatever loss they might bond over now, they were still strangers. There was no future with them.

She repeated this to herself as she made her way downstairs.

The sight of Eoghan with his dorky glasses and bedhead, wearing an apron and making breakfast, immediately broke her resolve to be cold and indifferent.

"Good morning," he said brightly, whisking something in a metal bowl. "Bacon's ready if you're hungry now."

Kian leapt upon a stool set at the kitchen island. He laid a heavy paw on the marble countertop and made a gruff sound.

Eoghan held out a thick slice of bacon to the cat, who took it and hopped down, trotting out of the room.

"He's spry for an old man."

"He's a snob, is what he is. Won't even eat with us. Where did you get all this food from?" Saoirse asked, nibbling on a slice of bacon of her own.

"I went into town early this morning," Eoghan said as he squeezed the juice from an orange into a pitcher.

"Nice of you," she said, trying not to be touched by his act of generosity.

"How are you?" he asked, giving her a penetrating gaze. She'd never been to a therapist before but this was exactly how she imagined one would look at her.

"A bit... overwhelmed."

"I'd imagine. What happened that night was why I eventually went into psychology, you know. The disturbing things we go through as kids affect us later as adults. I think each one of us was greatly affected by it.

"I'm sure each of our parents handled it differently, too," he continued. "Mine, for example, were more distant toward me after that. I don't know if it was the only way they knew to handle their guilt, but they avoided me, like I was... contaminated." He said it thoughtfully.

Saoirse stared at him with a mixture of horror and pity, her bacon quite forgotten. He smiled.

"I learned when I got older that none of that was about me. I imagine your parents were quite protective of you. Perhaps over-protective?"

She was astonished. "How do you know that?"

He turned toward the griddle, pouring pancake batter.

"You seemed embarrassed about your job yesterday. I can tell that you're not satisfied with how your life has turned out. Not proud of any accomplishments, not living with much passion. Am I right?"

Saoirse opened her mouth and closed it, her face warm.

"It's typical of overprotective parents to inadvertently make their children feel like they are incapable of achieving things," he said. "They end up handicapping them, in a way. It's hard to go after what you want in life when deep down you believe something fundamental about yourself is incompetent."

"Only my mom."

He raised an eyebrow.

"My dad was frustrated with me for giving up so much."

"It's also common for parents to take their kids' actions as a reflection of themselves and their parenting."

Saoirse snorted. "He was a motivational speaker."

"Exactly. He probably felt like a hypocrite for not being able to motivate his own daughter. And your mom felt guilty for not protecting you from Seamus and Melinda. They made it about them."

"That sucks," Saoirse said.

"This won't sound very clinical, but people suck."

Saoirse laughed in spite of herself.

"Or at least, people do sucky things when they're in pain," he said.

Saoirse gazed at her cousin. He seemed so wise and put-together. "What are *you* after here?"

"In this conversation?"

"In this house."

He peered at her. "What did *you* come here looking for?"

"I..." His turning around of the question startled her. "Answers. I want to know why they put a spell on us. Who killed my family. And why," she lied.

"As do I. I'm here for closure. So that I can move on."

"To what?" she asked before she could stop herself.

A shadow passed over his calm, composed, kind face. Sadness? "To whatever life has to offer me."

Before she could push him more, Linnaeus and Hawking walked into the kitchen, Linnaeus's hair a nest upon her head and Hawking pulling on a light jacket of hideous neon that reminded her of his truck.

"Pancakes, my man," Hawking said, slapping Eoghan on the back. "You put some protein powder in there?"

"Uh, no. I didn't get protein powder from the store."

"Eh, it's fine," Hawking said, tipping half the bacon onto his plate. "I prefer turkey bacon, but when in Rome. I can't believe it—this whole place and no home gym." He yawned. "Yeah, I was up late talking to Davie, she's getting antsy that I'm still here. My lady needs her man."

"It's too early for this," Linnaeus muttered. "Coffee?"

"Fresh-squeezed orange juice," Eoghan said. "Much better for you."

"That's debatable."

Eoghan joined them with a giant stack of pancakes. He winced when he leaned back in his chair.

"Bad back," he explained. "It's why I can't work out and look like you, Hawking. Maybe I'd have more luck with the ladies if I could."

No one spoke. Saoirse sensed sadness again in his self-deprecation.

"Anyway, what's the plan today?" He automatically looked at Linnaeus.

"I say one of us finishes up in the study, keep searching through the books," Linnaeus replied. "The rest of us can spread out in all the bedrooms, the attic, the garages, maybe someone brave wants to go in the crawlspace…"

"Hard pass," Saoirse said through a mouthful of pancake (which was quite good).

"Same," Hawking said. Linnaeus stared at him. "What? I don't want spiders and shit all over me."

His sister rolled her eyes. "Hopefully we find whatever it is the key unlocks before we have to go that route. But if we do, your ass is going in there. I don't care if it messes up your hair."

After a quick breakfast, they split up. Hawking offered to finish the study. Eoghan took the expansive garage while Saoirse began in the bedrooms. Linnaeus said she wanted to check the hallways, whatever that meant.

Saoirse had searched three of the bedrooms (finding nothing more than empty nightstands, closets, and dresser drawers) when Linnaeus shouted.

"Hey!"

Saoirse tore from the room and sprinted to the other wing. She found Linnaeus at the end of the hall, crouching on the floor before an old wardrobe.

"I might have found something," she said, her hair somehow even more frizzed and wild than before. She had pulled all the old coats and flung them over the hallway floor. Her phone flashlight pointed at something carved into the wooden bottom of the wardrobe. "It might be the manufacturer's symbol, but..."

Saoirse knelt down and peered at the shape. Her eyes widened.

"Hold on."

She left Linnaeus and sprinted back to the other wing. After grabbing one of the framed pictures from the wall of Seamus and Melinda's bedroom, she ran back.

Linnaeus gasped when she saw the picture of the three-armed spiral, exactly matching the image carved into the wood of the wardrobe.

"It was in their bedroom," Saoirse panted.

"So, it has to mean something," Linnaeus said. She took the picture and flipped it over. "*Triskelion: Forward Motion.*"

Forward motion... forward. Saoirse assumed that was a title, but... She stepped into the wardrobe and pressed against the back-wall panel.

It was a clue.

The wall gave way, so easily that Saoirse stumbled.

She turned back to Linnaeus, whose eyes were as wide as her own. Her cousin climbed into the wardrobe with her and together they stepped through the open panel.

"This is some C.S. Lewis shit," Linnaeus whispered. She held her phone flashlight up to show a lone flight of stairs.

"Let's get the guys," Saoirse said.

"Fuck that," Linnaeus replied and ascended the steps. They reached a heavy, wooden door at the top. Linnaeus tried the doorknob. Locked.

"This is what the key is for," Saoirse breathed.

Linnaeus sighed. "Well, now I guess we have to get the guys."

"Why?"

"Because Hawk has the key."

Moments later, they found Hawking sitting in the armchair of the study reading *The Passionate Marriage*. It took a few tries to get his attention.

"Oh—" he dropped the book and tried to shove it under the armchair with his foot. "Hi. Just taking a break. Did you find any—"

"Give me the key," Linnaeus demanded.

"Why?"

"Because we found it." Saoirse grinned.

He jumped up. "Let me get Eoghan—"

But Eoghan was there. "I came to check on everyone; did you say you found something?"

"Only a hidden passageway leading to a locked door," Linnaeus said offhandedly.

The group hurried back to the wardrobe.

"You find anything in the garage?" Hawking asked Eoghan.

"An arsenal of weapons."

Saoirse raised her eyebrows. "Like, guns?"

"No, a ton of swords and knives and stuff. Super old-looking. I had no idea Seamus collected them."

"No wonder we weren't allowed in there as kids," Linnaeus said. They made it to the staircase. Kian appeared, leaping up the steps behind them. Hawking fumbled with the key and Saoirse felt like her heart might burst if he didn't hurry up. He slid the key into the lock and turned it.

Sunshine fell from a tall window at the end of a long, triangular room made of wood so light it looked golden. At the end stood a large desk beneath a window, a bookshelf of identical black books, and a painting portraying green splotches that appeared to be abstract leaves.

Upon the desk sat an old computer and next to it, a pad of white paper.

Saoirse dashed across the beautiful room, hardly aware of the others. There were so many things to search and explore, but as she got closer to the pad of paper lying there, she could see that there was writing on it.

Her stomach dropped.

"Well, that's fucking perfect," Linnaeus said.

The writing on the paper—while in the same handwriting Saoirse recognized from Seamus's letter—was in another language.

"Someone look this up," Linnaeus snapped. Saoirse glanced at her cousins. Eoghan was already on his phone, the sunlight glinting in the thin golden frame of his glasses.

"Well?" Linnaeus said.

"No, I'm not—it's a client," Eoghan replied, looking pale and exhausted.

"*Now?*" Linnaeus demanded.

Eoghan stopped texting. "I'm done."

"It's okay, I've got it," Saoirse said. She pulled out her cell phone and entered a random word she saw: *Etliáhbás*.

"Nothing," she said. She tried a few more words with no results. "It's not a known language."

"But there are accent marks," Hawking said, pointing at the writing. "It's got to be Irish Gaelic written in code. The accents lean forward, not backward like in Scottish Gaelic."

Everyone stared at him.

"What? We're Irish, at least on Seamus's side, and we know he studied Gaelic, and Irish has those kinds of accent marks—"

Linnaeus gaped at her brother while Eoghan smiled, impressed.

"And you think it's written in a code? What code?"

Hawking ruffled his already carefully disheveled hair for a moment. "Let's look around the room, see if there are any clues of what it could be."

Since it seemed like as good a plan as any, Saoirse went to the computer. It didn't just look old, it looked *crude*, like someone had cobbled it together themselves. The monitor was a simple cube and, on the desk before it, was an odd sort of mouse—a flat black pad split into five sections. She felt all around the monitor and touched the black pad but was unable to turn it on.

"Ugh," Linnaeus exclaimed. She held a wooden box from the bookshelf. Inside was a glass case, and inside of that...

"Is that human hair?" Eoghan asked, fascinated.

A chunk of thick, black hair laid inside. Saoirse couldn't think who it could belong to; no one in the family had black hair (Linnaeus's was dyed).

Kian mewled as Linnaeus placed it back on the shelf, revolted.

"Any luck with the computer?" Eoghan asked Saoirse.

She shook her head. "What about those? Journals?"

"Yeah, but they're all blank."

"What the fuck was Seamus playing at?" Linnaeus said. "What about you, Hawk... Hawk?"

Hawking stared at the abstract painting of the leaves. Linnaeus walloped him on the shoulder.

"Ow, stop, I'm trying to focus."

"On what?"

But as Saoirse peered at the painting as well, she comprehended the logic to it. It wasn't only a random smattering of green leaves. Though not perfectly straight, in essence it was two lines of five leaves each in different sizes. On the first row of leaves, each leaf was slightly larger than the last, although almost imperceptibly so. On the second, the leaves descended from largest to smallest. This second row, however, jutted out past the first row, because it was indented by three leaves under the first row.

"There's something familiar about this," Hawking said.

"Like you've seen it before?" Linnaeus asked.

"No, but..."

"Flip it over," Saoirse said.

Hawking did so at once, and showed the group three words scrawled on the back.

Veni, Vidi, Vici.

"I came, I saw, I conquered," Eoghan said, leaning over Saoirse's shoulder. "Julius Caesar."

Hawking whipped out his phone. "Ha! I remember this from high school Latin."

He showed them where he had Googled *Julius Caesar code*. The search results all showed the same thing: The Caesar Cipher.

"Caesar invented a code? Interesting," Eoghan said. But Hawking was already at the desk, scribbling the alphabet on a fresh sheet of paper and then a second alphabet underneath it, indenting it by three letters. He drew lines connecting the A of the second line to the letter D on the first line and continued with the remaining letters of the two alphabets. Then he translated, turning back and forth from the encrypted paper to his.

"Linny, take my phone and use my translation app. I downloaded it when I went with Davie to Thailand for her shoot with elephants."

Linnaeus, bewildered, picked up Hawking's phone. Saoirse and Eoghan watched the twins, equally bemused.

"It's—no, it's not—it's still nothing."

"Let me see," Hawking said. He stared at his phone and frowned again. "Something's not right."

He lifted his gaze once more to the painting of leaves and Saoirse followed. Understanding hit both of them at the same time.

"It's backward," she said.

"The Caesar Cipher in reverse." Hawking crossed out his two alphabets and started over on a new sheet of paper. He wrote out the first alphabet, but the second indented one he began at Z.

"Here we go," he said as he started his rapid decoding again. Linnaeus typed in the words he created.

"Yes, yes, it's working."

Saoirse and Eoghan continued watching the twins work, Eoghan occasionally texting on his phone. She had to admire her cousin's dedication to his work and felt jealous. Maybe if she had something she loved to do, something where others depended on her, she would be able to accept her tragedy and move on. Get closure, like Eoghan had said.

But she didn't.

"What is it saying?" she asked Linnaeus to distract herself from this depressing thought.

"I don't know," Linnaeus said. "I'm working as fast as I can, I'm not really paying attention."

Saoirse stayed quiet, letting the brother and sister work. After what felt like eternity, Hawking stopped writing and looked up at Linnaeus. She entered the last word.

"It's ready."

They gathered around her and read.

My dear grandchildren,

I write this letter to you with tears in my eyes—tears of pride, knowing that your brilliant minds have undoubtedly worked out my clues, and tears of grief for the losses you've suffered. All I can hope to offer you now is an explanation of our actions.

Many years ago, your grandmother and I became aware of a serious danger to our family. We tried to convince your parents of this threat and of the solution to protecting them from it, but they didn't believe us. Finally, we decided we had to protect any of you that we could.

The magic we used to safeguard you from harm always asks a price. In this case, we could not take the same protection for ourselves if we administered it to you. This was, of course, a sacrifice that we were happy to make. However, the greatest loss was that it destroyed our relationships with our own children and ruined any hope we had of seeing you grow up. It also meant we could not protect any future children born into our family. We knew, though, that you four would be safe, and that was the best we could do.

As of writing this letter, we have been made aware that the time has come. We will die. Your families will die. And you will survive.

Those who are responsible for your parents' and siblings' deaths are cunning and vicious. Due to its own magic, this estate cannot be penetrated by anyone but those to whom it belongs and anyone they invite. However, these people appear to have an advantage we didn't anticipate. We know they will find us here, and we have taken great precautions to hide the things of value these evil people seek to take possession of.

Because they cannot harm you, you are free to live your lives in safety and peace.

We do not ask your forgiveness. We only ask

that you leave this place and find happiness. Create your own families. Enjoy the gift of life that has always been rightfully yours.

 Love,
 Granda and Nana

8

The ancient Druids, also known as the Fomorians, were followers of Balor of the Evil Eye and the original wielders of Scrios magic. However, evidence suggests that Balor was not their true master.

Seamus Dannan, *Lore: The True History of the Celts*

"No. No, this can't be it," Linnaeus said. Saoirse heard her own despair in her cousin's voice.

"Dammit," Hawking said, running a hand through his hair.

Saoirse didn't realize she had stepped away from the group until her back hit the slanted wall. Linnaeus flipped the original letter over, searched through the rest of the pad of paper. Hawking went back to the bookshelf, pulling out all the blank journals. Eoghan tried to turn the computer on. Each action was more frantic than the last, and none yielded results.

It was over. The excitement of the past two days, the

sense of purpose, of comradery, all washed away, leaving nothing.

No—*nothing* had been what Saoirse sought. *Nothing* was to be the reprieve from what actually lie before her.

Relentless and unending pain.

She sank to the floor. Kian slinked toward her and uncharacteristically bunted his body against her side with a light trill. She turned away from the cat.

After a few minutes, all the sounds of shuffling and searching ceased. Hawking sat on the floor across the room, in front of the bookshelf, his head in his hands. Linnaeus was slumped on the desk. Eoghan stood, his face pale.

"On the bright side," he said, his hands shoved into the pockets of his khaki pants, "we know we're safe."

"We can't die, but these people could be back anytime," Hawking countered.

"Why would they?" Linnaeus said. "They got what they came for."

"But Seamus said something about 'things of value.'"

"They probably already found them."

"But these people—"

"What fucking people?" Linnaeus said. "He didn't explain *anything*. How did they find out there was a threat in the first place? Where did fucking magic come from?"

There was silence as everyone appeared to ponder this except for Saoirse. Her mind was numb and muddled.

Eoghan took a deep breath.

"Look, Linnaeus is right. Seamus didn't really explain anything. The answers we wanted died with him. Maybe we should try to move on."

His words hung in the air.

"But if I may make a suggestion," he continued, "what would everyone think of staying one more night?"

He looked so earnest and young standing there with his hands in his pockets, his eyes magnified by his glasses. It didn't feel like a psychological recommendation, but a personal request. Saoirse wondered not for the first time if Eoghan was lonely. Especially spending most of his days in the company of people in various stages of psychosis.

"I've just enjoyed getting to know you all again," he finished awkwardly.

"Yeah, man," Hawking said at once. "Definitely."

"You sure? I thought Davie needs you back," Linnaeus said with bitterness.

Saoirse expected Hawking to fire back at her. But instead he gazed at his sister with such softness that Saoirse's heart ached. She could tell from the start that the twins hadn't seen each other much. But in that moment, she knew that Hawking regretted it.

"Fine," Linnaeus said. "Not much else to do."

Hawking stood. "Let's look around the grounds. Say goodbye to the place."

Linnaeus rose too and reached out her hand to Saoirse.

"Come on."

The four cousins traipsed down the sloping lawn toward the forest, Hawking in the lead. They took the same route, Saoirse recognized, that they had on the night of the ritual. It couldn't feel more different now, however: the sun warmed them from a cloudless sky as a pleasant breeze rustled the leaves of the barely changing leaves.

"You probably don't remember," Linnaeus said to Saoirse, swinging her thin arms as they walked. "But when we were little, I used to talk you into climbing so high in the trees that you couldn't get back down, and then I'd ditch you."

"That's right," Eoghan said. "And we would hear you screaming and have to help you down."

"I think I remember that," Saoirse said with a small chuckle. Sorrow pounding inside her, she thought of Patrick. How would she endure this? Would she live forever with no escape from it?

"Sorry I was a shithead," Linnaeus said.

"It's okay." They passed beyond the tree line. Sunlight filtered through the branches, making the forest dim and cool compared to the field they'd left. What Saoirse noticed the most was the change in sounds. The forest was full of chirps and rustling, like they'd entered a new world.

Hawking turned back to everyone and grinned. "Let's do it again."

"Do what?" Saoirse asked.

"Climb trees. Come on, how long has it been since you've climbed a tree?"

Saoirse and Eoghan glanced at each other.

"What did you guys have in mind to do, wallow?" Linnaeus sided with her brother. "We have the rest of our lives to do that. We're here now; let's climb a fucking tree."

Saoirse didn't need to ask where Hawking was leading them; if they were going to climb a tree, why not *the* tree?

Her breath caught when she saw it. All live oaks were beautiful, but this one... it was even more majestic than it was when she was a kid. Unlike the mansion, it was larger instead of smaller while viewed in her adult body. The trunk was taller than most but the branches were its most beautiful and unique feature. Enormous, gnarled, and covered in soft green moss, they spread from the trunk in a magnificent arch, from hanging low to the ground to reaching high above it. The leaves were still brilliant green, and Saoirse knew they would stay that way as long into the cold months as possible.

Before the tree, even wider in circumference after all these years, lie the mushroom ring.

"Kinda feel like an ass, not realizing all this shit was magical; I mean, look at it," Linnaeus said.

"Too bad it can't help us now," Saoirse said.

"Yeah, turns out it's all pretty useless, isn't it?" Hawking said as he stepped respectfully around the fat blossom mushrooms and climbed onto one of the low-hanging branches. Eoghan followed and Linnaeus went around to the other side of the tree.

"You better not start humming that fucking Carmun song again," she said.

"Yeah, yeah."

Saoirse followed her cousin, picking her own branch. Swaying on the slippery moss, she made her way up the branch toward the trunk.

Quick movement in the tree to her left made her head snap up. She thought of bears, but it was Kian, leaping up the tree on the other side of the trunk near the men. For some reason, this made her laugh.

"What?" Linnaeus asked, several branches above her.

"Kian," Saoirse giggled.

"I don't know how that old bag of bones can even climb up the porch steps, let alone up a whole tree," Linnaeus said, which made Saoirse laugh even harder. Was this actually funny, or was she on the brink of hysteria?

Did it matter?

She climbed to where Linnaeus chose a seat close to the top of the trunk where the high branches spread. Hawking and Eoghan sat on their own branches a bit higher than them, swinging their legs.

"Hey, you didn't get stuck this time," Hawking said, looking down at Saoirse.

"Not yet."

"We're all grown up," Eoghan said.

Silence fell.

"This tree really is amazing," Linnaeus said after a while. She picked up a small, smooth, white branch that was nestled at the top of the trunk and studied it.

With a growl, Kian appeared and took the branch from Linnaeus's hand in his mouth. He placed it gently back down on the trunk before settling there, like he was guarding it.

Hawking laughed. "I guess it belongs to him."

"Crusty old bastard," Linnaeus said to the cat, who closed his eyes.

Saoirse tried to let this moment distract her, tried to focus on what she heard and smelled and felt and saw. How the branch underneath her was so wide that it was comfortable to sit upon. The way the air chilled her skin. The scent of damp moss and leaves. After a while, she noticed the men speaking in low voices. Then they climbed down.

"We're headed back to the house," Eoghan said. "See you guys in a bit."

Saoirse turned to Linnaeus.

"I'm happy to stay here," her cousin replied. "It's nice." Linnaeus tilted her head back. She wore no makeup now, and Saoirse reflected that her cousin was more beautiful barefaced. Saoirse doubted Linnaeus knew.

When Hawking and Eoghan disappeared in the dark trees, Linnaeus spoke again. "When I was little, I always imagined that when I grew up I would bring my own kids here." She snorted. "What a nightmare. Me as a mother."

Saoirse knew what she meant. "Do you think you'll ever come back here?"

"I don't know," Linnaeus said. "I don't know where to go... now."

Neither woman spoke, and then Linnaeus said, "I found them."

"Your parents?"

Linnaeus nodded. "I was at the hospital and they'd just brought me home. I'd become something of a regular in the psych ward." She held out her pale forearm, showing the slashes there. "I remember that day my mom begging me to tell her what was wrong, how could she help. Why did this keep happening... I didn't know what to tell her. I had no answer. I felt like such a piece of shit, always scaring them and worrying them. Well, at least they had Hawk. He'd never had any issues: did well in school, popular, super successful in his career. My mom's only worry was that he was never going to settle down and get married. I got pissed and I left. And then when I got back..."

Saoirse couldn't speak.

"Why wouldn't he let us go after them?" Linnaeus asked, tears glittering in her eyes. "Granda. He must have known we would want revenge. 'Move on,' 'enjoy the gift of life.' Fucker," she added.

"He wanted us safe," Saoirse said lamely.

"He wanted his little grandchildren safe," Linnaeus said. "He didn't even pause to consider what we, as adults, would want. He made the choice for us."

Revenge. Of everything that went through Saoirse's mind after reading the letter, this was one that hadn't occurred to her. A new feeling rose in her gut. An active, scorching, energetic feeling. Rage. Hatred. A sudden need for violence.

But the sensation faded almost as quickly as it had come. Seamus was careful not to leave so much as a hint of who these people were. He implied the existence of other magic and mentioned those 'things of value' in the mansion —like the cup? But what did any of it matter if he kept his secrets locked as tightly away from his own progeny as he did his enemies?

The two women stayed in the tree until the sunlight faded before returning to the house. A mouth-watering aroma greeted them and Saoirse was astonished to see a sumptuous spread of food on the kitchen table: juicy steaks, fat lobster tails, crab legs (which she had never tried in her life), steaming bread, mashed potatoes, a large, crisp salad, and three bottles of wine.

"Did—did you—" Saoirse stammered, turning to Eoghan.

"It was all Hawking. He picked it up from a restaurant in town."

"My treat," the brawny, neon-clothed man said, grinning. "Come, let's eat."

They sat down and dug into the lavish meal. Saoirse bit into a springy slice of hot bread and groaned. How could just the bread be so good?

"This is generous of you, considering we're all absurdly wealthy now," Linnaeus said.

"I had to drive all the way to get it and now my truck smells like lobster," Hawking said, stung.

"Well. Thanks," Linnaeus said, ferreting through a crab leg. "So, anyone want to take anything from this place?"

Saoirse remembered the necklace, felt its metal weight against her chest. She didn't know why she still wore it. But for some reason, she didn't say anything.

Hawking shook his head. "Yeah, not really my style."

"I'm sure you'll be taking a certain book with you," Eoghan said innocently as he helped himself to the mashed potatoes.

Hawking glared at him while Linnaeus howled with laughter.

"So," Eoghan said when Linnaeus had calmed down. "What's everyone going to do now?"

Saoirse had been dreading this question, but Hawking spoke first.

"Surprise Davie in Baku," he said through a mouthful of steak.

"Is she good for you?" Linnaeus asked.

Hawking grinned. "Is my sister suddenly protective of me?"

"No, I've just never even met her."

"Yeah, well, how would you have? You never answer my calls," Hawking said.

Saoirse and Eoghan glanced at each other and Saoirse went back to concentrating on getting the meat out of her mystifying crab leg.

Linnaeus opened her mouth and closed it.

"Come to Baku with me," Hawking said with a smile. "It will blow your mind. We'll rent a yacht, sail the Caspian Sea."

To Saoirse's shock, the corner of Linnaeus's mouth twitched.

"Maybe."

"Well, this deserves a toast," Eoghan said cheerfully.

As he poured everyone wine, Saoirse stopped fiddling with her crab leg, her appetite gone. Eoghan had his life's work; Linnaeus and Hawking now had each other, it seemed. And she had nothing. She let the weight of that thought pull her down until she felt like she could sink through her chair. She remained quiet the rest of dinner.

Foregoing the chocolate mousse Hawking offered for dessert, she told her cousins she needed to go to bed so she could leave early the next morning.

"We'll all be up to say goodbye," Eoghan assured her. She tried to smile, and then made her way heavily upstairs.

Saoirse didn't shower or change or pack. She didn't even brush her teeth. She climbed under the bed covers and tried not to think.

A thump on the bed made her stifle a scream. The large black cat circled around in small steps before nestling himself in the covers at the foot of her bed.

Saoirse gazed at him for a while. "You're probably sad that you'll be alone again soon."

That cat huffed like he was resigned to his fate.

"You must not be long for this world, though," she said. "Probably kick the bucket sooner rather than later."

He peered at her with one yellow eye.

"Lucky," she said, and turned over.

She had just fallen asleep when a sound made her jump.

It was Kian, standing in the doorway, facing the hall. His back was arched and high-pitched growls rumbled from his body.

"What's up?" she said, rubbing her eyes.

He yowled louder, his fur raised.

Saoirse got out of bed groggily and tried to step past him to see what he was looking at, but he hissed and swiped out at her leg with one of his claws.

"Dammit—calm down, you lunatic—"

But then a strange sound came from down the hall. She pushed her bedroom door open wider and peered out.

The hallway was empty.

She heard a muffled thump.

"Hey, is everyone okay?"

Two dark shapes came stumbling out of the bedroom near the stairs. One dragged the other, who was fighting to get free.

The blood drained from her body. It was a strange man in dark clothing with a tattoo on his forehead and Hawking, still in his neon jacket.

The stranger wrestling with Hawking caught sight of her.

"Get her," he shouted.

Saoirse lost her head completely. She screamed and stumbled the opposite way down the hall, which was a dead-end.

The servants' stairs.

Wrenching open the door, which was narrower and plainer than the bedroom doors, she hurtled down the steps.

"Oh shit, oh shit, oh shit."

She tripped and fell the last few, landing on her knees.

"Ow, fuck."

Still panicking, she scrambled to her feet and flung open the porch door, running into the night.

Her knees were in agony and she could barely run. Where she was going to go? And why didn't the protective magic shield her poor knees?

This thought made her stagger to a stop in the wet grass.

She was protected from death, right? So why was she running? But then she supposed that people could cause her *pain* if they wanted to... could do *other* things to her... she blanched and made to start running again.

She was too late; stopping had cost her. In her periphery,

a dark shape raced toward her. The man slammed into her, knocking the wind out of her.

He grabbed her roughly off the ground. She pushed and struggled against him, one of her flailing fists making contact somewhere on his body. He gripped her tighter.

Saoirse stopped fighting. She fell limp, letting the man haul her over his shoulder and back up to the house. As she hung helplessly, she noted that they were going past the grand staircase to the opposite wing. He strode purposefully toward the open wardrobe, through the false panel, and up the hidden staircase—

The lights were on in the triangular room, making it look more golden than ever. The man dumped her on the floor. She pushed her hair back and found herself against one of the slanting walls next to Hawking and Eoghan. They gazed at her with a mixture of relief and alarm.

Three men dressed in black stood sentinel on the opposite side of the room. They were enormous, reminding Saoirse of pictures she'd seen of Navy Seals.

But what startled her most was the tattoo of a large eye across each man's forehead.

"Who are you?" Hawking asked, his voice hoarse. "What do you want from us?"

They said nothing.

Shouts and thuds came from the staircase.

"*Fuck you*—get—the *fuck*—off me—" And a man carrying Linnaeus stumbled through the doorway as she fought him like a feral cat.

"Got a feisty one," the man grinned at his fellows as he turned her around and slammed her back to his chest, pinning her arms. She attempted to head-butt him but he was too tall. Then she placed a well-aimed backward kick to his groin.

"Fuck—" the man said as he hunched over and let go of her.

"Enjoy, motherfucker," she spat as she joined her cousins against the wall.

Saoirse heard sharp footsteps coming up the stairs.

A woman of stunning beauty came into view, followed by another large man. She was tall, with sleek black hair and fair skin. Her skin-tight clothing showed off her slender body, her movements lithe and sensual as she strode forward. She, too, had a tattoo of an eye on her forehead, though her dark waves partially obscured it.

Then, as she gazed at Saoirse and her cousins, a smile spread across the woman's face; a smile so wide and predatory that it distorted her beauty and caused chills to crawl up Saoirse's spine.

"*Tua-day-danahn*," the woman said softly.

She walked to the desk and picked up the coded letter as well as the decoded one in Irish. This made her smile wider. She moved to the pile of blank journals on the floor and stooped to pick one up.

"I'm guessing none of you figured out the invisible ink?" she said. Then she jerked her head toward her men. "Figure out how to read these, the incantation is likely in there."

The woman turned back to Saoirse and her cousins. She walked slowly, her heels clicking and her hips swaying, and paused in front of Linnaeus. Then she moved to Saoirse. She had the darkest eyes Saoirse had ever seen, almost black, with thick eyelashes and perfectly arched eyebrows. She smirked at Saoirse, then moved on to Hawking.

Here, she paused longer. In her heels, she was almost as tall as him. Her eyes roamed up and down his body.

"I like this one," she purred. The men behind her chuckled. She put her hands on either side of the wall behind

Hawking and arched up on her toes. She pressed her body against his and the violation made Saoirse sick. Hawking shuddered as the woman slowly licked the sweat that trickled down the side of his face.

Hawking's eyes burned, his fists clenched with fury.

"Yes," the woman breathed. "You will be fun to play with..." She trailed a long finger down his chest, his stomach, and lower.

"Don't you fucking touch him, you cunt!"

Linnaeus held Saoirse's father's gun pointed at the woman.

Saoirse knew something was wrong the moment she saw a flash of silver in the woman's hand and no hum of energy filled the room.

The long blade swung through the air.

And sliced across Linnaeus's throat.

Hawking's howl of agony filled the room. Blood poured from the wound in Linnaeus's neck as she fell.

Hawking dropped to his sister. He cradled her head and pressed his hand to her neck. Blood drenched him as she gurgled and twitched.

"No, Linny, no," he sobbed as she stared into his eyes. "I'm so sorry. I'm so sorry."

Linnaeus continued to look at him as the minutes passed like seconds, until her eyes dimmed completely.

"Heartbreaking," the woman said. "Dispose of the body."

A man stepped forward to kick Hawking out of the way and take Linnaeus away. That too-wide, vulturine smile spread across the woman's face as she watched, the dagger dripping with blood. Hot rage flashed through Saoirse as she glared up at her.

"Another family member lost. I'm doing quite a good job of ridding the world of the Dannan family line, aren't I?"

Saoirse stared at her. This woman... this *bitch*... killed her parents... Patrick and Janey...

Vicious growls came the doorway. Saoirse whipped around.

Kian.

The woman's eyes widened at the sight of the cat. "*Cot-she*," she said, looking both shocked and delighted. "Seize him!"

Another man lunged forward and grabbed Kian, who screeched and fought with all his might. The woman wiped the dagger and sheathed it at her side.

"The King of Cats comes with me," she said, leering at Kian. "The other Deantan are here; the old fool says as much. His letter could be a decoy; surely, he's told his grandchildren more. Torture them until you find the artifacts, then kill them. Do it quickly; you must get back in time for the Beheading Game."

"Yes, Niamh," the largest and most brutal of the men said.

Niamh sauntered to the door and glanced back. Her black eyes locked on Saoirse's. "You should know, the magic your grandparents cast was binding to the four of you. Now that one of you is dead, the rest of you are mortal once more."

And she left the room, followed by the man holding Kian. The cat looked back at Saoirse with wide, yellow eyes, and was gone.

PART II

When the self-imposed prison walls in the mind of the magician finally fall, she becomes a wanderer in a world of great and mysterious possibility.

The writings of Seamus Dannan

9

The Deantan are comprised of four objects or artifacts: the Coire, the Tanist Stone, the Silver Bough, and the dagger Spellbreaker.

Seamus Dannan, *Lore: The True History of the Celts*

Saoirse didn't fight the man who took her from the triangular room and down the secret staircase. Eoghan plodding docilly in front of her. Hawking wept behind her.

She was in a daze; she knew she was in shock. The image of Linnaeus and the blood gushing from her throat replayed in her mind, mingled with images of her parents and Patrick and Janey. She was hollow inside. Linnaeus, so brave, so real. Cut down like she was made of paper, like she had never been real at all.

Saoirse was too numb to fear Niamh's command for the men to torture them. But deeper in her mind festered both an acknowledgment and a question.

Mortal once more.

The men brought them down to a place she had yet to visit in the house: one of the other kitchens. Whether it was the caterer's kitchen or the other, she didn't know. It was rougher and less refined, with industrial-looking appliances and a concrete floor.

The man who took Linnaeus's body joined them. Saoirse wondered what he had done with it.

Hawking had stopped crying. He now glared at the men through red eyes. Eoghan was on his other side, staring at the ground.

The largest of the three men searched the drawers in the kitchen until he held up a pair of plyers.

"Who's first?" he asked with a sick smile that reminded Saoirse of Niamh.

"We don't know anything," Hawking spat. "We don't know what that bitch was talking about."

The man with the plyers took three long strides toward Hawking and struck him across the face.

One of the other men sneered. "I think you have your volunteer."

"I think you're right," said the leader. "Hold him down."

Saoirse stared in horror as the two men behind him grabbed a chair from the table and forced Hawking into it. He struggled but these men were even larger than he was.

Hawking panted as sweat poured down his face, his entire front stained with his sister's blood. The leader knelt down before him and held out the plyers.

"We have no need for the cup. Where are the stone and the bough?"

A curious look passed across Hawking's face—recognition? The man must have seen it, too, for his leer grew wider.

He attached the plyers to the nail of Hawking's left pointer finger.

"You know. Tell me."

"I don't—I don't know—"

Saoirse shut her eyes just in time, but she couldn't block out Hawking's scream of agony. When he stopped, she opened her eyes. Blood streamed from his finger where his nail had been.

"Let's try that again. Where are the stone and the bough?"

"I told you, we don't know. Seamus didn't want us to know—" His words turned to another scream as the leader yanked on the next finger.

"And the Incantation," another man spoke behind them. "The old man probably told them about it. Can't do nothing with the Deantan without it."

"We don't have much time," the man next to him said. "Have to get back for the ceremony."

"He's right," the leader said to Hawking. "The artifacts are useless without the spell and you know that. Tell me."

Blood dripped from Hawking's hand. His face was pale and his whole body shook in anticipation of more pain. Saoirse couldn't stand it anymore. None of them knew what Niamh and her men were talking about, let alone where the things were.

But they could pretend to.

"Hawking."

"Shut up, Saoirse," he said, giving her a warning look.

"Ah," the leader said as he cocked his head at her and then back to Hawking. "You care for your little cousin. I see. This might be much more effective."

The giant man dropped the plyers and pulled her backwards against his chest. She heard the unsheathing of a knife. The blade was cold against her throat.

"No," Hawking said hoarsely.

"Yes. Tell me now, or I'll kill her."

Mortal once more.

Wasn't this what she came for? This man offered her oblivion. She only needed to press her throat to the knife, maybe put up a false struggle, and she would fade from this world as swiftly as Linnaeus.

Linnaeus.

She gazed at Hawking's pale face, at the agony in his eyes. He was about to lose someone else. And instead of longing for oblivion, Saoirse felt rage.

Not yet. Not like this.

She widened her eyes at Hawking.

Understanding passed over his face. If she'd learned one thing about him, it was that he was smart.

"I'll tell you. Just don't hurt her."

The man chuckled, the sound rumbling against Saoirse's back. "There we go. All it takes is finding a man's weak spot. Hurry, before I lose my patience."

"Seamus did leave us more information. We burned it after we read it, like he told us to. He said all three of the Deantan are hidden in the middle of the lake. He said not to seek them unless we absolutely had to. And he also said the Incantation is in the journals but we didn't figure out how to decode them in time."

The man's grip on her slackened.

"Was that so hard?"

Hawking glared at him in response.

The leader shoved Saoirse toward the others. "Lock them up. One of you stand guard. The other, meet me at the dock. Anthony should be working on decoding the journals as we speak." He paused and turned again to Hawking. "If you've lied to me, she will die very slowly while you watch." He left the room.

The men grabbed Saoirse and Eoghan and marched them up to the main floor and back up the stairs. They didn't stop until they reached a bedroom on the third floor and shoved the three of them inside. The man who had cut Hawking free now stood in the doorway, brandishing his knife.

"I'll be right outside, shitheads." He slammed the door.

Saoirse at once took Hawking to the adjoining bathroom. She turned on the faucet and told him to hold his fingers under the stream of water.

"That was quick thinking," she said as she tore a washcloth into strips.

"Hopefully it'll keep them occupied for a while," he said, wincing as she wrapped a strip of cloth around each of his fingers. "Give us a chance to figure out how to get the fuck out of here." When she was finished, he bent over the faucet and drank.

There was only a small window above the tub in the bathroom. The bedroom itself was windowless and bare besides the lamps on the nightstands. Eoghan sat on the bed, still staring at the floor.

"Are you okay?" she said, putting a hand on his shoulder.

He jumped. "I..." He looked haunted. For all his expertise in helping others with their traumas, Eoghan seemed just as fragile as she was, maybe more so.

"It's going to be okay," she said, even though she saw no possible way to escape from this room.

"Well," Hawking said, coming in from the bathroom. "You heard that woman. They're going to kill us anyway, even if we did know where the Deantan are. Finish the job she started with everyone else."

Saoirse trembled with fury. Niamh. Her family's killer, via one of her henchmen. She was the one who coordinated it all.

"How did she have Melinda and Seamus killed?" Saoirse said, trying to contain herself. "I thought Granda said they couldn't get in the house."

"Obviously, they found a way. Some advantage like Seamus said," he said, settling himself on the floor. He looked so different now—bloodstained and beat up, his hair a true mess instead of a carefully constructed one, no longer posing and preening. "The Cult of Balor," he murmured.

"What?"

Hawking stared absently and motioned to his own forehead. "That eye thing they have, that's Balor's symbol. He was supposedly half-demon, half-man, and had one eye in the middle of his face. It makes sense."

"What makes sense?"

"There were things Niamh—" he said her name bitterly, "said. Tuatha dé Danann, Cait Sídhe. The second one sounds familiar. I can't remember why. But the Tuatha dé Danann—she called us that. If she meant what I think she did…"

"You're not making any sense," Saoirse said, feeling more desperate with each moment. "Hawking, what the hell are we going to *do*?"

"I don't know. I wish Seamus *had* told us where the Deantan are. Then we could use them."

"Yeah, right," Saoirse said. "We don't even know what they do."

"I do," Hawking said seriously.

Even Eoghan looked up.

True Lore

"How the hell do you know?" Saoirse said.

Hawking shrugged, his face flushed. "From Seamus's book. When we found it in the study I kept it and read it."

"When?"

"At night and stuff," he said, his face still red. "I like to read, alright? Anyway, his whole book was about how true Gaelic lore was passed from generation to generation orally. That we can't trust the written accounts. But apparently, our family had passed down the true mythology, even after moving to the States. His book put the traditional myths and what he thought was the true lore side by side. He wrote about the Deantan, items imbued with magic using Scrios, which was a type of costly magic; nothing done with it is done for free. Anyway, he said right there in the book what the Deantan are and what they do."

"Which is?"

Hawking took a deep breath. "The Coire, which is a cup that grants mortal protection. Obviously, that's the one Seamus and Melinda used to protect us, and the price for its use was that they couldn't use it to protect themselves."

"Obviously," Saoirse said, rolling her eyes at Eoghan, who didn't react.

"It's concerning that they aren't interested in it—that huge asshole said they don't need it. I wonder why they wouldn't want protection." He chewed his lip. "Anyway, then there's Spellbreaker, which is a dagger that, well, breaks spells. I'm certain it's what Niamh used to—"

To kill Linnaeus, Saoirse thought.

Hawking cleared his throat and went on.

"It broke the immortality spell Seamus and Melinda cast on us. I'm not sure about the price to use it, and it was also rumored to have other powers but Seamus didn't say what.

"Then there's the Silver Bough, which can transport the user to the land of Tír na nÓg—"

"The land of *what*?"

"It means *The Land of Youth*. In the myths, people thought it was a fairy land or a paradise we go after we die. Seamus said it's simply another world with a different race of beings. A good place," he added.

"And the Silver Bough takes you there?"

"So he said. Its cost is time. Time passes differently there than it does on earth. I can't understand why the Cult of Balor would want it." He paused. "Then there's the Tanist Stone, which would really come in useful right about now."

"Why?"

"Seamus said it does the bidding of whoever holds it. Anything. It has all power."

All power. Saoirse shivered. She could certainly see why the cult would want that, and why Seamus worked so hard to prevent them from getting it. "Where could he have hidden them?"

"I don't know. Maybe more secret hiding places, deep inside the house. Or they could be hidden in plain sight, which would also be smart."

Something nagged at Saoirse. *Hidden in plain sight...*

"What did they look like, exactly?"

"We know about the cup and the dagger because we've seen them. Bough means branch and apparently, it's silver. As for the stone, Seamus described it not as a gemstone—not a jewel or a mineral crystal—but as hewn from plain rock. That would make it very easy to hide, but probably also easy to lose."

But Saoirse was no longer listening. She reached into her shirt with trembling fingers and pulled out the necklace.

"I... I found..."

Hawking jumped up from the floor and grabbed the amulet of stone framed by gold. Eoghan stared at it with wide eyes, a vein popping in his neck, and spoke for the first time.

"Where did you find it?"

"In the study. It was shoved into a drawer and I kept it because I remember Melinda letting me play with it..."

"This has to be it," Hawking said, staring at it in wonder. "The Tanist Stone, disguised as a necklace."

"Are you sure?" Saoirse asked. "It could be just a necklace."

"I've dated a lot; I know jewelry. Why would someone set such an ugly, plain stone in a beautiful, gold necklace?"

He had a point. The stone really did look like a rock one could find lying on the ground. This was all-powerful?

"So, I can give it a command?"

"Not without the Incantation. You heard them. The Deantan are useless without it. We need to find the spell, and I bet I know where it is.

"We need to get those journals."

10

The Cait Sídhe, or King of Cats, had many names and rumored purposes. His true identity will surprise many.

Seamus Dannan, *Lore: The True History of the Celts*

They spent some time formulating a plan, and Saoirse did not like it.

"You can do this," Hawking said, his eyes dark and intense. "You can, Saoirse."

She nodded, trembling already, and turned to Eoghan.

"Eoghan, are you sure...?" Saoirse thought he looked more petrified than she did, hardly capable of carrying out his part.

"Yes," he whispered.

She and Hawking glanced at each other again.

"Come here," he said, and threw his arms around both of them. Caught in an embrace between her two taller cousins, Saoirse thought this was the closest thing she could have to older brothers. Warmth spread through her chest. She wanted to tell them...

"I..." she said as they pulled away. She swallowed. "Good luck."

"You too," Hawking said significantly. "Go. Now."

Saoirse dashed into the bathroom and climbed into the tub, used the soap niche as a foothold, and pulled herself up to the window. Hawking and Eoghan had used their combined strength to shove it open; it had been stuck from lack of use. She pushed her shoulders through the small opening.

The cold night air hit her like ice water. The sky was still black. She struggled to get through, and with the combination of shimmying and flexibility that was purely genetic, she made it onto the ledge below. Hawking and Eoghan stood at the bedroom door, each wielding a lamp from the nightstands. Hawking nodded to her, and she nodded back before dropping out of sight.

"Shit," she hissed as she turned around on the narrow ledge. Gone was the feeling of absolute protection she'd resented. No surging energy would catch her if she fell. And the fall to the patio below would certainly kill her. She gripped the rough brick of the house, finding barely enough hold for her fingertips to grip. There was a sudden slam, a yell, and a thud. She had to get moving.

Cursing in a steady flow, she inched her way across the wall, pressing herself close and keeping her gaze fixed on the drainage pipe ten feet away. It was Hawking who had mapped out this route for her. Apparently as a boy he'd scaled most of the ledges and balconies of this house. *This is why women live longer than men,* she thought.

The drainage pipe had held Hawking's weight as a child but what if it couldn't hold hers? What if Hawking and

Eoghan's diversion didn't work? Had they even gotten past the door guard, or had she heard *him* immobilizing *them*?

"Fuck this plan."

She moved closer to the pipe.

There was no way to test it out. Either it would hold her, or it would not.

Her breath came in sharp gasps. "No, no, no," she panted. "Calm down. Do it, Saoirse."

She jumped from the ledge, grasping the pipe but her hands were slick with sweat.

Terror pounded through her as she slid down several feet. Then she found traction on the rough brick. She stopped sliding. The pipe held.

"Okay," she breathed. "Okay. Now for the hard part."

It took all her willpower not to start crying.

She had to scale up the pipe until she reached a high balcony. She quickly realized that the only way was not to cling to the pipe like she wanted to, but to lean back, keeping her grip on the bricks with her feet, and pull herself up using mostly her legs.

The pipe creaked ominously.

"Don't think, just fucking do it."

Steadily she went, trying to keep her panic in check. Not too slow but not too fast. She thought back to her attempt to jump off the lookout to her death. What had she been thinking? There was nothing worse than heights.

After several agonizing minutes, she reached a point where the pipe broke off in two directions, forming a Y. She would have to hoist herself from the top of that Y to the balcony above it.

She knew she didn't have the upper-body strength to pull herself up onto the balcony. She would have to jump.

"One," she counted, rattling the pipe with her shaking

after positioning herself on the top of the Y. "Two. *Three.*"

She sprang upward with as much strength as she could, hearing the pipe break beneath the pressure of her jump. Arms flung out desperately, she caught two of the stone spindles. Her chest slammed into the solid rock beneath the balustrade. Saoirse dangled there, trying to inch her arms up the spindles. It was no use. She was losing strength.

"No," she panted. "You're almost there—"

She swung her leg up. Her foot reached the balcony between two spindles and wedged there. Yelping with the pain of exertion, she pulled herself up to standing outside the balustrade.

Saoirse climbed over, fell to the ground of the balcony, and cried.

She gave herself thirty seconds.

Then she got up, wiped her eyes, and looked across to the third balcony, above which, high in the peaked turret, glowed the window she knew belonged to the triangular room.

The balconies were reasonably close together, but climbing onto the balustrade and jumping onto the next balcony wasn't fun. However, after everything she'd just done, her body coursed with adrenaline. Adrenaline and a sense of satisfaction.

I actually did that, she thought as she leapt through the air, landing clumsily on the second balcony. If things had gone to plan, the window here in this middle balcony should now be unlocked for her to use later...

She made it to the third balcony. The climb from the balustrade to the ledge of the window was short, but she had no way to peek inside to see if Hawking and Eoghan's diversion had worked. So much rode on whether or not they had gotten past the man guarding the bedroom door.

They have, she told herself. Two against one, the element of surprise... it had to have worked.

Taking a deep breath, she heaved herself onto the window ledge.

The room was empty.

She exhaled with relief and tried to open it. Locked, as Hawking had told her it likely would be. Gripping the frame with one hand, she drew her elbow back and bashed it into the window as hard as she could.

The glass exploded. She covered her hand with her sleeve and cleared out the shards still clinging to the frame, then lowered herself inside.

Immediately, a man shouted from somewhere down below.

Saoirse rushed to the desk. The small, black journals were strewn across it, along with thick, odd-looking leaves from which a clear substance oozed. Shaking, she pulled the trash bag Hawking had taken from the bathroom can out of her pocket, then swept everything on the desk into it, including the leaves. She had scrabbled back out the window when heavy footsteps raced up the stairs.

"Dammit." She jumped back down to the balcony, landing painfully, then climbed up the balustrade and leapt to the middle balcony. She tried the window. It was unlocked. Grinning in spite of her terror, she shoved it open and crept inside.

She was in the middle of the hallway that lead to the wardrobe. The false wall inside was open, and she could hear a man shouting from the triangular room. Swift with fear, she sprinted down the hall, the bag of journals flung over her back.

Heavy pounding of footfalls came from the hidden staircase.

Saoirse looked around in a panic. She wouldn't be able to outrun him. Flinging the bag of journals over her shoulder, she slipped behind a tall, mahogany cabinet next to the staircase.

Footsteps sounded nearer.

She held her breath, slick hands clutched on the bag strap.

Skidding around the corner, he spotted her.

Saoirse flung the heavy bag as hard as she could and slammed him in the head. The man pitched forward and rolled down the marble staircase, his body making sickening slaps as it hit each step. Landing in a heap at the bottom, he lay still.

One man had been in the triangular room. Two men should still be out at the lake. And the other was hopefully knocked out in front of the bedroom where they had been kept prisoner.

Exhaling, she ran down the stairs, not looking too closely at the body. Once again blasted by the cold, night air, she raced across the lawn to the enormous detached garage. The distant sound of a boat motor rumbled.

She swore. They didn't have much time.

Saoirse ran around the side door to the carriage house and slipped inside.

The garage wasn't really a garage. Two sensible, old people cars were parked immediately inside, but the rest was as large as a warehouse and looked like a museum of ancient weaponry.

"Hell yeah," she breathed. It was as Eoghan had described it. Old swords and knives were displayed on the walls, although some were missing. And crouching on the ground in the opposite corner of the vast room was—

"Hawking, Eoghan," she cried.

"Saoirse," Hawking said as he stumbled away from their cache of blades and pulled her into a hug. "You made it."

Eoghan smiled weakly from the floor, holding two knives in his hands.

"Yeah, and I got—"

"The journals. You're amazing," Hawking beamed.

She tried to hide her grin, embarrassed. "They're already back from the lake, we've got to hurry—"

She poured the contents of the trash bag onto the dusty floor.

"What's with the leaves?" Hawking asked as he bent over the pile with a flashlight.

"I don't know," she replied. "They were all over the desk."

Kneeling down, she flipped through the journals. Some had writing on them, but some were still blank.

"Hang on," Hawking said, handing her the flashlight. He picked up one of the thick leaves, where the clear, aloe-like substance was still gushing out. He put some on his fingertips, then smeared it onto one of the blank pages.

Dark writing faded into view.

"I bet we can thank Melinda's botany expertise for this," he said.

The revealed ink read like a script.

ME: WHAT EXACTLY DID THEY SAY?

KIAN: THAT "SHE" WAS CLOSE TO HAVING ENOUGH POWER TO KILL THE DANNANS.
NIAMH
MUST HAVE FIGURED OUT SOME KIND OF MAGIC.

ME: A FIFTH DEANTAN?

KIAN: IT MUST BE. THERE'S NO WAY SHE COULD USE CRUTHU.

"What is this?" Hawking said.

"Kian... like... there's another Kian?" Saoirse asked, confused.

Hawking sat back and rubbed his eyes.

"Of course," he breathed. "Cait Sídhe."

What he said sounded like what Niamh had said when she saw Kian the cat in the secret room. "What is that?"

"It was in Seamus's book. The Cait Sídhe or King of Cats, was a cat with all sorts of legends. Some thought it was an evil fairy who took the form of a cat and stole people's souls; other said it was a witch who could transform into a cat nine times—that's where the saying that cats have nine lives probably comes from. But in all the myths about it, the Cait Sídhe is described the same way: enormous, with black fur except for a patch of white on his chest."

Saoirse shook her head, not following. Hawking continued, looking haunted.

"Seamus said the truth was that he was actually an ancient Druid who defected and had transformed himself into a cat."

"What's a Druid?"

"They were leaders in ancient Celtic culture, thousands of years ago. Seamus said they were evil, synonymous with the Fomorians."

"The Fom—what does any of this have to do with—"

"Saoirse, Kian is not a cat."

She stared at him. "He's not? Then what is he?"

Hawking gazed back intensely.

"A very old man."

11

The Tanist Stone, perhaps the most formidable of the Deantan, was created with a failsafe to prevent the wielder from becoming more powerful than its maker.

Seamus Dannan, *Lore: The True History of the Celts*

Saoirse stared at him in astonishment as her mind worked.

Kian was... a man?

But the more she thought about it, the more it fit. Kian's impossible age, the way he never allowed any of them to pet him, how he had always lingered around as they plotted and planned and searched...

And how he had come to curl up at the foot of her bed tonight when she was in despair. His rage in the secret room after Linnaeus was killed.

"And that's why Niamh took him?"

"He must be important," Hawking said, chewing his lip again. "I wonder how he and Seamus communicated."

Saoirse gave the flashlight to Eoghan, who took it wordlessly, and flipped through the journals that already had the ink exposed.

> KIAN: HELP ME TRANSFORM. THEN I CAN USE CRUTHU TO DESTROY THEM.
>
> ME: MY FRIEND, MELINDA HAS BEEN STUDYING CRUTHU INCESSANTLY. EVEN YOU DON'T KNOW HOW IT WORKS EXACTLY. WE'RE FUMBLING AROUND, BLIND IN THE DARK.
>
> KIAN: I REFUSE TO ACCEPT THAT. CRUTHU IS HUMANITY'S BIRTHRIGHT. THERE MUST BE A WAY.

"Cruthu. So, it is real," Hawking said.

"What—"

"It's the antithesis to Scrios magic. Magic that isn't dependent on artifacts, like the Deantan. Magic that asks no price."

Saoirse frowned, flipping through the pages more.

"It's all recordings of Seamus and Kian. I don't see anything else, no spell."

"We'll search them all, it's got to be in one of these—"

The door to the carriage house burst open. The fluorescent lamps overhead came on, flooding them with light.

"Get back," Hawking roared to Saoirse as he shoved her behind him. Eoghan leapt to his feet, gripping the large knives in his hands, and Hawking stooped to pick up a sword.

The tall, brutal leader stood in the doorway, the other man by his side.

"You're dead."

"Keep looking," Hawking hissed to Saoirse. "Find the Incantation. We'll hold them off."

"The girl is first," the leader said from across the room. "I'll make you watch as we all take her in turns, skin her alive, then cut her from her cunt to her throat."

Saoirse's eyes widened and she tried not to think about what he said as she smeared the plant substance on more blank pages. Only dialogue, nothing that looked like a spell... find the spell...

"You won't touch her!" a voice screamed, and Saoirse saw not Hawking, but Eoghan race toward the men with his daggers held high.

"Shit," Hawking shouted as he too ran forward, and the battle began.

Saoirse forced herself back to her search, trying to ignore the shouts and yells of pain. She flipped the pages faster and faster, still finding nothing...

"Come on, Saoirse," Hawking yelled.

"I'm trying, it's not anywhere."

"It has to be," Hawking shouted. He was in a violent tussle with one of the men, his sword discarded on the ground. Eoghan paced back and forth with the leader, his knives held aloft and his pale face set.

"No," came a strangled cry, and Saoirse whipped back to find Hawking pinned to the ground, the man he was fighting choking him.

She leapt to her feet and kicked Hawking's sword to him. He grasped the hilt and shoved the blade into the man's side.

The man howled with pain as he fell off Hawking.

"Keep looking," Hawking shouted at her as he bent over

double, catching his breath. "Seamus must have known it, he had to use it to activate the—the cup—"

Hawking stared at her with wide eyes and she stared back, the realization hitting them both. Then the stabbed man got back to his feet, a large blade in his hand.

"Hawk, look out!"

Hawking turned just in time to block the man's attack. Saoirse gasped as the knife sliced into Hawking's arm.

"Carmun," Hawking bellowed as he brought up his sword to block another attack. "It's the Song of Carmun, sing it!"

Saoirse seized the necklace from under her shirt, held it in her hand, and sang.

"*Tra ghuthaan fasaah agas speraan rotea...*" Her voice rang out tremulously in the cavernous garage. The leader dodged around Eoghan and sprinted toward her.

Saoirse sang faster.

"*...thas miir aair adh cuiir guaa baas...*"

The stone exploded with light and a shockwave burst from it, making everyone stumble back. The man recovered and hurtled toward her as the stone's brightness faded. He was inches from her, his arms reaching out—

"Get me out of here!"

At once, the sight of the man and the garage disappeared. She was ripped backward through a tunnel of light. She screamed in terror—

It stopped almost as suddenly as it had started.

Saoirse knelt, panting, in tall, dewy grass. She lifted her gaze. It was still night. In front of her was a meadow of more tall grasses, which ended in the tree line of a forest.

"Where the hell am I?" she said, sluggish and dizzy.

The sound of water lapping made her turn around. She

was on the shore of a lake. And far across, on the other side, was the silhouette of a mansion.

"Hawking, Eoghan," she whispered desperately. She glanced down at the necklace hanging past her chest.

All power.

She used it to escape in a panic. But she could have ordered the stone to do anything—kill the men, for instance. With this stone, she was more than invincible, like the ritual with the cup had made her. She was all-powerful.

Grasping the amulet once more, she raised it to her lips. Did she have to sing the Song of Carmun again, or was it now "activated"? She could go back in an instant and save her cousins; she could destroy Niamh and everyone that was involved in the deaths of so many people she loved...

But something made her stop. A nagging in her mind that she was missing something important. Something to do with the cup. The cup. What was it about the cup, about the protection spell?

Seamus and Melinda hadn't been able to protect themselves with the cup. Yes—that was it. But why? What had Hawking said about the Deantan?

Scrios. Costly magic. It always asks a price.

She looked once again at the stone she held in her hand. She dropped it as if it had burned her. *Always asks a price.*

What price had she paid by using it to escape?

With a keen sense of foreboding, she decided she must only use the stone in moments of desperation until she could figure out what cost it would exact.

Saoirse navigated her way through the tall grass, her bare feet freezing. She wanted to go faster, but her fatigue made it difficult. With every moment that went by, her dread grew greater and greater. Were Hawking and Eoghan able to fight them off? The men were obviously highly skilled and trained in combat. Hawking would have likely died if she hadn't kicked his sword to him. And he was already injured.

She continued slogging around the lake as fast as she could. Finally, breathing hard and longing for water, she made it to the carriage house.

Even as she stood outside, she knew something was wrong.

It was silent.

As Saoirse reached for the door, an instinctive part of her told her to close her eyes.

She didn't. She looked.

And then fell to her knees and vomited.

Bloody heaps were scattered all over the concrete floor. Severed limbs. Bits of clothing. The ground stained red. That sick, coppery smell she was coming to know all too well...

And then she saw something that jolted her to her feet.

A flash of bright yellow underneath all the red. She stumbled forward to pick it up...

It was Hawking's neon jacket, ripped in half.

"No..."

She dropped it, fighting another wave of nausea.

Ten feet away lie Eoghan's thin-framed glasses, the glass shattered, the frame twisted.

"No... *no*..." She stumbled through the carnage, past chunks of flesh flayed from the bone... the blood...

Her horror grew as she understood that with all the bloody pieces of human bodies spread across the vast room, she was really only looking at two bodies.

It was too much. She scrambled backward, slipping on blood, stepping on something that squished horribly under her bare feet, until she stumbled outside into the frigid air.

She turned from the carriage house and ran, ran even though her heart and lungs were about to give out—

Saoirse fell in the grass of the great lawn and wept. She cried for a long time. Alone. The last in her family to survive.

It was over. No more hope. No more chances. They failed.

She failed.

After a while, Saoirse rolled to her side and gazed up at the mansion. The window of the secret room was alit with a warm glow. The room where her father's gun still lie on the floor after Linnaeus tried to use it to save Hawking. Before she was murdered.

Saoirse didn't know who she mourned the most for, who she missed the most, but it was probably Linnaeus. Strong, brave, foul-mouthed Linnaeus. She thought of how they talked in the oak tree mere hours earlier. How Linnaeus told her what a piece of shit she thought she was, and how Saoirse felt at the time that her cousin was anything but that. For how many suicide attempts Linnaeus had, Saoirse couldn't think of her as a failure. She was a survivor.

What would Linnaeus do now if she were here?

The answer came to her swiftly and certainly. It was the very next thing they had talked about in that old tree. Linnaeus would want revenge.

Saoirse sat up.

Something lit inside her. Something she hadn't considered until now. In the tree, it had kindled and quickly burnt out. But the concept of revenge and the scorching rage it ignited in her belly now only grew with every passing moment.

She wanted it. She wanted to make them pay. All of them, but especially Niamh.

She had the Tanist Stone, the stone of all power. She still didn't know the price, but it made sense to her that the bigger the act the stone performed, the larger the cost would be. What if every time she used the stone, it made her enemies stronger? How would that work if she tried to use it against them?

Is that why they'd been able to slaughter Eoghan and Hawking while she was gone?

Hot tears threatened to spill again, but she swallowed them down, letting her rage keep her other emotions at bay. She had to think.

Could there be a way to use it as little as possible to minimize the damage but enough to get her to her goal? If only she could leverage it, use it to get another type of weapon, one that could replace the power of the stone...

Her mouth fell open. Of course.

Kian.

What had she read in the journal, the conversation he'd had with Seamus? He said that if he could be transformed, he could use his own magic to destroy them. Seamus and Melinda couldn't figure it out, but maybe with the stone she could do it. Maybe it wouldn't exact too big a price...

Her scorching rage changed to icy determination. She didn't want to die a failure, giving up when there was something she could do. Why not try? She had nothing more to lose.

Saoirse grasped the amulet once again and raised it to her lips.

"Take me to Kian."

12

The Fomorians, or Cult of Balor, had many rituals to benefit themselves, all done at the ultimate expense of others outside the group.

Seamus Dannan, *Lore: The True History of the Celts*

Saoirse was jerked backwards once more through a tunnel of rushing light. It lasted a bit longer this time. Just when she felt like she was about to vomit again, it stopped. She fell, panting, on damp ground.

Light still blinded her. Then, blinking, she saw that she had landed in front of a vast and brightly lit mansion.

It was quite different from the one she had just left. This an was opulent, luxurious, Mediterranean-style house. Creamy and intricately embellished stone was offset by a dark tile roof. Palm trees grew around it, lit by the house and swaying in a gentle night breeze, which was welcome in the sudden suffocating humidity. A huge fountain stood before her, and she crept closer, staying hidden behind it.

From this view, she could tell some sort of party was happening inside. Beautifully dressed people laughed and drank on the terrace. Two armed guards stood at the open entrance, which sat above a long, sweeping staircase.

Not a typical party.

This must be where Niamh and the others lived. Where the Cult of Balor was headquartered. For Niamh to make it back here so soon, Saoirse guessed she was somewhere on the coast of the Carolinas, maybe Georgia.

Kian was in there... if he was still alive.

She shuddered, then shook her head. No. He had to be alive. He was her last hope.

Saoirse crept back from the fountain and circled the property from the shadows of the grounds surrounding it. There must be many other entrances. Indeed, there were—and heavily-armed guards stood there, too.

By the time she had gone around the entire home, she was faint, her heart beating too fast. It must be a side effect of the traveling, she thought. Or could *that* be the price of using the stone? Sapping her of her energy?

"Okay, Saoirse," she whispered to herself as she stared at the mansion from the shadows. "Think."

She had the Tanist Stone. She didn't want to tell it to save Kian because that seemed rather a large job and she still didn't know its price. Traveling at near-light speed had been risk enough.

What could she ask the stone to do that would allow her to enter the mansion and find Kian without being caught?

She looked down, not realizing she was once again holding it in her hand. If this idea didn't work, she was dead.

And there was no way to know it had worked without walking straight up to the mansion.

All power, she reminded herself.

Raising the stone to her mouth, she whispered, "Make me invisible."

Gazing down at herself, she looked as solid as before. Besides the sensation that she'd just run a marathon, she felt no different.

The people were gone from view now; perhaps they had all moved into a certain part of the home for food or entertainment. But the guards remained.

She gripped the stone, fully intending to use it to save her own life if this didn't work. "Here we go," she muttered.

Saoirse stepped around the fountain and into full view. The guards continued peering around the grounds behind her. She exhaled, and walked closer, ascending the smooth stone stairs.

Slick with sweat, she lost her footing and tripped, her knee slamming onto the stone. She swore.

At once, the guards sprang forward.

She scrambled to the side of the wide staircase. *They can't see you but they can hear you, you idiot*, she cursed herself. She pressed against the stone railing as one guard, holding a very large and aggressive-looking gun, descended the stairs. He gazed around with keen eyes. She tried to hold her breath, which was coming quick and shallow, as he peered directly at her. Then he moved on.

Exhaling again as slowly and as silently as possible, she got to her feet and crept the rest of the way up the stairs and onto the terrace. Warm light glowed beyond the open doors to the house. The remaining guard was also scanning the area, fingering his gun, and she slipped past him and into the mansion.

The foyer was staggering with its tall pillars and stunning chandelier; it made her family's estate look puny and shabby in contrast. She saw no one, but an eerie sort of string music echoed through the marble foyer, coming from deeper inside the house. Saoirse followed the sound, glad she was barefoot as she crept along the cold marble floor. She walked past a library, a ballroom, and a vast dining room, but all were empty. The music grew ever louder until she recognized it wasn't strings playing, but the singing of a live choir. Finally, she arrived at a stone archway, beyond which she could see nothing but a few steps and then darkness.

Breathless, she descended the stairs. *I'm invisible*, she reminded herself. *I'm safe*. Her eyes took time to adjust to the dark. Soon, she perceived faint lights lining the place where the wall met the floor as she went farther and farther down. At the last step, the walls widened into a larger tunnel of the black stone. The walls were inlaid with more glowing lights.

Saoirse crept down the tunnel, and a new sound, almost drowned out by the singing, made the hair on her arms stand on end.

Small, frantic cries of terror.

Light pulsated and flickered at the end of the tunnel where another archway stood. Saoirse walked through it.

What she saw made her stagger back.

The room beyond the tunnel was immense and lit by hundreds of flaming torches. In the middle of the room stood a human figure, at least twenty feet tall, made of splintered wood. Dozens of people faced away from the effigy in a large arch. They were shrouded in black cloaks and hoods with tall, conical hats ending in sharp points that reminded her of the Ku Klux Klan. Their faces were covered, with only holes for their eyes. The singing came from these people—a high wavering melody from female voices and a deep rhythmic hum from the males.

Standing in front of the effigy, clinging to one another, was a man, woman, and small child.

The music stopped in ringing silence and a figure stepped through the arch of people in black. This one wore the same cloak and capirote, but in white. A female voice rang from the figure, a voice so familiar that Saoirse clenched her jaw.

"Welcome to *Ceaann Cluuic Getthraa*. The Beheading Game," Niamh said. "We begin with Balor's submission to Carmun, from which spread forth throughout the earth the scourge of our people."

One figure in black stepped forward while two came from the sides to flank Niamh. Saoirse recoiled as the two on either side of her undid the clasps of her white robes and let them fall to the ground, exposing her naked body. The figure in black in front of her did the same to his own robes until the two stood nude before each other, their faces still shrouded by the hoods and capirotes.

"Submit yourself to me," Niamh commanded in a purr and the man lied on the stone ground before her. The parents shielded the child—which Saoirse could now see was a small boy, only a little older than Patrick—from the sight.

Niamh mounted the man and as she moved, the black-cloaked crowd made gasping moans in rhythm with her rising and falling hips. Saoirse looked away. It was sick, perverse, twisted beyond anything she had ever seen or imagined. The depraved sounds quickened into a frenzy. Saoirse wanted to leave, to get away from this repulsive act. Unable to stop herself, Saoirse glanced at Niamh, who was now moving violently upon the man. Finally, the sounds reached an apex and with a final cry of pleasure, Niamh stopped. She dismounted the man and her aides came to her sides, putting her white robes upon her once more. The man on the floor also stood, dressed himself, then faded back into the crowd.

Niamh stood for a few moments, her breast heaving under her cloak. Then she turned toward the trembling family, the boy's face still pressed to his parents' bodies, and raised her arms.

"Let the Beheading Game begin."

Cloaked figures seized the father and mother and ripped them away from their child. They were dragged, thrashing and shrieking, to the wood effigy. A man tied the end of a rope hanging from the ceiling to the boy's feet. Pale and shaking, the child fell to the ground as the rope rose. The eerie singing began again.

The mother and father were forced into the effigy. They screamed and tried to reach their hands through the cracks in the wood toward their son.

The boy rose higher, the rope holding him upside down in the air, and then stopped. His head was level with Niamh's. A large, golden bowl was placed beneath him. Niamh took a dagger from her cloak, and Saoirse recognized it as Spellbreaker.

A cloaked figure took a torch from the wall and stood close to the effigy. The eerie singing and humming began once again.

Niamh stepped closer to the boy. He no longer cried. The blankness on his face and in his eyes was worse than his tears.

"Your parents will burn." Her voice rang through the cavern over the screams of his parents and the singing mob.

"Let terror and grief course through your veins. It will make your blood taste sweet to us as it safeguards our youth and wholeness."

Niamh drew back the dagger as the man raised his torch to the effigy.

"No," Saoirse screamed.

The singing ceased at once.

Everyone turned toward the sound of her voice.

"Who was that?" Niamh shrieked. "Find them!"

Shit.

Slipping through gaps in the crowd, she darted toward Niamh and the boy. Niamh was staring around, her face livid. Saoirse formed a fist, raised her arm, then swung in a wide circle. Her fist connected with Niamh's face and knocked her to the floor. Spellbreaker clattered away and Saoirse seized it even though her hand felt broken. She clutched the boy, who yelped at her touch, and held his body to her as she sliced the dagger through the rope binding his feet. As she turned to carry him toward the effigy, she saw the mob of cloaked figures sprinting toward her. She grasped the necklace.

"Freeze them," she ordered the stone. The mass of people halted in place with sudden silence. Saoirse swayed on the spot, weak and lightheaded.

"What the fuck?" the man with the torch shouted. He stared at the boy seemingly floating toward him. She put the child on the ground, grabbed the torch, and forced it on the man.

His hood caught fire. The man roared and thrashed as he fell backward, the flames spreading rapidly over his body.

From the splintered wooden effigy, the man and woman stared in shock. Several feet away, Niamh stirred.

"Open the hatch," Saoirse told the Tanist stone. The man and woman jumped down and grabbed their son, looking wildly around for their savior.

A few of the immobile people twitched. Saoirse frowned, dizzy and confused. The spell wasn't holding and she didn't know why.

"You need to run," Saoirse told the parents.

"Who are—"

"Run. *Now.*"

The man took his son in his arms and sprinted back up the passage, the woman on his heels. Saoirse followed, disconcerted by the movements of the slowly unfreezing mob. Weak and heavy, she pushed on. She had to make sure the family was safe.

They raced back through the tunnel, up the stairs, and down the blinding marble hallway. When they reached the foyer, the guards at the door turned.

"*Freeze the guards,*" she screamed, and doubled over in pain. Something was wrong. She shoved this thought aside as she pushed the man and woman toward the exit.

"Run as far away from here as you can," she panted. "Don't stop."

They complied, the woman glancing back toward Saoirse's voice. Her eyes widened. Saoirse knew then that she was no longer invisible. The family disappeared into the night.

Panting and shaking, Saoirse raised the stone once more. "Lead me to Kian."

At once, she felt a magnetic tug from the stone. It pulled her up the left side of the grand foyer stairway. She moved as fast as she could, holding onto the bannister with her left hand while clutching the stone in her right. Shouts sounded from the main hall.

"Come on," she urged herself as the stone pulled her down a long hall lined with doors, similar to those in her grandparents' mansion, but brighter and more lavish. She was about to pass a fifth door when the necklace suddenly yanked her to the left. She stumbled into the door, then turned the knob.

Inside was a dark, empty room save for a small cage, inside of which laid a large cat.

"Kian," she breathed. The cat didn't move.

She dropped to her knees and fumbled with the latch. Then she pulled the cat into her lap.

He was limp in her arms. Gashes ran all over his body, blood congealed in his fur. She felt his belly, which rose and fell faintly.

"Revive him," she whispered to the stone. Kian's large, yellow eyes flickered open and he let out a soft mewl. Saoirse leaned to the side and vomited.

This time, it was bright red. Blood.

Kian hissed.

"Not doing too well, are you?" a female voice said from the doorway.

Saoirse whipped around. Niamh stood in her white cloak, her hood removed, her dark hair spilling down her shoulders. Blood trickled from her eyebrow where Saoirse had hit her.

"I'd say using the Tanist Stone again might finish you off."

"What are you talking about?" Saoirse croaked, her stomach cramping and her chest aching.

"Scrios always asks a price, and it appears this one you're paying with your life." Niamh scowled. "You cost me a child."

"Good. They're long gone now."

A muscle in her jaw twitched, but Niamh shrugged. "I'll easily find another. Give me the stone."

"No." Saoirse raised it to her mouth.

"I'd be careful if I were you," Niamh warned.

"Fuck your advice," Saoirse retorted, clutching the cat close to her.

Niamh's eyes flashed. She pulled Spellbreaker out of her robes and Saoirse cursed herself for not taking it.

Niamh gripped the blade and drew her arm back.

"Take us somewhere safe," Saoirse said.

At that precise moment, Niamh let the dagger fly.

It was an inch away from her when her body was jerked backward. Niamh and the blade disappeared. All was light.

Then everything went black.

13

The Silver Bough is a Deantan made to cross into other worlds. However, as no use of Scrios magic is given for free, the cost of using the Silver Bough is time.

Seamus Dannan, *Lore: The True History of the Celts*

Hawking knew how to get what he wanted from situations. He had a gift for understanding people: what they wanted, what they were afraid of. This sense of peoples' motivations gave him a certain self-assurance. He always knew how to proceed, how to create win-win situations. And if not win-win, then at least a win for himself.

But at this moment, as he streaked through the dark forest in a panic, stumbling over roots and barely missing trees, he had no idea what to do. He didn't even know why he was running away.

I'm trying to find Saoirse, he told himself. *Yeah. I'm not running* away *from anything. I'm running to help her.*

The lie made him feel better. He slowed down and stopped to lean against a tree, gasping for breath. Why, in all the hours he spent at the gym, didn't he ever do some running? Maybe learn how to fight? All the advice he lived by on building muscle for aesthetics didn't do jack shit in a real-life situation of survival. *Lift heavy. Power-walk on the treadmill.* All hulking muscle and chiseled abs had gotten him was almost killed. Stupid asshole.

Then again, how could he have ever known, back when he was hustling for sales and women, that he would end up fighting for his life?

He leaned his forehead against the mossy trunk. His life had been so normal and predictable. All excitement had been manufactured by himself. A newer, faster car. Some high-thrill trip with his buddies. The pursuit of a new girl. He had the control. Nothing blindsided him.

Until the day he got the call from Linnaeus that their parents were dead.

Linnaeus.

He crumbled, all six feet of him, to his knees.

Hawking hadn't cried when he found out his parents had died. Just like he'd never cried about a break up or even during an inspiring sports movie. He probably hadn't cried since he was five-years-old. He loathed himself for doing it now—sniveling, snot dripping from his nose, while Saoirse was out there somewhere and Eoghan was—

Don't think about Eoghan.

For a moment, he wished he had his phone with him to call Davie, but he hadn't been honest with his sister about her. He'd seen social media evidence the night before of her cheating on him. It was blatant; she hadn't even cared to hide it. She was sending him a message. *You've been gone too long and I'm forgetting about you.* Davie had shown barely any sympathy when his parents died. What did he expect her to offer him now?

"Get up," he commanded himself. "Stop being such a damn baby."

But sobs wracked his body as he knelt in the dirt, his thoughts turning back to his twin. Linnaeus was always the outsider. Rebellious, a screw-up, acting like she hated everyone. He'd given up trying to help her be normal a long time ago. In fact, they hadn't seen each other in years before coming to the manor. He lived far away, enjoying his huge commissions, expensive toys, and model girlfriends. It was easy to leave her behind. After all, he wasn't responsible for her. He'd deserved to live his own life.

Bitterness welled in him. When he'd seen her scarred arms that first day, had seen the evidence of the hell she'd been living in...

When it came time to act, she was so brave. Braver than he'd ever been. And smart. He'd always assumed she wasn't intelligent because she'd dropped out of high school. In how many ways had he written her off?

And when she tried to protect his dignity from that *bitch*—

"I should have protected you," he moaned, curling on his side in the dirt. He meant more than protecting her from Niamh. All those years, he should have been there for her. He could have listened to her, tried to understand her. The one person he had gotten wrong.

Instead, he'd left her alone while he pursued his own bullshit life. That life was still waiting for him. But nothing waited for Linnaeus.

He hated himself for that.

After a while, Hawking decided he'd had enough self-pity. Taking a deep, shuddering breath, he wiped his face. He had to *do something*, like find Saoirse. When she'd told the stone to get her out of there, where had it taken her?

And what was its price?

He looked around the forest, even though he could barely discern the trees from the darkness. Could the stone have brought her in here?

"*Saoirse!*" he shouted. "*Saoirse!*"

Only night sounds answered him. He shivered. Were there wolves in here? He'd never seen any as a kid. Bears? A hungry animal would finish him off, injured as he was. A grim reminder of his loss of mortal protection.

For the first time since he fled from the carriage house, he glanced down at his arm.

Blood poured from the wound there. It looked deep and in danger of infection. He couldn't clean it but he could at least stop the bleeding.

Tearing a strip from the bottom of his shirt (annoyed at how easily it tore; he'd paid $200 for this shirt), he wrapped it around his arm. His fingers still throbbed from having his nails torn off. His head ached from being hit, and he was sure ugly bruises were blooming on his throat where he'd nearly been choked to death. A slash across his back stung where a knife had torn his favorite jacket in two. After running his uninjured hand across his back, he tried to look at it in the darkness. Not much blood there.

The most logical move was to go back to the manor in case Saoirse had returned. Especially if Eoghan was still there...

Hawking had been using all of his willpower to resist thinking about Eoghan. It ran out. A slew of images of his cousin rose to his consciousness.

He doubled over and vomited on the forest floor.

Eoghan had snapped. There was no other way to put it. Hawking watched with his own eyes as the nice, geeky psychologist transformed into a vicious monster.

Hawking had never seen such carnage in his life.

At first, when the leader turned back to attack Eoghan after Saoirse disappeared, he thought his cousin was a goner. Eoghan had fallen to the ground; all Hawking could see were the whites of his eyes. Hawking shouted his name. Then Eoghan sprung back up, grabbed the leader, and bit a chunk out of the guy's neck like a fucking vampire.

The look in his eyes—that wasn't Eoghan anymore. Hawking thought of what Eoghan had said about his patient with multiple personalities. That's what it had been like— like Eoghan was someone else.

His own attacker had left him and gone to the leader's aid because Eoghan was slashing and stabbing and biting. It wasn't like his cousin had suddenly grown stronger or more skilled. He was on a level of violent insanity that reminded Hawking of people having a bad trip on LSD and committing unimaginable atrocities.

The breaking point for Hawking had been when he saw Eoghan hacking away at a one of the men's faces with a knife. He bolted from the garage and ran until he could no longer hear the screams.

A horrible thought occurred to him. If Saoirse was there and she met this monster-version of Eoghan, she could already be gone.

"Fuck," Hawking said, his head in his hands. "Fuck, fuck, fuck." He slumped back down to the ground, pain shooting through his back as he leaned against a tree.

Linnaeus was dead. Saoirse was missing at best. Eoghan was a fucking psycho. And Niamh was still out there, with many others, he was sure. The men that had accompanied her here surely weren't her only henchmen. They would come back to find the other Deantan.

The thought of what Niamh and the Cult of Balor would do with the Tanist Stone made him sick. From what he'd read in *Lore: The True History of the Celts*, the cult was depraved and psychotic, performing child sacrifice and ritualistic rape, among other things. They were obsessed with power and domination. If they got hold of the stone...

They wanted the Tanist Stone *and* the Silver Bough, he reminded himself, though hell if he knew why the cult wanted the latter.

He remembered the wonder with which he'd read about the bough. A closely-guarded secret of his, Hawking had always nursed a particular liking of fantasy things, rereading *The Lord of the Rings* dozens of times and playing *World of Warcraft* late into the night after girlfriends had fallen asleep...

The Silver Bough, transporter to Tír na nÓg. There were so many names for the place, so many other meanings. *The Land of Youth, The Land of Promise, The Land of Colors.* In his book, Seamus had described the race of people there as peaceful, strong, and good. He said they possessed their own magic...

Hawking opened his eyes. He didn't know why Niamh wanted access to Tír na nÓg, but he knew why he did.

Because what he needed most right now was *help*.

He scrambled to his feet. If he could find the bough, travel to Tír na nÓg, appeal to the people there, he could come back with an army. He could do something for his family, for Linnaeus, for the world, because the world was fucked if the Cult of Balor wielded the Tanist Stone.

Where could Seamus and Melinda have hidden it? The

Tanist Stone was set into a necklace and shoved in a drawer. It hadn't been the worst idea, although if anyone else had ransacked the place like they had, they would have found it just as easily. Seamus had assumed that would likely never happen...

A disconcerting thought struck him, not for the first time. How *had* Niamh found them? In his letter, Seamus said that the estate couldn't be found by any outsiders. How confident had he been that no one else would be able to find the Deantan?

However, he had taken precautions, like making them go on a damn treasure hunt to find his last letter. The picture of the triskelion with the hint written on the back so they'd known to go through the false panel in the wardrobe...

Wait.

The picture of the triple spirals had been a clue. What about the *other* picture on the wall in Seamus and Melinda's bedroom? The symbol of the tree. *The Oak.*

He'd told Saoirse that a bough was a branch. On that picture, there had been an old yellow stain. But what if it wasn't a stain? What it if was a highlight, pointing out one of the branches of an oak tree?

Not an oak tree. *The* oak tree.

Hawking began to walk.

He followed the faintest shift in the darkness far in the distance. A place where the forest was less shadowed, where the dense woods cleared to make space for one enormous, sprawling tree.

A trancelike calm settled over him. Hawking breathed in the scent of the woods, let in the sounds of night creatures.

When the trees cleared, the oak tree spread before him, illuminated by starlight.

He approached it reverently, reaching out to touch a soft,

mossy branch. He knew he wasn't looking for a large branch. And he knew it wouldn't be attached to the tree because it was a Deantan—not part of the tree, but hidden there. The Silver Bough wouldn't be mossy or dark because of its name. It would be... different.

He scanned the gnarled branches as he walked around when he remembered.

When they sat in this tree yesterday, Linnaeus picked up a small white branch. And Kian the cat, who was never really a cat, took it from her and protected it with his body. Like it was something important to him. Something sacred.

Kian knew all along where the Silver Bough hid.

And now Hawking did, too.

He climbed swiftly, reaching the apex of the trunk where the branches spread high. He knelt over the top, brushing fallen leaves aside.

And there it was.

Small, soft, smooth to the touch, and stark white against the tangle of dark branches.

Hawking knew what to do. He climbed back down the tree, holding the branch carefully, and stepped in the circle of mushrooms. He didn't know why he entered the fairy ring, didn't know if it was necessary (it hadn't been for Saoirse to use the Tanist Stone), but it felt right.

The Song of Carmun came to him as it had subconsciously from the moment he'd arrived at the manor. Always there, embedded in his mind.

As soon as the last note left his lips, a particle of pure light appeared in front of him, hovering in the air, tiny as the head of a pin. He stared as it grew. The larger it got, the more orblike it became. And the more he could distinguish inside the orb, like he was gazing through a window framed in radiance.

He saw colors.

The sphere grew until it expanded large enough for him to fit inside. A portal.

And Hawking, with the Silver Bough clutched in his hand, stepped through.

14

While Scrios magic is destructive magic, Cruthu is magic that is of creation and asks no price of the wielder.

Seamus Dannan, *Lore: The True History of the Celts*

Saoirse awakened slowly, her awareness of sensations and sounds dim and muddled. Something rough and wet on her cheek. A soft thumping on her chest. Mews and yowls echoing in her ears.

But when something sharp nipped her nose, Saoirse opened her eyes.

A large black cat pounced on her in a frenzy. Faint and dizzy, she closed her eyes again.

The cat sunk sharp claws into her chest through her shirt.

"Hey," she yelled, her eyes flying open.

Kian sat back, a long, low whine coming from him. Saoirse tried to sit up and couldn't. Her chest hurt like she'd been hit there with a battering ram. Her heart raced even though she'd barely moved. Something cold and solid touched her arm. She turned her head, almost passing out again, and saw Kian pushing a bottle of water against her. It took all of her effort to lift the bottle, untwist the cap, and lift it to her mouth. She drank deeply.

Kian hissed. The cat batted at the bottle with his paw. Saoirse took it from her lips, wondering what he was fussing about. Then she rolled to the side and doubled over. She vomited all the water she had drunk, but it was tinged with red. She stared at it for a moment, then passed out again.

When she came to a little while later, Kian was again anxiously pushing a cold plastic bottle against her. This one was new, the old one having drained when she dropped it after fainting. Kian had apparently dragged some kitchen towels over this mess to keep the cold water from soaking her.

She fumbled with this new bottle, the thirst almost as bad as when she had been purposefully dehydrating herself. When she was about to drink, Kian put a paw on her hand and growled.

Drink slowly.

She'd made the same mistake as she had when she had tried to kill herself by dehydration. Even though she wanted to chug the whole thing, she took a small sip and put it back down. After a few minutes she took another sip. Saoirse was amazed when, after about fifteen minutes, her head was much clearer.

They were in the small kitchen of a cabin. Every surface —from the ceiling to the cabinets—was covered in kitschy fake wood. A white sky and drifting snow peeked through the curtains covering a tiny window over the sink. She gazed as Kian trotted over to the refrigerator, pulled open the door, and dragged out a loaf of bread with his mouth. Clever cat.

No, she thought. Not a cat.

"Are we alone?" she croaked.

He gave a low trill. She assumed, by his casual attitude as he dragged the loaf of bread to her, that meant yes. He placed one of his big paws upon the loaf.

Eat.

She unwrapped the bag and tore off a small piece of bread while he went back to the fridge. The stone had fulfilled its command well. A remote cabin, deserted but filled with food and water? Too bad it was so damn cold, she thought as she shivered.

Kian dropped the bag of lunchmeat he had taken from the fridge at once and loped out of the room. A couple of minutes later, he came back in, dragging a large wool blanket clenched in his sharp teeth.

"Thank you," she rasped as she pulled it over herself. "Why don't you take care of yourself now? You look like shit."

He did indeed. In addition to the wounds and matted blood in his fur, he also looked thin and wobbly on his feet. He nudged the lunchmeat toward her with his paw, and then leapt up onto the wooden counter. As he prodded the handle of the water faucet and lapped the water greedily, she wondered if he had attended to her needs first before worrying about his own.

The saltiness of the lunchmeat was marvelous on her tongue. She alternated between small bites of meat and bread with more sips of water. After a while she felt well enough to hoist herself up by her elbows and sit up, leaning against the kitchen wall. Even this small bit of exertion left her panting.

Kian joined her and they ate in silence for a while.

"Any idea where we are?" she asked.

He shook his head, and the movement was so awkward and exaggerated that she smiled.

"I can't believe you're a person."

He looked up at her with his wide, yellow eyes.

"What, did you think I rescued you because you were my grandparents' favorite cat?"

He continued to stare at her.

"We figured out how to read the journals. The transcripts of your conversations with Seamus. Between that and Hawking—" She swallowed at the grief that pummeled through her. "H-Hawking reading Seamus's book, we figured out who you are."

He gave a small meow.

"We found the Tanist Stone. And figured out the spell. But the others..."

Kian paced around. Then he scurried over to the kitchen drawers, pawing them open and then groping through them. At the last drawer, he picked up a pen in his mouth and clawed at something until it floated down to the floor.

Paper.

Saoirse stretched out and grabbed the pen and paper, knowing what he was after. Unable to think of a better way to do it, Saoirse wrote out the entire alphabet at the top of the paper. She pointed to each letter in turn.

Kian slammed his paw down on the paper almost at once. *B.*

Then again about halfway through. *L.*

At the second *O* she understood.

"Blood?"

He hissed and batted at the necklace hanging from her neck.

"Blood..." Her eyes widened. "It's taking my *blood?*"

He dropped his head down. *Yes.*

What Niamh said in the room where Kian was held captive suddenly made sense. "That's its price? Eventually, it will kill me?"

Yes.

She looked down at the plain, gray stone set into the gold necklace. She wanted to rip it off. Resisting the urge, she turned back to the cat.

"Kian, you're... you're my only hope. The others are dead." Her eyes welled with tears, her mouth trembling. "I saved you because you told Seamus that if you could transform back into a human, you could use magic to defeat Niamh. Is that true?"

The cat nodded. *Yes.* Then he placed a paw on her arm and lowered his face. He closed his eyes.

"Thank you," she said, and reached out a hand to stroke his face.

He straightened at once and leapt back.

"Sorry," she said. She kept forgetting he was actually an old man.

He gave a trill, shaking himself a little.

"I-I want revenge. And I want to stop them. They're evil; they were about to kill a kid—"

Kian indicated the paper with a paw. She went back to the alphabet.

Youth.

She frowned and shook her head, confused. He pawed at the paper again. After some time...

Ritual. Cult.

And then she understood. Killing the child...Niamh's words came back to her: *...as your blood safeguards our youth and wholeness...*

"They kill children with Spellbreaker and drink their blood to stay young?"

Yes.

Bile rose in her throat as she thought of the boy and imagined Patrick or Janey in his place. The old grief welled up, almost immediately hardened by rage. "We have to stop them. They've taken everything from me," she said. "But I can't let them kill more children. How do I help you transform?"

He indicated the paper once more.

Cruthu.

"Cruthu?" It sounded familiar but she couldn't place where. "What is that?"

Magic.

"What kind of a magic? Another Deantan?"

Kian shook his head.

Nature. Science.

Saoirse laughed in spite of herself. "Nature magic? Science magic?"

Kian huffed irritably and nudged the paper again.

Go back. Need hair.

Saoirse rubbed her eyes. "I'm lost. Go back? To Niamh?"

No.

"To Seamus and Melinda's?"

Yes.

"Because you need... hair?"

My DNA.

"Where—" But she knew where. They had found hair—human hair—in a box in the triangle room. Kian's hair. Preserved for thousands of years...

"How do we get there? We don't even know where we are, pal. We're both injured. And the cult is probably there, waiting for us to show up."

The cat slumped, shivering.

"You're cold," she said. She was too, in spite of the blanket. "Does this place have heat? A thermostat?"

No.

"A fireplace?"

He chirped, turning toward the next room.

"Alright. You bring the food." And she gingerly shifted to her hands and knees, knowing she still couldn't stand. Feeling only a little foolish, Saoirse crawled into the tiny living room, dragging the blanket with her.

A fireplace was indeed there, along with an old plaid couch and not much else. She edged to the hearth and pulled open the chainmail curtains. The wood inside was mostly ash, but there was a small pile of fresh, dry wood on the hearth along with a box of matches and another box of white cubes labeled *Firelighters*. She heaved several pieces of wood inside the grate, trying to hide from Kian how dizzy it made her. Then she tossed a few of the white cubes on top, fumbled with the matches, and sighed as the fire blazed into life.

She pushed herself back to lean against the couch, clutching the wool blanket to her and enjoying the warmth. Kian curled on the threadbare rug in front of her.

"Come here," she said.

The cat turned his luminous eyes to her.

"Come on. We need all the warmth we can get."

She could tell he was uncomfortable. But his large body was soft and heavy and warm as he settled in her lap. He closed his eyes as she put her arms around him.

"Don't worry, we won't cuddle when you're human again," she yawned. He purred in answer. Saoirse leaned her head back against the couch and fell asleep.

She awoke some time later to a loud pop from the fire.

She jumped, confused for a moment as to where she was. The light from the window was almost gone now. Kian still dozed in her lap, a red scar across the top of his head stark against his black fur. She relaxed.

Fucking Niamh.

She could imagine what the witch would do with the Tanist Stone if she got hold of it. Probably force others to give it commands on her behalf to preserve her own health. Murder all the children she wanted.

The stone was tucked back inside her shirt. She pulled it out, careful not to wake Kian. The gold of the necklace glinted in the firelight and she turned it around in her fingers.

"Why the hell did you take my blood?" she murmured.

Scrios requires a price.

She jumped again, so badly that Kian woke; however, he immediately closed his eyes and went limp once more.

A voice had spoken inside her head that was not her own.

"Y-you can talk to me?" Saoirse whispered.

Yes, said the voice. It was old, genderless, and faint, like an echo.

"Who are you?"

I am not a who.

Saoirse blinked at this. "*What* are you?"

A conduit of Scrios power.

A thought made her blanch. "Does me talking with you require a price?"

No.

Saoirse exhaled in relief. "What is Scrios?" Hadn't Niamh mentioned that word?

A type of magic.

"Like Cruthu?"

The opposite of Cruthu. Scrios takes. Cruthu gives.

And then Saoirse remembered where she had first heard about Cruthu. From Hawking.

"Cruthu gives... what does that mean?"

Cruthu can be used freely. There is no cost.

"Then why use Deantan? Why doesn't Niamh use Cruthu?"

One like Niamh cannot use Cruthu.

Saoirse sat up straighter. "Why?"

Niamh seeks to consume. To destroy. Cruthu is of creation.

"And Scrios?"

Is an imitation of Cruthu. It is of destruction.

"Does that—bother you?"

I am not a who.

Right. "Can I use Cruthu?"

Only you can know the motivations of your heart.

Saoirse frowned. Maybe Kian could tell her what that meant. "Is Cruthu more powerful than Scrios?"

Scrios and Cruthu can be of equal power.

"What would happen then?"

It would create a more complex situation. Other laws would come into play.

"What laws?"

Laws of order. Of balance. The Law of Opposing Magic.

"And what is that? What's the law?"

An exchange of sacrifice. The greater sacrifice wins.

Saoirse stared at the stone. She didn't understand most of what it was talking about, but she knew now more than ever that she had to help Kian transform. Even if she could figure out how to use a little bit of this Cruthu magic to help him, he would be restored to full power. He would be able to stop Niamh.

They had to get back to the estate.

"I'm going to have to use you again to get us back to Seamus and Melinda's mansion," Saoirse said. "Can you—would you be willing to tell me when I've recovered enough to use you to travel there without dying?"

Yes.

She wasn't expecting that. For being "of destruction," the tone sure was helpful.

"Thank you."

She paused, about to ask where Scrios and Cruthu had come from in the first place, when she saw Kian staring at her, his body tense. He glanced to the necklace and growled.

"Calm down, I'm okay. It said I could talk to it without it taking more of my blood."

Kian hissed and leapt from her lap, his back arching as he spit at the stone.

"It's okay," Saoirse exclaimed. The cat continued to bare his teeth and hiss at the necklace. "I'll take it off, okay? I'll stop talking to it." She lifted the chain over her head and tossed the necklace onto the farthest couch cushion. "Happy?"

The cat mewled and settled down on the rug, staring at the couch.

"For your information, it told me I could ask when I was ready to use it to get back to the manor without it taking enough blood to kill me—" The cat sprang to his feet, his back arching again. "Which is really helpful," she continued loudly, "because it's the only way we have a hope of getting back to the estate."

The cat moved his head from side to side.

"No—don't shake your head. Kian, I *have* to use it again. Look outside. Where does it snow in October? We're probably in Canada or Alaska or even somewhere overseas."

Kian stopped his frantic pacing and stared at her.

Finally, he flopped to the ground again, huffing in resignation.

"Good," Saoirse said. "We'll take some more time to rest and recover and I'll check in with the stone and I promise we won't leave until I can do it safely. Okay?"

The cat chuffed in answer and refused to leave his spot on the floor. Rolling her eyes, Saoirse climbed onto the sofa, settled herself on one of its pillows (the Tanist Stone lying on the cushion at her feet) and slept once more.

The next morning, after many hours of sleep and more water and food, Saoirse felt much better. Kian eyed her while she held the stone and asked if she was ready.

Yes, came the strange voice into her mind. *You can make the journey without risking death or serious illness.*

"Is the cult there?"

I cannot answer.

Saoirse raised her eyebrows. So, there were limits to its helpfulness.

"It won't tell me if the cult is still there. We'll have to wing it."

She said it with more bravado than she felt. Who was she? Since when did she wing anything? But when she thought of the rather heroic (albeit violent) things she'd done the other night, she knew a small spark of pride.

The cat shifted.

"Well," she said to Kian. "It says I'm ready. Are you ready?" She knelt down and held an arm out to the cat. He whined in protest but allowed her to gather him close.

"Alright. Here we go." She turned to the stone. "Take us back to the estate."

15

Scrios magic was created as an imitation and opponent of the original magic, Cruthu.

Seamus Dannan, *Lore: The True History of the Celts*

"Dammit," Saoirse swore as she stumbled on wobbly knees and fell on the dewy grass in front of the mansion. "I should have asked it to take us inside."

Kian peered into her face, his yellow eyes wide.

"I'm fine, a bit weak and lightheaded, that's all." She shivered. No matter how helpful and candid the stone was, she'd never get over the fact that it was stealing her blood. She peered with trepidation at the lawn sloping up to the stone steps that led to the back terrace.

"Don't make fun of me for crawling," she said.

Kian cocked his head to the side and made an amusing mix between a purr and a trill. Saoirse burst into laughter.

"Okay, let's make a deal. You don't make fun of me for crawling up to the house and I won't make fun of you for spending thousands of years as a cat."

Kian chirped in an irritated sort of way and proceeded in front of her, his ears perked. She was glad Kian was on alert; his feline hearing would tell them if anyone was here before hers would.

At last, Saoirse made it into the main kitchen and collapsed. Kian set to work retrieving water as he'd done in the cabin. While she drank, he slinked out of the room, his body tense. By the time he got back, looking more relaxed, she was able to climb into a chair at the table.

"No one here?"

He shook his head in his awkward way. The cat trotted over and put a paw on her leg.

"I'm fine. It's amazing how much better I feel after some water." She stood shakily and grabbed a banana off the island. With a pang, she thought of Eoghan. He'd purchased these the morning he made them all breakfast. She forced back tears. It was bullshit that out of the whole group of them, she was the only one who survived. Linnaeus and her courage. Eoghan and his kindness. Hawking and his (albeit surprising) intelligence. She was simply the lucky one; the one who'd found the stone.

She put the banana down, no longer hungry.

"I can get around," she addressed Kian who peered at her. "What now? Get the hair?"

He chirruped and led the way to the secret room. He looked tense and agitated again and when she passed the bottom of the grand staircase and the body of the man she had knocked down the stairs wasn't there, she didn't blame the cat. Had he lived? Had the men who killed Hawking and Eoghan taken his body?

Saoirse tried to go as fast as she could—she had to grip the bannisters and walls for support and take frequent breaks to rest—but finally they made it back to the triangular room. Light from the window cascaded down, emphasizing the stain of Linnaeus's blood on the wood floor. Saoirse looked away.

Instead of retrieving the box of his hair from the bookshelf, the cat was pawing at something underneath the desk, directly above which was the old computer.

"What are you—"

A sudden whirring sounded and the screen on the computer came to life. She bent over and peeked under the desk. The wood had been cut out, and there it was: the bottom of the monitor, with an on/off switch built into it.

"Clever," she muttered, feeling stupid.

Kian had already leapt up to the desk and was moving his paw upon the square black pad that sat next to the computer. When she straightened and saw the screen, her face broke into a smile.

This was how Kian and Seamus had communicated. A program similar to those used to help people who'd been paralyzed and deprived of speech to communicate. A cursor moved across the alphabet, and Kian commanded it down to a list of what must be frequently used words. After using the device for less than a minute, he had constructed a sentence.

THIS IS HOW I'LL TEACH YOU ABOUT CRUTHU.

Saoirse nodded enthusiastically, marveling at the genius of the device.

CRUTHU USES THE FUNDAMENTAL BUILDING BLOCKS OF LIFE AND REALITY.

She frowned, thinking of what he had said in the cabin. *Nature. Science.* "Is it like controlling nature?"

Kian chuffed, looking affronted, and slammed his paw on the pads with more vigor.

> IT IS NOT CONTROL. IT IS NOT FORCE. TO USE CRUTHU, ONE MUST GAIN THE ALLEGIANCE OF THE VERY ESSENCE OF THE NATURAL WORLD, THE MOST FUNDAMENTAL ELEMENTS OF REALITY.

"Gain their allegiance?"

> THEY HAVE TO TRUST YOU.

Saoirse laughed. "Trust me? Like, the cells and atoms and all that have feelings? They make decisions?"

Kian glared at her as he slammed a paw down.

> YES.

Saoirse raised her eyebrows. He was serious. "How do you know this?"

> NO TIME TO EXPLAIN.

Saoirse rubbed her forehead. "How do I gain their allegiance?"

Kian hesitated, his paw in the air. Then he touched the pad.

> I THINK THE ELEMENTS CAN SENSE AND UNDERSTAND A PERSON'S CHARACTER. THEIR FEARS, THEIR DESIRES. THEIR NATURE. THEY WON'T SERVE SOMEONE WHO SEEKS POWER, DOMINION, CONTROL, OR GAIN.

Saoirse felt judged by these elements already. It made sense now why the stone had said Niamh couldn't use Cruthu. *Only you can know the motivations of your heart.*

Did she even know what those were?

"Wait—I read in the journals that my grandparents

couldn't figure out how to use it and that's why they never transformed you."

Kian hesitated once more before he wrote.

> THEY COULD CONCEIVE OF WHAT TO DO, ESPECIALLY MELINDA. THAT'S ALSO IMPORTANT—THE ACCEPTANCE OF THE POSSIBILITY. BUT FOR SOME REASON THEY COULDN'T GAIN THE ELEMENTS' ALLEGIANCE. WE TRIED FOR MANY YEARS.

Saoirse laughed again, this time with bitterness. "What the hell makes you think *I'm* good enough if they weren't?"

Kian gazed at her for a long time.

> THEY WERE GOOD PEOPLE BUT THEY CRAVED RECOGNITION AND PRESTIGE. IT ALMOST GOT THEM KILLED. IT'S WHAT ALERTED THE CULT TO THEIR EXISTENCE IN THE FIRST PLACE. THEIR PUBLISHED WORKS AND LECTURES. THEY GOT CAUGHT UP IN THEIR OWN GENIUS. I THINK THAT IS WHY.

"Well, obviously I'm not 'caught up in my own genius,' seeing as I haven't got any."

> YOUR OBSTACLE WILL BE YOUR SELF-DOUBT. BELIEVE IN YOURSELF, SAOIRSE.

She scoffed. "You sound like my dad."

> MAYBE HE WAS RIGHT. EAT SOME FOOD. THEN WE WILL GO TO THE WOODS. BRING THE BOX OF MY HAIR. WHEN WE'RE THERE, I WANT YOU TO CONNECT WITH THE NATURAL ELEMENTS AROUND YOU. FEEL THEM. HEAR THEM. SEE THEM AS THEY ARE. CALM YOURSELF, ENVISION YOURSELF AS PART OF REALITY, NOT SEPARATE FROM IT. YOU DON'T NEED TO KNOW HOW TO TRANSFORM THE FUNDAMENTALS OF MY PHYSICAL FORM; YOU ONLY NEED TO ASK FOR IT TO HAPPEN.

"I'm sorry but that sounds like hippie bullshit. You want

me to commune with nature? Meditate in the woods? Should I eat some special mushrooms first?"

The cat hissed.

THIS ISN'T HIPPIE BULLSHIT. IT'S SCIENCE.

"I thought it was magic?"

THEY ARE ONE AND THE SAME. YOU MUST TAKE THIS SERIOUSLY. WE'RE RUNNING OUT OF TIME. I DON'T KNOW WHY THE CULT OF BALOR ISN'T HERE YET, BUT THEY WILL COME TO FIND THE OTHER DEANTAN. PLEASE, SAOIRSE. CONCENTRATE. OPEN YOUR MIND. NOTICE WHY YOU FEEL SO RESISTANT TO THIS AND LET IT GO. YOUR HEART IS GOOD; IT'S YOUR MIND THAT STRUGGLES.

Saoirse scowled, offended and something worse that she didn't want to admit to herself. "Why can't you do it yourself?"

THIS FORM LIMITS ME. IN MANY WAYS.

If a cat could look sad, he certainly did with the slight droop to his head. She wondered what he meant and forgot her irritation with him.

"I'll do my best. I promise."

THANK YOU.

Kian leapt off the desk while Saoirse took the box from the bookshelf and followed him out of the room.

After finally eating the banana, as well as some cheese and more bread, Saoirse and Kian headed for the forest. It was late afternoon now. The day was warmer than usual, the sky clear and vibrantly blue. Sunlight gleamed off the cat's handsome coat as he trotted through the grass in front of her. *This form limits me.* What must it be like to spend so many millennia trapped as an animal? What had he done for all those years? He must have been lonely. She wondered how he even came to find her grandparents in the first place.

How would it feel to have the consciousness of a human but be trapped in a body that can't be human at all?

The forest was cooler, but more beautiful than ever. Light filtered through the electric green leaves. Saoirse continued to follow the cat, who strode along with such purpose that she wasn't surprised when they arrived.

The oak. Of course. What was it about this tree?

Kian stepped into the circle of mushrooms and looked at her expectantly. She followed him, thinking less of the ritual her grandparents performed when she was a kid and more about climbing the oak with her cousins days earlier. This was for them, she reminded herself. Defeating Niamh and the cult so that their deaths weren't for nothing.

Nervous, she sat down in the dirt and opened the wooden box to reveal the glass case that held the hair. This one proved harder to open but finally she pried it apart. Kian gingerly took the lock of hair from the box in his mouth, lied down in the dirt, and set it upon his paws. Then he gazed at her, waiting.

"Okay, so feel the nature, commune with it, ask it to transform you. Yeah?"

The cat chuffed, irritated, and closed his eyes.

She was glad he wasn't looking at her anymore; she felt more foolish now than when she'd had to crawl her way into the house. Saoirse took a deep breath. *Feel them, hear them, see them as they are.*

She sat cross-legged, noticing how her feet were still bare, how the cold dirt felt. She placed her palms in the dirt and sifted it through her fingers. Then she considered what insects and spiders might be crawling through it and jerked her hands back at once.

Calm down and take this seriously, she chastened herself. *We may not have much time. This is what you saved Kian for. This is what you almost died for.*

Sober once more, she tried to focus on the sounds of the forest. Light wind rustling the leaves. A euphony of bird songs. Chirps and twitters that surely belonged to more insects. Her skin crawled and her eyes flew open. This wasn't working.

She wished she could talk to Kian now and ask him for more advice. What else had he said in the secret room?

Envision yourself as part of reality, not separate from it....

Saoirse took another deep breath, closed her eyes, and tried to clear her mind of all thoughts of flying and crawling insects and arachnids. Perhaps once she had the elements' allegiance, she could ask them to keep all bugs away from her. That was a welcome thought.

She sat, trying to breathe and stay calm. *Part of reality, not separate from it...*

She tried to imagine sinking into the ground, fading into the wind, becoming as transparent as the sunlight. The sunlight which was swiftly fading. She opened her eyes, shocked. How long had they sat here? It must be early evening by now. She glanced at Kian, who laid with his head resting upon the human hair. Was he asleep? Or was he trying to concentrate on her behalf even though he couldn't use Cruthu himself? Was he cheering her on? Did he know how much time had passed? Was he giving up on her?

The beginnings of panic churned. What if she couldn't do this?

She felt the heaviness of the Tanist Stone against her

chest again. If she spoke to it, Kian would hear. Could she talk to it only in her mind?

Careful not to make a sound, she lifted it out of her shirt and thought the words, *Can I speak to you like this?*

Yes, came the peculiar, echoing voice.

Are you able to transform Kian back into his human form?

Yes. I can do all things that are possible.

If I ask you to do it, will I die?

Yes.

Despair joined the panic inside her as she let the necklace hang back down over her shirt. She had no idea how to even begin to use Cruthu. Nothing Kian had said about it made any sense to her, except for one thing:

It's your mind that struggles.

She'd always known that. Her mother's fault or not, Saoirse believed in her own incompetence deep in her core. No accomplishments over the last few days had been on her own; it had all been with the help of the stone.

She was a failure, had always been a failure, but she could do this one thing.

Saoirse took a shaky breath and grasped the Tanist Stone within its gold necklace once more. Terror coursed through her along with deep, inexplicable sadness. Mere days ago, she had wanted to die with all her heart. Now, sitting in this beautiful forest, she wanted to weep.

Do it now.

Saoirse gripped the stone, took one last look at the cat, and closed her eyes.

Transform Kian back into a human.

Kian was ripped into a place of extraordinary light. He roared as bone-breaking, flesh-tearing pain consumed him.

He would have feared death had he not known this feeling so well. It was working. She was doing it.

This destruction and reforming of his physical self was as familiar as he remembered it.

No fear this time. The light, the energy, surged through him as the very foundations of him decayed and reformed. He was being changed at the subatomic level. Taken from the elements in his human hair, just as it had from the elements in the cat hair Ciar had given him.

Even in the midst of agony and the imprisoning feeling of being controlled by a force other than his own will, he marveled at the power of Cruthu. Of creation.

He had no sense of time or space. He simply was, and he experienced it fully. This was true magic.

And then, it happened.

The light sparked out, and he was in darkness. Not the darkness of nothingness. The darkness of night.

He opened his eyes and knew, by the changes in his sight, that he was human once more. Everything was less sharp, less distinct. But the *color*. Tears rose to his eyes. One beauty traded for another. How he'd missed this.

His body was bare and cold. Relishing it, he shifted onto his back and gazed up at the moonlight pouring down into the clearing. Smell was muted, taste was subdued, but he didn't care. He was human.

"Saoirse," he breathed, and his own voice startled him. He could barely contain the emotion as he turned toward her, to thank her, to see her with his new eyes—

No.

She laid still and pale, her red hair vivid, her lips blue, her eyelids fluttering. He felt for her pulse—her skin was cold. There it was—slow, too slow. Why, how could this—

Then he recognized it lying against her shirt and knew at once what she had done.

"*No!*" he bellowed and ripped the necklace from her. He held the vile thing in his hand. "Tell me how to save her."

A voice entered his mind. *I can do as you wish, but your life will be the price.*

He faltered. He would do it, of course, but then she would be left alone. How would she survive? He couldn't abandon her.

"Pick—pick another price," he stammered. He didn't know if it was even possible; to his knowledge no one had ever tried it. "Pick something else. Please."

You seek to bargain with me?

"Will you? Can—can you save her and exact a different cost from me?" Her pulse beat slower and slower against his fingers. "I'll pay it. Anything."

You will not like it.

"Tell me!" he shouted.

I will save her in exchange for your access to Cruthu magic. An impenetrable wall will exist between you and the powers of creation.

Kian sat, stunned. Then he took a deep breath. "Do it."

As you wish.

Saoirse's eyes flew open and she drew in a sharp breath. She wasn't weak or faint. No pain crushed her chest or twisted in her stomach. Her head was clear.

She was alive.

Then, out of her periphery—

"*Who the fuck are you?*" she screamed as she scrambled away from the stranger. Her back hit the oak. She grasped for the Tanist Stone but it was no longer there.

"Saoirse, it's okay. It's me—Kian."

Her mouth fell open. "*Kian?*"

But—but no, Kian was supposed to be an old man. This person standing before her was *young*—her age or a little older. And not only was he not old, he was quite frankly the most beautiful man she'd ever seen.

Tall and muscular, a shock of black hair fell against his fair skin. *Black hair, not gray or white, you idiot*, Saoirse cursed herself.

He peered at her with green eyes. "You're okay, right?"

While his accent sounded American, there was something lilting in the way he talked. He was also, she comprehended with another shock, completely and utterly—

"Naked," she whispered.

"What?" he asked, stepping closer.

"Kian, you're naked!"

He looked down at himself and back up at her, unconcerned. "Cats don't wear clothes."

She suppressed a wild laugh, which felt inappropriate at the present moment. As she was trying to avoid his groin area, she caught sight of something dangling from his hand. The long chain of a necklace.

She pointed a shaking finger at it. "Did—did you—"

"Saoirse," he said, crouching down before her so they were eye-level, his movements feline. From this angle she had to concentrate even harder not to look at his nether region. "You used the Tanist Stone to transform me."

"I know. I couldn't use Cruthu; it wasn't working."

Kian stared at her. A lock of his hair, almost blue in the moonlight, fell onto his forehead. "You were willing to die?"

"Well, yeah," she said defensively. "They're coming back for the Deantan and you need to transform so you can use

Cruthu to defeat them. I couldn't use Cruthu—Kian, you're our only hope. The world's only hope."

"Not anymore," he said, holding her gaze. "Now it's you."

Saoirse blanched. For a moment she couldn't breathe. "What—what do you mean?"

"I used the stone to save your life. Don't you wonder why I'm still alive, why it didn't kill me in order to save you?"

She stared at him, unable to answer.

"I bargained with it."

"With the *stone*?"

"I used it to save your life... in exchange for my ability to use Cruthu."

"*What*," she screeched, springing to her feet. "No—why—why didn't you let me die?"

"Why didn't you use Cruthu?" Kian retorted, standing as well.

"I *couldn't*."

"Well, I couldn't let you die."

Her mind raced. She had to fix this, she had to undo what he'd done. "Kian, I *wanted* to sacrifice myself for this. It was at least *something* I could do."

"Are you sure it wasn't because you're still suicidal?" he asked, his face hard.

His comment knocked the wind out of her. She opened her mouth and closed it again.

His face softened. "I'm sorry. I shouldn't have said that." He took a step forward and she backed away.

"What now?" she glared at him, fighting back tears. "I screwed up. So, here we are, both alive and mortal, and neither of us can use Cruthu against Niamh."

"You *can* use Cruthu, Saoirse, and you will," he said. "I'll teach you. I have complete faith in you. It is your birthright as a human."

She covered her face with her hands. "Kian, I *can't*. I'm telling you, I tried. I don't have it. The—elements and shit—they don't trust me. My motivations or desires or whatever are off—"

She stopped talking abruptly. Kian had crossed the distance between them. His face was so close to hers that she could feel his breath. He raised a hand and placed it on her chest. Her mouth fell open and she gazed up into his green eyes as he spoke.

"Your problem isn't in here," he murmured, increasing the pressure of his hand over her heart. Then he raised it to gently touch the hair next to her temple. "It's in here."

She gulped. "In my hair?"

His green eyes twinkled. "In your head."

They gazed at each other for a few breathless moments, Saoirse unable to move. Then he stepped away, his face serious again.

"By the way, I'm keeping this." He opened his other palm to show the stone. "You're officially banned from using it."

He turned and walked away, Saoirse gaping after him.

After pulling herself together, she followed him through the forest, her mind racing again. Everything had suddenly and completely changed.

Kian had transformed, but not into an old, gross Druid man. And his ability to use Cruthu was gone. *Why* had he done it? When he was the one person alive who knew how to use this magic?

This *damn* magic. It made no sense to her. And what the hell was that, the whole "your problem isn't in here, it's in here" nonsense (as much as she'd enjoyed his touch, particularly when his hand had hovered over her left breast...)

She shook her head. *Focus, Saoirse.*

How did she fix a problem that was in her *head?* He really *did* sound like her dad.

What had been that thing Dad always said? It drove her crazy because she knew he was trying to drill it into her, as if him repeating it enough times would cause it to finally sink in and change the way she thought about things.

You can't do this yet. *Yet.* It had been his favorite word. And also, the always irritating, *Don't give up when you're running uphill.*

The memories of his words didn't inspire her. They made her feel worse. Dad had always said these things, and it hadn't mattered. She still gave up, over and over again, no matter what the task was. And then Mom would come to her rescue, telling him that she couldn't help it, she was so fragile after what had happened...

Funny, now that she knew nothing bad had happened to her. Strange, sure, and impossible to understand as a child. But it was her parents' fear of what her grandparents had done that traumatized her, not the act itself.

Did it even matter? Sure, she hadn't been abused, wasn't left fragile and incapable from it. But she had proven she was incapable anyway. Maybe it was who she was.

She swallowed painfully at the thought.

But then there was Kian... he seemed to believe she could do it. Why? Because it was her "birthright?"

Or did he see more in her?

She thought back to what he'd said during their argument, before that humiliating exposure of her past self-destructive desires.

I couldn't let you die.

He'd cared whether she lived or died, had sacrificed his *own* birthright powers to save her.

She gazed at his inky black hair, which fell to his shoulders, and at the muscles moving in his back as he walked.

She took a deep breath. This was it. This was her situation. She hated it, it terrified her, but there was no changing it. Especially when he was guarding the Tanist Stone, as if he knew she was already thinking about reversing the bargain.

I couldn't let you die.

No more whining, no more wallowing. She had to listen to Kian, learn from him, and trust that there was a way for her to wield this power.

Saoirse let out a long breath and allowed herself to be distracted from her unease as she gazed at the most marvelous male backside she had ever seen.

PART III

As the magician learns to harness the secrets of reality unencumbered by her own denials of it, she changes from the simple wanderer to warrior.

The writings of Seamus Dannan

16

Much legend surrounds the land of Tír na nÓg. It is often described as a paradisiacal land of eternal youth and beauty, and dangerous to the human traveler.

Seamus Dannan, *Lore: The True History of the Celts*

"Holy shit," Hawking whispered.

The Costa Rican Cloud Forest. The Azores in Portugal. Bamboo forests in Japan. The Amazon, Machu Pichu, Vietnam, New Zealand... He had traveled to the most stunning places in the world. But what spread before him brought tears to his eyes, which made him feel like a douche bag.

He stood on a hill with a jungle of the largest trees he had ever seen to his left and fields of flowers to his right. But what rose in front of him made him sink to the ground.

There was nothing like this on earth.

It was an immense, impossibly tall mountain of the most

vivid green. It rose higher than the clouds; he could not see where it ended. He would have thought this mountain was a wall if he couldn't see where it sloped from valley to peak. More colors materialized in the midst of the green: blues and purples and reds. Brightly colored birds soared here and there. It was like this world had a permanent Instagram filter.

When Hawking regained some of his bearings, he noticed other things. How soft the springy grass was underneath him. How the perfect warmth from the sun combined with a gentle breeze was better than the best Hawaiian day. He wanted to strip naked and roll down this hill. He didn't even feel this good on 'shrooms.

The rainforest caught his eye. The trees seemed prehistoric: twice the size and height of sequoias, with splashes of color on the trunks that reminded him of rainbow eucalypti he had seen in Indonesia. The leaves were gargantuan and as vivid as the green on the mountains. Mossy darkness, shadowy but not uninviting, waited beyond them.

Standing up, he craned his neck and saw sparkling blue beyond the rainforest. A lake? An ocean?

The fields to his right were a sea of blueish purple flowers. He took a deep breath and in the clear air, he caught a hint of their perfume. Hawking never wanted to leave.

Then he glanced down at the white branch in his hand.

He hadn't come here to sightsee.

About to climb down the hill, Hawking stopped when he spotted figures in the valley between his hill and where the land sloped up again. He couldn't make out much about them besides that they appeared to be men with long hair.

"Hey," he shouted, waving the branch in the air.

The group—five of them—moved. They saw him. He grinned, waving again as they ran toward him. He had done it. He had found Tír na nÓg and would bring back help. It was all going to be okay.

But when they got close enough for him to see them clearly, he froze.

Their long hair flew behind them as the men raced across the land. Their faces were hard with fury; their muscular bodies barely covered by scraps of animal hide. But what shocked him the most, what filled him with dread and a sense of wrongness he couldn't explain, was their eyes.

Their irises and pupils were white: completely, vacantly white.

One was much faster than the others. Hawking braced himself but the man dodged around him and tore past. Hawking turned to watch—

The portal was still open. The man—with his creepy-ass eyes—had sprinted right through the other side and into Earth.

Hawking leapt away and the portal closed. It had been his body on the threshold that kept it open. The other four men staggered to a halt. One's eyes widened. His mouth moved, speaking a language Hawking didn't recognize, but the man's words were translated in his mind.

"It's the bough. Seize him!"

Hawking turned and ran with everything he had toward the trees. The temperature dropped when he entered the dark jungle. He threw himself behind a massive tree. Trying to breathe as quietly as possible was a tall task, but his panting was masked by the sounds of the rainforest. He hunched over, a stitch in his side, his many injuries throbbing with pain he hadn't noticed when he was taking in the landscape.

Risking a glance around the side of the tree, he saw

nothing save for a thick, wet mist. Had they not followed him in here? Why?

What the hell had Seamus been talking about? Yes, Tír na nÓg was beautiful, but these were not good people; he sensed their coldness and malice. And he had let one through the portal, what a fucking *idiot*.

Despair overwhelmed him. He swallowed hard and gripped the bough. He had to get back to Earth. Coming here had only made things worse; he had to go back and stop the man who had gotten through—

An earsplitting crack sounded above his head. He looked up. An arrow was buried in the vibrant trunk.

Leaping over giant roots, whipping through thick leaves as big as his body, Hawking ran. He was going the opposite way of the hill, deeper into the jungle. He tried to cut over, hoping to race around and back out. Arrows hit the trees to his left and right with deafening cracks, forcing him to keep running forward—

And then a sound made his stomach sink. Laughter. Cruel, mocking laughter.

He wasn't escaping. He was being taunted. Herded.

Could he climb? Would that make him an easier target for their arrows?

Fuck's sake, Hawking, think.

His heart leapt with fear as glowing, white eyes peered at him through the trees and mist. Still, he ran, ignoring his own exhaustion. He couldn't stop, he couldn't fight, he had no weapon—

The trees opened up and blue sky spread before him. He raced through the mist toward it—

Hawking yelped as he barely staggered to a stop in time. Beyond the trees was a short stretch of ground that ended in a cliff hundreds of feet above a vast, turquoise body of water.

He turned around. The trees were filled with hundreds of those glowing, white eyes.

A man with dark hair stepped out of the jungle. He bared his teeth.

"Thank you for bringing the Silver Bough to us."

"We've been waiting for quite some time," a woman with brilliant red hair smirked, coming to stand beside him. The animal skins barely covered her body.

Hawking looked around in panic. The drop-off was behind him and next to him stood one of the immense trees. He shifted next to it, glancing up, trying to think fast. Could he—

"He thinks to climb the tree," the first man chuckled, stalking toward Hawking.

The crowd laughed. Dozens of them were coming out of the shadows now.

"Give me the bough, Earth-born. I'm tired of playing. Hand it over and we may wait until you're dead to begin devouring you..."

Hawking glanced down at the white branch clutched in his hand.

"Stop." He thrust the Silver Bough behind him, over the side of the cliff. The man froze. "One step closer and I'll drop it." *And then what, genius?* But he had to stall for time, he had to think—

"You would destroy your only way back to Earth?" the woman scoffed.

"If it meant you shitheads couldn't get through, yeah," Hawking said, and he meant it. He edged backward an inch. This was it. His only choice. He couldn't let them get the bough, and to hell with letting these cannibals get their hands on him. He would jump. Better to be splattered on the rocks below than eaten alive.

"Even if you manage to escape us, which you won't, you'll be stuck here forever," the man hissed.

"I don't know, this place doesn't seem so bad," Hawking said. Now. He had to jump. He had to do it, *now*—

"Oh, it is," a hoarse female voice whispered close to him. "It's bad."

And before he could find the source of the voice, the ground beneath him disappeared.

Everything went black. As he free-fell, he thought for a wild moment that he had stumbled off the cliff and gone blind at the same time.

But then the pungent scent of damp wood filled his nose and his legs and back met something solid. He shouted and clutched the bough to him. He was sliding down some kind of chute. The slick surface beneath him abruptly leveled out and he came to a halt.

Scrambling to his feet, he jumped as he backed into something hard. A wall.

"Relax," came the same croaky female voice. And then a bright, warm light came to life before him.

It took him a few seconds to adjust to the sudden brilliance, which looked like a ball of fire but emitted no warmth. An ancient woman held the light in her hand. Her loose skin, as dark as the skin of those who chased him, sagged from her face. Her hair was a wispy cloud atop her head.

Hawking gasped. Her eyes, shimmering in the imposter fire, milky white—

"Ah. My eyes. Don't worry, I'm just blind as night. Not one of them."

He heard her voice in his head, but her mouth moved differently, not matching the words he heard.

"You're safe. They cannot harm you here."

She looked frail and stooped. Not a threat, although she did conjure light out of nowhere...

"Where are we?"

"Inside a tree," she replied.

He took in what he could see of his surroundings. A wooden tunnel, tall enough to stand in and wide enough for them both to walk through. To his left was the sloping slide he'd come down.

"More specifically," she said, "inside the roots of a tree."

Hawking shook his head in awe. "This is unreal."

"You don't dwell in roots on Earth, I take it?"

"You know I'm from Earth?"

"I heard you come through to our realm on the Hill of Tarscha. I opened the ground for you to enter the roots. You must have the key, the Silver Bough. The means to travel between realms. It only exists between our two, although I must suppose there are others." The woman peered at him. "Have you come to help us?"

Hawking's breath caught. "Wait—what?"

"Did you come from Earth to help us?" she repeated.

"Help *you*?" Hawking asked, bewildered. "I came because Earth needs help."

The woman closed her milky eyes and shook her head. She muttered something that didn't translate but Hawking had a fair idea what it meant. Finally, she spoke.

"Then both our worlds appear to be in trouble."

It couldn't be true. But he remembered those people with their glowing white eyes and mocking laughter...

He sagged against the wall, then hissed at the contact with the cut on his back.

"You're wounded," the old woman said. "I can smell your blood." With her free hand, she felt his face, his head, his neck, down to his arms and hands. She motioned for him to turn around and delicately touched his back.

"Ooh, you're in bad shape. That didn't all happen to you here, did it?"

"No, before—"

"I figured. If one of those—" she spat a word he didn't recognize— "had gotten hold of you, you wouldn't have made it out alive."

"What *are* they?"

"We call them the Changed." She did not elaborate. "Come."

She flicked her wrist, and the ball of light moved from her hand to hover in the wood tunnel in front of them. He followed the old woman as she shuffled forward, apparently knowing where to go without the need of sight. She wore clothing made of a soft-looking material, different from the animal hide the others wore.

"The roots are connected," she explained as they walked. "All the trees in Tír na nÓg share the same root system."

Another wooden tunnel opened to their right. They walked for a long time, Hawking feeling suddenly weak and feverish.

"Does everyone live in the roots?"

She chuckled. "No. Before, we all lived together above ground. But my family has sought shelter here for many years. My name is Una. What is yours?"

"Hawking. Thank you for saving me, Una."

"Well," Una chuckled again, "it isn't every day an Earthborn comes to Tír na nÓg."

"How are we able to speak? It's like your words are translated in my mind."

"Another feature of the connection between our worlds, I assume. It is quite convenient, is it not?"

Hawking marveled at this, at everything he had experienced of Tír na nÓg so far. It was like Earth but better. Except for the white-eyed cannibals.

"And the—Changed—can't get in here?" he asked.

"They are unaware of this tunnel system. We built it and we open and close the entrances at will. I opened one for you, then closed it after."

"How did you find me?" Hawking asked as they took another turn.

"I was monitoring the Hill of Tarscha," Una replied. "As were they. I do not know why the Changed wish to enter Earth. As you know, my desire was to find help for our people here. My family, as well as the Changed, have been waiting at the Hill for someone to come through for a long time."

Hawking's heart sunk further.

"Almost there," Una said, and Hawking could see warm light far down the tunnel.

It was a large, beautiful room, with vines and small roots twining down the walls. He saw some kind of furniture—

Suddenly, he was slammed against the wall by an invisible force.

"Kipp! No!" Una shouted.

A young woman with a mane of blonde hair that shone brilliantly against her dark skin stalked toward him, her face set with fury. Her eyes weren't white: they were a startling blue, like the turquoise lake beyond the rainforest.

Hawking couldn't breathe, like the air around him had disappeared. He dropped the bough, fighting against the invisible bonds that held him to the wall. He desperately needed to inhale, his head flooded with panic—

"Enough," Una said.

Abruptly, he was able to gulp in fresh air. His unseen bonds disappeared. He stumbled to the ground, gasping.

"I brought him. He is from Earth. Look at his eyes. He is no threat."

Hawking looked to Una and the young woman she had called Kipp. Kipp glared at him. She wore the same neutral-colored clothing as Una, though not nearly as much of it. Hawking could see her muscular physique balanced with feminine curves.

"The Changed had him cornered. They were going to kill him and take the Silver Bough. Imagine how disastrous if they made their way into Earth—"

"One did," he said. "One got past me before the portal closed."

Una closed her eyes once again and muttered an untranslated oath. Hawking felt his status drop from letdown to moron.

An old man appeared from a doorway covered in hanging vines. He looked as old and frail as Una and blinked at Hawking with polite curiosity.

"Alasdar, this is Hawking, he comes from Earth," Una explained in a loud voice. "I saved him from the Changed and now he's going to stay with us."

"How nice," the old man said with a vacant smile.

"He's not quite all there," Una explained to Hawking.

"Excuse me," Kipp spoke for the first time, still glaring at Hawking. "Why is the Earth-born going to stay with us?"

"Because he's injured, for one," Una said. "He needs food, water, and help with his wounds."

Kipp stood her ground, her arms folded. Una hobbled close to her and put a hand on her arm.

"Thank you for protecting us, Daughter. But I sense goodness in him. You have no need to worry."

Kipp softened fractionally at her mother's touch. She nodded, still eyeing Hawking, and left the room.

"Come, sit," Una said. Lit by more spheres of glowing light, the space was adorned with wooden furniture that resembled what he was accustomed to on Earth, except it was... different. The smoothness of the angles, the practicality of the fabrics covering them... he sat on what he supposed was a chair, marveling at the softness of the material. It molded to his form and as he sat back, he acutely felt his own exhaustion.

Kipp reappeared holding a wooden tray. She set it on a surface next to him and stepped back. His fatigue, his thirst, his hunger—all pummeled him as he reached for a wooden cup, which also molded to his grip. It was delicious, cold water. He drank deeply and set it down.

On the tray was food he couldn't adequately describe. He figured one hunk of something must be similar to bread, another like meat, although it was a deep purple in color. Juicy-looking colorful orbs he assumed were fruits made up half the spread.

He hesitated. Hawking considered himself adventurous with food, always trying exotic dishes on his travels. But this was food from another planet. He closed his eyes, felt around for the purple meat, and took a bite.

A groan escaped him. The texture and taste were better than the finest filet mignon.

"Is everything better here?" he said through a mouthful.

"If you say it is," Una said, amused. "None of us have been to Earth."

He took a large bite of the bread-like substance. It was dense and delicious. Hawking ate, not caring about the three people watching him (Alasdar still smiled at him blankly) until he couldn't fit even one more of the intoxicating fruits.

"Finished?" Kipp said coldly.

He wiped his mouth and nodded.

She knelt before him, scanning his body. Up close, he appreciated her fine, dark skin and the unique bone structure she shared with her parents. He couldn't decide if she was beautiful or not. Typically, he was attracted to very thin girls, although he preferred them to have great tits and ass —whether through augmentation or endowed naturally, he didn't care. This woman before him was not thin—she was curvaceous and strong, could even be equal to himself in strength. The idea made him feel odd.

She motioned for him to hold out his arm. She unwrapped the bloodstained cloth and he inhaled sharply at the sight.

The cut in his arm was no longer bleeding. It was covered in a greenish yellow, wet scab. The skin surrounding the wound was dark red and throbbing. He caught a whiff of a repulsive smell.

"How is it already—"

"The time lapse between here and Earth," Una said, and he figured she could smell the rotting stench of his arm as well. How much time had already passed on Earth?

Kipp closed her eyes and took in a deep breath.

Hawking's arm tingled. The red around the injury faded, as if absorbed by the wound itself. The gaping cut shrank, the greenish scab fading until normal skin grew over.

Hawking raised his arm, astonished. It was like the wound was never there.

"What is this magic?"

"Something that is rumored to have been lost from your

world," Kipp said, feeling around his head. "Now I know the rumors are true."

"Cruthu," he breathed. "That's how you made all of this?" He motioned to the dwelling.

Una nodded at his side. "And the Changed no longer have access to the magic."

Hawking frowned. "The Changed can't do magic? Then why don't you just kill them?"

Kipp's gaze snapped to his, her eyes so fierce that he leaned back.

"Because they are our people. They belong to us, and we to them. If they were Changed, then it stands to reason they can be... *un*changed. We hide from them and defend ourselves if necessary but we do not kill them."

He remained silent as she closed her eyes and worked on the rest of his injuries. By the time she was done, his fingernails had regrown, his head and throat no longer hurt, and the cut on his back was healed. He felt energized and rested.

"Thank you."

She glanced away from him and moved to sit across the room, her expression guarded.

"How many of your people have been Changed?"

"To our knowledge, those who remained like us were killed by them," said Una. "We are likely the only ones left."

Something weighted the air at her words. Sadness. Loneliness.

"I'm sorry," Hawking said. "I thought when I came here I would find a good place. That's how our legends speak of Tír na nÓg. What happened? What Changed them?"

"Might be best to show him," Una said to her daughter. "Perhaps his world suffers from something similar."

Kipp stood. "Come," she said to Hawking.

He followed Kipp through the expanse of their dwelling, wanting to stop and examine more details, but trying to keep up. She was a lot taller than he usually desired, almost as tall as he. She knelt on the ground at the end of a room. Before her was a small curtain of vines, which she swept aside to reveal a tunnel large enough for a person to crawl through.

No spheres of light lit the way, but as the tunnel sloped upward he saw a different kind of light. Daylight.

"I thought you closed the openings?" Hawking asked.

"We keep some open for oxygen," Kipp replied. "They are hidden from the Changed."

The tunnel angled vertically with wooden steps molded to it. Hawking followed Kipp as she climbed. His endurance was still shit, but at least all the time he spent building his legs made the climb easier work. Kipp reached the top and moved to the side, allowing him to join her on the top steps.

What he saw hit him like a punch to his gut.

Far in the distance, a gathering storm of inky black clouds obscured the brilliant blue sky.

Some sort of lightning flashed there, but instead of long lines of electricity, the lights exploded in deadly sparks. They reminded him of a something amiss, like a damaged power line. A mistake. Something unnatural.

There was a deadness to it.

Below, the green of the mountain and valley were faded to brown, rotted and decayed.

Not only was this at odds with the beauty of Tír na nÓg, Hawking felt, in every cell of his body, complete and utter wrongness.

"This is not a good place, Earth-born," Kipp said softly as she gazed ahead. "Not anymore."

17

A close proximity with Scrios magic can have an undesirable effect on an already psychically vulnerable person.

Seamus Dannan, *Lore: The True History of the Celts*

Eoghan was caked in dried blood and none of it was his own. A pill bottle rattled in his hand.

Psychogenic tremors. Don't focus on it. Breathe slow. Don't let panic overtake you.

Each breath filled his nose with the coppery scent of annihilation.

"What have I done," he rasped as he let the pill bottle fall from his hand. "What have I done, what have I done?"

Rumination. Obsessive thinking. Stop it. Change it. Change the course of your thoughts. Action for distraction.

Eoghan heaved himself off of a scratchy, thin comforter, springs popping as he rose from the cheap motel bed. In a frenzy, he ripped off his bloody clothing. His naked form stared back from the filthy mirror, his teeth bared.

Internalization of guilt. Self-hatred. Identify cognitive distortions. Reframe positively.

"Reframe... reframe..." Eoghan laughed, falling backwards on the ratty bed and didn't stop until his abdomen hurt.

Appropriate response to irony. Self-validate. Self-disclose. Denial of a distasteful truth. State the truth.

"I liked it," he whispered. The shock in their eyes as he slashed and flayed. Cutting into them like hunks of meat. Hacking away at their faces until they were mere raw hamburger instead of human. He sighed in contentment.

Then his stomach twisted.

"What have I done..." He curled on his side in a fetal position.

If his colleagues knew, if his patients knew what an imposter he was...

Psychotic aggression can be treated and controlled with psychostimulants, mood stabilizers, and antipsychotics.

"Obviously not," Eoghan's voice broke and he wept. He grabbed a sandpaper pillow and held it to him.

Catharsis. Let it run its course.

He wanted... he wanted... his mother. He cried harder.

Her face. He only ever saw it two ways. Blank and cold, or contorted with rage.

Never a smile for him.

Never.

Child ego-state engaged. Disorganized attachment stemming from abusive main caregiver. Fright without solution. Look for positive models of safety, security, affection.

Not Dad. Dad was scared. He would drink and fade into the background... Dad was nowhere, no one.

Recall times of warmth, times of care, times of genuine human connection.

Nana. He moaned into the pillow. Being held in Melinda's arms, rocked as she sang softly into his hair. She'd loved him. He knew she'd loved him.

And then that night, he was ripped from her forever...

He let go of the pillow, grasped around on the comforter for the pill bottle. Oxycontin. He'd prescribed it himself.

Desire to dissociate as a defense mechanism, need stronger coping skills.

He unscrewed the cap. One. He swallowed. Two. Again. Three.

Suicidal ideation, stop and call for help.

Four. Swallow. Five.

This was the only way. The only way to stop it all.

As Eoghan picked up the sixth pill, his brain zapped.

He cried out, dropped the bottle. Pills spilled onto the threadbare floor as another wave shocked his brain.

Pain. The idea of pain. The memory of pain. The immersion in all that is meant by pain, all the pain that has ever been felt or will be felt in the world. Every muscle rent, every bone snapped in two—

"Okay. I won't. That's enough." His words came out through his clamped teeth in a strangled scream. "*I won't.*"

Wrenching his teeth apart, he shoved a finger down his throat and vomited over the side of the bed.

Eoghan staggered to the small shower. His feet were shredded and clotted from the miles he'd walked barefoot after leaving the manor. He yanked on the shower spray. This place (which had taken his stack of cash, no questions asked about his gruesome appearance) probably didn't have hot water but it didn't matter; he needed it cold.

He stood in a waterfall of ice until he shivered so

violently that he almost fell. Grabbing a washcloth—more sandpaper—he scrubbed at himself until he was clean. Well, until he looked clean.

He would never be clean.

Eoghan stumbled out of his room and to the office, wrapped in a thin towel. He requested fresh clothes, offered more cash, and took what he was given.

The clinical voice inside his head was gone now. Only one thought dominated his mind.

He had to go back. He had to fix this.

"I have to go back. I have to fix this."

18

Danu created Cruthu for the dwellers of Earth and Tír na nÓg. While created for their benefit and development, the magic included an intrinsic safeguard. One had to possess certain personal qualities in order to use it.

Seamus Dannan, *Lore: The True History of the Celts*

When they broke through the tree line, Kian whooped for joy.

"Shh," Saoirse hissed. "The cult might be back."

"You're right," he said, turning to face her as he walked backward. He raised his face to the moonlight. "You have no idea how good this feels."

Or looks, she thought and glanced away. *Get a grip; quit drooling over him like a horny teenager.*

Kian stumbled and sprawled on the ground. He threw

back his head and laughed. "I'm still getting used to it. My body is so clunky now."

Saoirse smiled in spite of herself. Even through her shame and anxiety about what lie ahead, she couldn't help finding Kian's happiness endearing.

"You're going to be a mess if the Cult of Balor is here. No help to me at all," she said, helping him up. As his hand wrapped around hers, she shuddered. Even his hands were amazing— strong and smooth and—she shook her head.

"I think I need a cold shower."

"Ah, a shower." he said. "I haven't enjoyed being submerged in water in—well, you know."

And then the image of this new Kian standing under a stream of water, rivulets running down his muscled body…

"Okay, why don't you stay hidden out here and I'll see if the cult is back," Saoirse said harshly.

"Why you?"

She didn't answer, leaving him behind the overgrown hedges and sneaking in through the solarium. Peering out the windowed wall that faced the driveway, she saw no cars there.

The house beyond was dark. Saoirse held still, listening for any sounds. Nothing.

"Kian?" she called from the doorway to the solarium.

He rose from behind the hedge, his eyes bright under his dark brows, the hollows under his cheekbones emphasized by the moonlight. His movements weren't clumsy now. Not once breaking their gaze, he climbed the stairs in a graceful prowl. By the time he reached the top, Saoirse could no longer breathe.

"All clear?"

She swallowed and nodded.

"Good. I'm starving." And he moved past her into the house.

Saoirse closed her eyes and took a few deep breaths before following him inside.

Kian worked in the kitchen with vigor. Saoirse sat at the table, grateful that everything below his waist was obscured by the island.

"You may not remember, but Seamus was an excellent cook. Not Melinda; she was a disaster. Which is ironic because she was a talented chemist," he said as he pulled out spices and other ingredients. "All of my senses are duller now, but my range of taste as a cat was very limited."

"How... long?" Saoirse asked tentatively. What she really meant was, *how old are you?*

"How long was I a cat? Five thousand years."

Her mouth fell open.

"I spent centuries watching humans invent all kinds of foods I didn't want as a cat."

He made himself a feast of mashed potatoes, macaroni and cheese, barbecued chicken, pop tarts, and an enormous salad filled with all kinds of vegetables (courtesy of Eoghan's shopping trip). He particularly loved the pop tarts.

"I couldn't taste anything sweet as a cat," he explained through a mouthful.

This is the weirdest thing I've experienced yet, Saoirse thought fervently.

"We can start at dawn," he said, chewing. "I thought of a place that might be good to practice. This will go a lot better now that I can actually talk to you."

He grinned, and the smile only made his face more achingly handsome. When he finally finished (Saoirse having declined all of his offers to share) and washed everything down with a cartonful of orange juice, he suggested that they take night watches in case the cult came back.

"I think we should sleep in the solarium. That way we can see the driveway and hear if anything is happening inside the house. It's also the best spot to make a run for it."

"Um, Kian?" she said as he made to walk back into the beautiful sunroom.

"Yes?" He turned his entire body toward her.

"Do you think you might want to put on some clothes?"

"Oh." He glanced down at himself. "Yes, I guess I should. I can take that shower. You should, too. Your clothes are caked in all sorts of stuff."

She blanched. With the whirlwind of the past few days, she hadn't even thought of how she must look and smell.

When they reached the top of the stairs together, he headed for the room Hawking had stayed in and she went to her own. Saoirse tried to wipe her mind of all thought as she peeled off her filthy clothes and stood under the hot running water. Particularly of Kian taking his own shower only a few rooms away…

"Stop it," she growled at herself. It was a part of herself that she had shut down years ago. Why was it emerging now, uncontrollably?

She switched the water to cold and shrieked.

After the shower, Saoirse contemplated her reflection for the first time since her family died. Malnourishment made her pale and thin, sickly-looking. Her breasts and rear were smaller, her ribs showed. Kian looked healthy and strong. She looked terminally ill.

She would eat more, she swore to herself.

Feeling increasingly foolish, she snuck into Linnaeus's bathroom and fiddled around with her cousin's vast amount of makeup. She dried her hair some, thankful that her waves, weighed down by length, tended to look good regardless of what she did to it.

"What are you doing?" She glared at herself in the mirror. "An evil cult has killed off your family and you're responsible for stopping them from hurting anyone else and you're worried about looking cute for a guy?"

In defiance of this silliness, she threw on a pair of leggings and a large t-shirt and marched downstairs.

When she entered the giant glass room filled with plants, she stopped short.

"Heaven help me."

Kian stood in the middle of the room. He hadn't put on a shirt at all, only a pair of Hawking's dark gray sweatpants that hung low on his hips. His hair was wet and water glistened on his muscular chest.

"Sorry, I took longer in the shower than I meant to," he grinned.

She made some kind of noise in response.

"Are you okay?" He peered at her. "You're so quiet now. You never stopped talking when I was a cat."

Saoirse flushed. "I ..." She waved her hands around helplessly. "It's a lot."

"Of course," he said with concern. "Why don't you lie down? I'll take the first watch; I'm not tired at all."

Saoirse climbed onto one of the cushy lounge-chairs. She felt exposed in the large, windowed room. But Kian was right that this was the best place to keep a lookout and escape if the Cult of Balor came back.

She thought with a pang of the other night, so recent yet a lifetime ago, when she and her cousins had smoked pot in here. It was all so overwhelming—the grief, the threat, the expectations on her, Kian's unexpected youth and beauty. She tried not to look at him and gazed out the far window where the carriage house stood at the end of the driveway. Her stomach twisted with nausea as she remembered the carnage she had seen in there, at the unrecognizable bodies of her poor cousins...

"I've been thinking," Kian said, sitting down on the chair next to hers, his thick black hair now dry and soft-looking. "It's odd that they haven't come back for the other Deantan yet. That's the first thing I expected them to do after you rescued me, and they had plenty of time to get here while we were recovering in that cabin."

A thought struck Saoirse.

"Kian, what if they did? What if they found them? The bough?"

To her surprise, he smiled.

"There's no way they would find it. They would still be here looking for it, trust me. But there's still the issue of how they got here in the first place. The magic that protects this place has been impenetrable."

"They must have something we don't know about. Maybe another type of Deantan, like Seamus thought. He said that in one of the transcripts."

"He did think that, and I bet he's right. They have something."

"Why did my grandparents have the Deantan in the first place?"

Kian raised his eyebrows. "Your family line has protected the Deantan and the truth for thousands of years. The Tuatha dé Danann. They were wielders of Cruthu."

"My family line?"

Kian nodded. "The practice of Cruthu faded long ago, but your ancestors still passed on their knowledge for generations. In the last couple of centuries, around the time they immigrated to America, they stopped believing. They merely told the stories as fairy tales, passing the Deantan on as heirlooms.

"Seamus grew up here," he continued. "This has been your family's estate since they immigrated, but the Dannans had dwindled down until it was only Seamus and his parents. They died while he was in high school, leaving him the only survivor."

"Wow," Saoirse said. "Seamus lost his family, too. I never knew."

"He understood perhaps more than anyone how painful it would be for you." Kian gazed at her with sadness in his bright green eyes.

She was touched. It made her think back to the restrained affection he had shown her in his cat form. He could have been bitter, being stuck as a cat for so long—and maybe he had been. But he chose to be kind.

"You too," she said. "You had to watch them all die while you were trapped as a cat."

The light in his face died out and he averted his gaze. "I didn't really have a family."

She waited for him to continue but he looked so tense that she changed the subject.

"Were you already with Seamus and his family?" *My family,* she thought.

"Yes," Kian said, his eyes refocusing on her. "But not to their knowledge. They thought I was a stray cat on the property. I had tried to reveal myself to their predecessors only to be attacked, so I contented myself with at least knowing where the Deantan were. Things changed, however, after Seamus published his book.

"You see, the Cult of Balor—another family line, called the Fomorians—had been around for as long as the Tuatha dé Danann. For millennia they've searched for the Deantan.

And enjoyed their prolonged lives," he added darkly. "You saw the ritual. That's the cost of using Spellbreaker for renewed youth. It must be taken from the blood of a child."

Saoirse shuddered and wondered if Niamh had already found another one to replace the child she'd saved.

"They're evil people," Kian continued. "Always have been. They believe themselves superior to all others, and worthy of taking everything they want. They raise their children with brutality and follow the whims of their every lust. A wholly destructive and consuming society."

Saoirse thought of something.

"Why were they searching for the Deantan if they already had a way to stay immortal? Why do they want them so badly?"

He shrugged. "More power, I assume. And they believe the Deantan belong to them."

She could understand about the Tanist Stone, although with such a steep price it was hardly ideal. She wouldn't put it past Niamh to force others to use it for her so that her blood was never taken. With the Coire cup they could gain their immortality that way, although they would still have aged. And the Silver Bough—maybe there was something in Tír na nÓg they wanted.

"Anyway, Seamus left for college shortly after his parents died to study Celtic history and there he met and married Melinda. She was unique. Brilliant—had been in college since she was fifteen. She was in a doctorate program when they met. While she had begun her education focused on botany, she came to be obsessed with physics. Specifically, quantum physics."

He said this with such enthusiasm that she felt like she was supposed to have a reaction. When she continued to look at him blankly, he continued.

"Quantum physics is the study of nature—matter and light and such—at the atomic and subatomic levels. There have been some remarkable discoveries in quantum physics. None of it was a surprise to me as someone who had knowledge of Cruthu. But Melinda was bright and openminded enough to sense these discoveries' connection to the supernatural."

Saoirse snorted. This shit was supernatural, alright.

"Seamus came to some interesting conclusions of his own. The silly stories he'd been told as a child seemed to actually be different interpretations of Celtic mythology. Through his research, he concluded the *correct* interpretations. He also began to have suspicions about certain family heirlooms he had grown up with."

"Had you revealed yourself by then?" Saoirse asked.

"No, not until he published his book. It made him somewhat famous. That was how the cult found him. They attacked but he and Melinda managed to escape, to flee back to his childhood home. It was then that I revealed myself to him—Cait Sídhe, the King of Cats," he laughed bitterly. "I told them about the protection on the Dannan property that had been cast generations before by an ancestor who still had access to Cruthu—a tricky bit of magic to do, to make it last so long into the future, but it proved effective. As long as they stayed here and allowed themselves to fade into obscurity, they were safe."

"And they didn't like that," Saoirse said.

"It was hard for them. Both orphans—Melinda having been raised in foster care until her genius was finally recognized—both brilliant, they wanted recognition. Like I said, they were good people but they were proud."

Her dad must have gotten that from them. Though he loved helping people, he also loved the spotlight.

Saoirse suddenly felt profoundly exhausted. Her head drooped.

"Alright," Kian said. "Enough bedtime stories. You need to get some sleep. We have a big day ahead. I need to get you up to speed as soon as possible."

Before they come back, she thought.

Kian rose as she curled on her side on the lounge chair. The heavy softness of a blanket covered her. She glanced around for him but he was already staring out the vast window, his dark silhouette illuminated by starlight.

Saoirse awoke to warm light against her eyelids. She sat up with a start. Sitting across from her was a smiling Kian holding a plate of food.

"What—" It was far past dawn. "You let me sleep all night."

"You needed it," he said, holding out the plate.

"What about you?"

"I was too excited. It's like I've been reunited with a long-lost friend. I'm myself again. Besides, I slept constantly as a cat."

"Fair enough," Saoirse said. He'd let her sleep all night, had gotten her a blanket, and now made her breakfast. Kind *and* thoughtful.

"Go ahead and eat. I have an idea for today and it's going to take some physical exertion."

The way his green eyes twinkled made her blossoming appetite shut down.

Get a grip, Saoirse, he doesn't mean sex. Right?

She forced herself to eat the eggs, sausage, toast, and fruit he made her. For a man who spent the last five thousand years without opposable thumbs, he was a good cook.

Once she was finished Kian revealed his plan for their day's training.

It was definitely not sex.

"You want us to go all the way up *there*?"

He nodded, the wind tousling his midnight hair as he smiled down at her. They stood on the back terrace, a backpack filled with bottled water slung over Kian's shoulders. "We'll take our time. Getting there will be part of the process."

Saoirse looked on helplessly. He intended them to cross through the forest, which was miles long, and then climb to the top of a distant peak. While not a mountain—the area didn't have any of those—it was at least a very large hill.

Exercise hadn't been part of Saoirse's life before all of this, and spending time in nature was limited to the kid-friendly weekend hikes with her parents and the twins. She had refused their invitations to camp, insisting on more than a primitive bed and bathroom situation.

What if I have to go to the bathroom? she thought in a panic as she surveyed the distant peak.

And then a slew of memories she'd kept at bay rushed into her mind. This man, when he was a cat, when she thought his human form was to be old and decrepit, had seen her covered in blood, vomit, pass out... she had pet him... *he had lain in her lap.*

Her face burned.

"Let's get on with it," she said irritably and Kian chuckled.

He led her through the woods as if by a natural compass —or maybe he had the area memorized from many feline wanderings. The forest was a sea of green tinged with yellow and red as it began to yield to autumn. Saoirse drank water frequently as they picked their way through the mossy roots and fallen branches. She was still recovering from blood loss. Her feet hurt already and she was starting to sweat in spite of the cool day.

"Just breathe," Kian said.

She glanced at him as he walked along with easy grace, looking obnoxiously peaceful and content. He hadn't worn shoes, which was somehow fitting. He also once again neglected to put on a shirt.

"This is a way to get out of your head. Try to let go of thoughts and focus on the ground beneath your feet, the breeze on your skin. Your heart beating, your breath. Use your senses. Ignore the prattling of your mind."

"*Prattling*—" she started, offended.

"You're human," he said. "All of our minds prattle. It can be a good thing, of course, but it can also block us from hearing the whispers all around us. There's so much information. Try to take it in. Sense it with other parts of you."

Saoirse clenched her jaw. All of this reminded her distastefully of the New Age phase her parents had gone through when she was young. She remembered them inviting all sorts of astrologers and energy healers and other charlatans into the house and forcing her to meditate for what felt like hours. All it did for her was bore her out of her mind.

"This is how you turned yourself into a cat? Nature walks?"

He raised his eyebrows. "I didn't turn myself into a cat. My aunt Ciar did it."

"I thought you said you didn't have any family?"

"I had her," he said shortly.

She had more questions but, as before, his tone of voice

at the mention of his family made her decide against it. She sighed, frustrated with herself. Whatever she was supposed to be learning during this exercise, she was failing again. Her mind apparently enjoyed prattling more than the average person's.

However, when the forest transitioned to an incline, she found it easier to ignore her thoughts. Indeed, the hike upward, with no discernible path, was so difficult that it took all her effort to continue climbing. Sweat poured down her face now and her breath came in sharp gasps. She couldn't even spare a glance for Kian or be turned on by the sound of his panting. Well, maybe a little.

When they finally reached the top, the sun was at its highest point in the sky. The land was barer here, exposed to the constant sunlight, and she collapsed onto the hard dirt. She dimly registered that Kian had lain down beside her. But when a shadow passed over her eyes, she opened them to see that he shielded her from the sun with his arm. With the other, he thrust a cold bottle of water into her hand.

There it was again. The kindness. The thoughtfulness.

She drank, deep and slow, until she could talk. She passed the bottle to him.

"Seamus said in his letter that he knew somehow that they were about to die soon. How?"

Kian gave her a sad smile, still shielding her eyes from the sun's glare.

"They knew because of me."

"You? How?"

"Even though they were safe here at the estate, they asked me to spy on the cult," Kian said, the dirt they lie in dusting his black hair. "They were paranoid, wanted to make sure the cult couldn't get to them. I would travel to their headquarters to observe them and their practices. I was never able to get close to Niamh, but I heard the conversations of others. It was during one of these missions that I overheard members talking about 'her' and how 'she' was getting stronger and would be able to find the descendants of the Tuatha dé Danann no matter where they were hid. So they could destroy them."

"That confirms it," Saoirse exclaimed, turning to him more. "Niamh does have some other power—"

"But not something she has access to all the time. She likely has to grow in strength, as it took many years from that conversation for her to do it. But that was why your grandparents used the Coire to try to protect everyone. Because of the information I gave them. And then, when I went back and heard that she was almost strong enough, that was when we knew your family's deaths were imminent. Why Seamus knew to write that letter. He suspected Niamh would have a way to break the protection on the estate." Kian hesitated, avoiding her gaze again. "I was gone when it happened, sent to gather more intel. When I got back…" He exhaled. "Not that I would have been able to do anything to stop it, but…"

"It's not your fault. In fact, you saved us."

"Not all of you," he said.

Saoirse wanted to touch him, to thank him for being so protective of her family, but she kept her hands to herself.

"You think this power that Niamh has is how she got into the manor?"

"Maybe she was finally powerful enough. And maybe they aren't back because she has to regain her strength again." He frowned. "It doesn't make sense. I know Cruthu. I know Scrios and the Deantan. There's never been any hint of any other kind of magic, or of a fifth Deantan."

After a few moments' silence, Kian pushed himself into a sitting position. "Check out the view."

It was worth the effort it took Saoirse to sit up. The lake she'd grown up with spread before her in a maze that wound through the green, forested land. The water glittered deep blue, far out to the horizon.

"It's beautiful."

"It was made for you," Kian said close to her, "and you for it. You feel separate from it, but in truth you are connected at every level. It waits for you, Saoirse."

She turned her head and met his eyes, vivid green as the forests below.

"What is it waiting for me to do?"

"To recognize it. To ask it. What do you want it to do?"

"The lake?"

"Nature."

Sweat poured down her face. Her clothes clung to her, sticky and damp, as the sun beat down.

"A cool wind would be nice," she joked.

"Then ask it."

"Ask it—out loud?"

"Ask it from a place that isn't separate from it. A place that acknowledges how deep and inseparable your connection is."

She tried to understand, she really did. But then she blurted, "What the hell are you talking about?"

She expected him to be annoyed with her, but he laughed and to her shock, took her by the shoulders and shifted her to face him.

"Here, like this," he said as he moved closer to her and gently lifted her legs to rest over his. She stopped breathing. Any closer and she would be in his lap.

She doubted he'd ever done *this* with his aunt.

"Take us, for example," he said as he pressed one of her hands to his chest. Then he placed his other hand over her chest the way he had by the oak. His eyes bore into hers. Her lips parted.

"We seem separate but feel how connected we are now. Where our bodies touch. The way my heart beats like yours; the way yours beats like mine. Breathe deep. Close your eyes and feel it."

She felt it, alright. Kian's slick, hard muscle under her hand. His hand, right above her breast, strong yet gentle. There was no way her heart beat slow and steady like his. Hers was wild. She felt intensely alive and aware of her thighs resting upon his, of how close his body was to the part of her that was flooding with heat and wanting.

This—how she felt right now—couldn't possibly be what he was trying to accomplish.

"It's been so long since I've touched another person," he murmured. "You know, as a person."

She made an odd, strangled noise in response.

Kian opened his eyes. They were molten green. He didn't speak as he gazed at her. She held perfectly still. He bit his bottom lip.

Then he dropped their hands. "This isn't working, is it?"

He leaned back and Saoirse scrambled away from him. She let out a long exhale. What *was* that? Never in her life had she experienced such desire. She was weaker now than she had been after the hike.

Had he felt it, too?

"I think," he said and she turned to see him eyeing her critically, "that we're going about this the wrong way. I've been trying to bring you out of your head, but maybe inside your head is where you need to be."

He may as well have been speaking another language for all she understood him, but he leapt to his feet.

"Come. Let's go back. I want to show you something."

"What?" she said as she stood, unable to handle any more surprises.

"Something you never knew existed in that house."

19

When Scrios was created in contrast to Cruthu, certain consequential laws manifested in order to govern the interaction of the two magics.

Seamus Dannan, *Lore: The True History of the Celts*

"What is it?" Hawking asked. "How long has it been there?"

They were back in what he supposed was the living area of their dwelling, sitting in a circle while Alasdar played with little lights of his own making.

"We call that area Briosun," Una said. "It has existed since before my own time, although the darkness began much later. We were always told to avoid Briosun. According to legend, beings from Earth called the Tuatha dé Danann came to our land long ago and placed something there. We do not know what, but we always assumed it was dangerous. Does that ring a bell to you?"

"No, but I do know of the Tuatha dé Danann. I have reason to suspect they were my ancestors."

He thought he saw a swift look of satisfaction pass over her face, but for how quickly it passed, he might have imagined it.

"A number of years ago, the rot and the darkness began."

"Why?" Hawking asked.

"We don't know that either. But that was when our people began to Change."

"Why didn't you Change?"

Una opened her mouth but it was Kipp who scoffed. "Aren't you listening, Earth-born? We don't know anything. We don't have answers for you."

Hawking frowned. He was getting irritated with the way she kept calling him *Earth-born*. In her mouth it sounded like an insult.

"Hasn't anyone gone to this Briosun?"

Kipp scoffed again. "And risk becoming Changed?"

"Is that likely to happen?" he asked. "Did the others who Changed go there, or did they Change even being far away from it?"

Kipp glanced at her mother.

"He has a point," Una said.

"No, he doesn't," Kipp snapped. "Why would we go to Briosun? It's a death sentence."

"No," Una said, ignoring her daughter and turning her brown, lined face to Hawking. "None of us has ventured there."

"Sounds like the next move to me," he said. "Maybe there's a way to defeat it."

"You're mad," Kipp said, looking furious again. "You just got here, you don't know a thing about what we've dealt with in Tír na nÓg. For you to make suggestions—"

"Actually," Hawking cut across her, "things have gone to shit on Earth, too. You're not the only one with problems. I can't go back; I have to do something."

"What is it, Hawking? What is happening on Earth?" Una asked.

He hesitated. How did he explain it? "There's a group of evil people that attacked my family but their true aim is to collect artifacts of more power, like the bough." He thought of what he had read in Seamus's book about the Cult of Balor. "They want power, domination. I can only imagine what they would do with more magic. I have to find a way to stop them, and maybe what's happening in our worlds is connected; maybe Briosun is the answer—"

"Enough," Kipp said, standing and shaking her mane of blonde hair. "Time is passing much more slowly here for you than it does on Earth. We need to get you back to the Hill of Tarscha."

Hawking hadn't thought about that. How much time had already passed on Earth? How long had he been here, a few hours?

But still. He couldn't come back empty-handed, no matter how much time had passed.

"Kipp, what is the alternative? Live underground, hiding from the Changed until we die?" her mother asked.

"At least we're alive."

"Darling, what sort of life is this?"

When Kipp didn't reply, Una rose to her feet. Although her ancient body was unsteady, her milky eyes were fierce.

"For years, we've waited for Earth-borns to come and save us. To hear that Earth is also under threat is a blow, I won't deny it. But all is not lost. All cannot be lost." She turned her head in Hawking's direction. "He is here. An

Earth-born. A descendent of those who came long ago. This is not a coincidence."

To Hawking's shock, Kipp's face crumpled, a single tear falling down her cheek.

"All cannot be lost," Una repeated, taking her daughter's hands. "Going to Briosun was always a possibility, a last resort. The day has come."

Kipp cried in earnest and Hawking looked away from this vulnerable scene, feeling like an intruder.

"But—" Kipp said after taking a steadying breath. "Mother, how—"

And then Hawking heard it. People shouting. In the tunnels.

He launched to his feet.

"No," Kipp gasped. "It cannot be—"

Una raised her arm and the lights in the room went out. Hawking grabbed the Silver Bough from the table next to him.

"I will hold them off. Go." Una commanded.

"Mother—"

Hawking couldn't see Una but he felt the power radiating off of her.

"You know this isn't the end, my love. We cannot end. Go to Briosun. Save our world."

Kipp sounded like she choked off a sob and then Hawking felt her hand around his arm. Shoving the bough into the waistband of his pants he staggered with her in the dark, the voices of the Changed growing louder and louder.

Kipp stopped suddenly and Hawking stumbled into her. She swore an oath.

The shadows of three figures were illuminated in the soft light coming from the vertical tunnel. Kipp jerked him to the left and into a room where he could make out a woven tapestry. She ripped it down and shoved him through the dark opening.

The sensation of the ground falling from beneath him hit Hawking again. He slid down another wooden chute, Kipp following behind him. A ball of warm light appeared before him but all he saw was an endless slide before him.

"Where are we going?" he shouted.

"You'll see. We built in some escape routes just in case."

"That was smart. Are they following us?"

"Yes," she said. "But we're faster."

Hawking knew this was not true, at least for himself, and was about to say so when the ground leveled out. He scrambled to his feet; more tunnel stretched out before him. He jumped as Kipp's arms wrapped around his middle.

"I'm going to give us some help," she said, and then his feet lifted off the ground.

"What the—"

He choked on his words when he glided forward at breakneck speed, Kipp's arms clutched tight around him. Her blonde head looked over his shoulder. Glancing at his feet, he began to panic and sway—

"Don't fight it, you idiot!"

"I'm sorry, I—" He swallowed the urge to vomit. He felt like girls seemed when he would take them for rides on his motorcycle. Tense and freaked out, leaning the wrong way in spite of his instruction. What did he always tell them?

Close your eyes and trust me. I've got you.

He loved the feeling of them grabbing him tight like Kipp was now, their breasts against his back and their thighs pressed against his. But right now, trying not to lose it, he felt immense sympathy for those girls. Closing his eyes, he forced himself to breathe and concentrated on her arms around him, holding him steady.

"Keep your eyes closed," Kipp ordered.

Sunlight burst against his eyelids and he was suddenly free-falling— and not down a chute that would catch him. His eyes flew open.

And Hawking screamed.

They were falling through the air over the sea, hurtling toward the sparkling turquoise water. He had skydived, bungee jumped, even base jumped once, but there was nothing holding him this time, nothing to slow his plunge—

Kipp let go of him with one arm, looking wholly unconcerned, and made swift motions with her hand toward the water. As they dropped closer, dark pieces of wood joined together, fitting like a puzzle—

"Kipp," he gasped, "we're going to—"

And then air rushed around him in a different way. It pressed against him, all around his body like a cushion. He slowed...

When they reached the makeshift raft, Hawking dropped lightly onto it. While Kipp stayed standing, he crouched to the wooden ground, shaking.

Your status as an adrenaline junkie is revoked, you big stupid baby, he scolded himself.

Kipp knelt next to him. The raft lurched forward and Hawking felt the urge to vomit so imminent that he closed his eyes. He felt something against his forehead and looked to see Kipp gazing back at him as she touched him lightly. His nausea disappeared and she turned back to the vast blue water.

"Thank you," he said.

She didn't answer.

They were moving at a decent speed, much more slowly than they had through the tunnel, but with purpose. Shouts behind them made Hawking whip his head around.

Half a dozen of the Changed, both men and women, were leaping from the hole in the cliff where he and Kipp had fallen. Their brown bodies fell hundreds of feet and hit the water with sickening slaps. They didn't move after that.

"Shit," Hawking said. "Didn't they know that fall would kill them?"

Kipp looked away, but not before Hawking saw pain in her blue eyes.

"They don't appear to think rationally. They are single-minded on a goal and act with bloodthirsty aggression."

"Yeah, I saw a bit of that. How did they find us?"

"Something to do with you."

"Me?"

"They haven't found us in all these years. You're the only thing that's different."

Hawking considered this. "And you know the Changed don't have any power?"

"At first, we were worried. We didn't want to trigger the Law of Opposing magic. But they've shown no signs. They're vicious, insane with violence and stronger because of it."

"The law of what?" Hawking asked.

"It's something that goes into effect if two people meet in battle with equal magical force. They must each choose a sacrifice and the greater sacrifice wins."

"A sacrifice? Like what?"

"I've never been in that situation. I suppose any kind."

It sounded like a dangerous bluffing game. How would you know if your sacrifice was enough? Should you sacrifice the biggest thing you could think of? What if they chickened out and had a much smaller sacrifice and you made your huge sacrifice for nothing? He could see why Kipp and her people wanted to avoid this.

"If they had no magic and you had Cruthu, how did your people lose the war?"

She turned around to look at him. She had a little wrinkle between her eyes that he was now accustomed to seeing whenever she was annoyed with him.

"I've already explained this. We couldn't kill them. Obviously, you don't have the same bond with your people on Earth if you even have to ask. They're ours. We're theirs. We could not kill them."

At first offended at her assumption, he realized she was right. People on Earth definitely didn't have this bond. They murdered each other over parking spots.

They didn't speak for several minutes as they sped across the remarkably calm water. Hawking trailed his fingers over the side of the raft, enjoying the sea's coolness. Dark shapes moved underneath. He wondered what kind of marine life existed on Tír na nÓg.

He risked a glance up at Kipp. He had only seen her in the soft light of the root dwelling. Here in the sun, her rich, warm brown skin had golden tones that were brought out even more by her honey-blonde hair.

"Are you worried about your parents?" he asked after a while.

Kipp shook her head. "Una is extremely powerful." But she glanced back behind them. "Besides, even if they don't survive, I know I'll be with them again."

"Really?" he asked. Did the people of Tír na nÓg have religion, or did they know something he didn't about the afterlife? "How?"

"We belong to each other," she said simply, as if that settled the matter.

Hawking didn't know what to say. He thought of his parents and Linnaeus. He hoped Kipp was right.

"How long will it take us to get to Briosun?"

"An hour by sea at this speed."

"Do you know exactly how time passes differently between here and Earth?"

"No. Only that it's slower here. I don't know by how much."

The sun was making its descent. *Their* sun. Not his sun.

"I wonder how far away our planets are."

Kipp giggled. The sound astonished Hawking.

"What?"

"You think so linearly. It's not as simple as 'far.'"

"What does that mean?"

"There are more layers to reality than merely distance. This is another realm. We may not exist in the same universe."

"You're saying the bough could be a way to pass between different *universes*?"

"It's rumored that Cruthu can accomplish the same thing," Kipp said. "Rumor—I've never known anyone to do it. There is still so much we don't know about Cruthu and its possibilities."

Hawking glanced at the setting sun, then found the moon—a pale, crescent ghost in the deep blue sky.

"Could Earth and Tír na nÓg be the same place but in different dimensions?"

Kipp glanced at him with her turquoise eyes and nodded appraisingly. "Now you're thinking the right way."

"How many different realms are there?"

"I only know that Danu created our two," she replied, moving from her kneeling position to sit cross-legged next to him. "I'm sure more worlds were created by others."

"Danu," Hawking murmured. He remembered the name from Seamus's book, but it was barely mentioned. Just a passing story about her and a battle with someone named Carmun.

"Tuatha dé Danann. *The people of Danu.* You're a descendent of the ones who worshipped her, Earth-born. She's the being who made our worlds and gave us magic."

"Cruthu?"

"Yes. It means 'creation.' Danu created Earth first and then Tír na nÓg as an improvement. According to our legends," she added.

"That's convenient."

She chuckled. "You can't deny the evidence supporting it. Before the Changed, our people never warred. We never lost our worthiness to use Cruthu. We're a peaceful world, free from the chains of greed. We take care of each other."

Looking at her beautiful dark skin, he amused himself wondering what white supremacists on Earth would make of the master race not being white at all.

"Where is Danu now?"

Kipp's face darkened. "Gone. Destroyed long ago."

"How could a goddess be destroyed?"

"Who said she was a goddess? She created our worlds and us but she wasn't a deity. She was simply more advanced." The wind blew her hair back from her face. "Theoretically, we will all be advanced enough to one day create worlds and life of our own. I think Cruthu was given to us so we could learn how to become more advanced creators."

Hawking was impressed. Kipp was wise and pensive. He wondered why she was opening up to him like this.

"Kipp is a cute name," he blurted. *What the hell are you doing? Are you trying to flirt?*

She raised an eyebrow.

"To me, at least." His face burned. He had so much game

when it came to women, but with this one he was a complete ass. Why? He wasn't even attracted to her.

"And what is Hawking?"

It was odd to hear her say it. He had assumed she'd forgotten his name. "I was named after Stephen Hawking. He was a scientist who studied how things in outer space work. Gravity, black holes..." He trailed off. That was all he knew about his namesake.

Kipp raised her eyebrow again with the same appraising look she'd given him earlier. "Well, it sounds like at least some of you Earth-borns understand what's going on."

He opened his mouth to reply but Kipp's face was suddenly tense.

"What?" he asked, following her gaze. "What is it?"

She swore, moving into a crouch. Then Hawking noticed something on the horizon. Small specks of black, far in the distance.

All around them.

"Is it—"

"Yes," Kipp said.

"How did they—"

"I don't know."

He could now see that the specks were ships, growing larger and larger as they raced toward them at impossible speed. They were enormous vessels, like nothing he had seen on earth. How were they fueled to move so fast?

Kipp was frozen.

"Do something." He was pathetic, had nothing whatsoever to offer to get them out of this situation.

"I can't hurt them—"

"Then don't, just get us the hell out of here!"

Kipp nodded, her chest rising and falling rapidly, and stretched out her hands. As she parted them, great waves come from the sea in a small space between two of the ships. She gritted her teeth. He knew the waves were only meant to push the boats apart so they could speed through, but both vessels tipped as the massive waves crashed upon them.

"No!"

"*Kipp,*" a voice roared behind them.

Kipp and Hawking whipped around. One of the ships was dangerously close and Hawking could see one of the Changed at the helm: a man with golden hair like Kipp's and those white, blank eyes.

"Ris," Kipp whispered, and the sound of her voice scared Hawking more than anything.

"Give me the bough," the man commanded in a deep voice.

"Ris, it's me. It's Kipp. Let me help you."

The man named Ris sneered at her. "Kill them."

"No! Ris, please, it's me..."

Kipp was sobbing now. Dozens of men and women nocked arrows and cocked knives back, ready to throw.

Hawking grabbed Kipp by the waist and threw them off the side of the raft. Muffled

thuds hit the raft and he knew dozens of deadly blades had penetrated the water. He kicked downward with all his might to get them out of range.

Kipp came to herself. Wrestling out of his grasp, she took firm hold of his arm. She pulled him at rapid speed through the water—not deeper, but forward. The gigantic shadows of the ships came closer but Hawking needed air, he couldn't hold his breath much longer. He signaled to Kipp and she nodded, looking frightened, but took them upward between two of the ships.

As soon as his head broke above the water, strong hands

grasped him under the shoulders. He fought them but it was no use. These people were herculean in strength. They dragged him onto the wooden deck and threw him to the ground next to Kipp.

The man she knew, Ris, stalked toward them.

"Please... please..." she cried out.

Ris kicked her aside as he bent over Hawking. Tearing his shirt from him, Ris smirked. The bough laid upon Hawking's stomach, still lodged into the waistband of his pants. He reached down to grab it—

Suddenly, Ris was blasted backward by an invisible force.

"You dare," he roared as he got to his feet.

Kipp had her hand out. "Ris, Ris, brother—"

Brother, Hawking thought with a jolt.

"Take her," Ris said to the others, who seized her by the arms and hauled her to her feet. "Take whatever pleasure you want from her and kill her."

Ris didn't spare a glance for Kipp. He only stared at Hawking, at the bough he now clutched to his chest.

Hawking looked desperately to Kipp. Tears poured down her face.

"I'm sorry," she whispered.

Those holding her flew from her, the same as Ris had when he had tried to grab the bough. Then Kipp closed her eyes.

Everything around Hawking blazed with sudden, bright heat. Screams filled the air.

She had set them all on fire.

Kipp collapsed and Hawking grabbed her with one hand, his other still clutching the bough, and yanked her over the side of the ship.

Flaming figures screamed and stumbled overboard,

landing around them, but Hawking used all his strength to drag Kipp's limp form through the water. The sun had set now but the fire illuminated what he was looking for. A smaller boat attached to the side of the ship.

The tender was low to the water and propped up upon slats of wood. Hawking climbed onto one of the slats and heaved Kipp into the small boat. Then he shoved the tender off the slats and jumped in as it landed in the water.

Grabbing the oars, he rowed away from fire and death and into the starlit night.

20

While the Tuatha dé Danann were a people of creative magic and goodness, the Fomorians followed the basest of human desires, raising their children generation after generation in greed and consumption that could never be satiated.

Seamus Dannan, *Lore: The True History of the Celts*

"Harder," Niamh hissed.

The man pushed down cruelly, kneading his knuckles into her back muscles. The one at her legs gripped and stroked her calves. At the top of the bed, another plunged his fingers into her hair and pulled with punishing strength.

"Good," she said, gritting her teeth. The men working on her body were naked. So was she.

"You're very tense," the one kneading her scalp said.

"No shit." She wasn't tense. She was fucking pissed. Her thoughts spun in the circles as they had for days.

The Cait Sídhe. She'd *had him*. The creature that served the Tuatha dé Danann, her ancient enemies. The information she could have extracted from him, had she had more time... And that worthless girl had taken him.

She couldn't wait to kill that little bitch. This one would be done by her own hand. Indeed, Niamh regretted not annihilating the other Dannans herself.

The man at her back dug in his elbow, making her cry out. He didn't stop. He knew this was how she liked it.

The girl had the Tanist Stone. That she'd dared to wield it, had not even understood its power... Niamh's only hope was that in her foolishness she had gotten herself killed.

And then there were her men at the Dannan manor, slaughtered...

Niamh forced herself to breathe as strong hands kneaded down the soles of her feet. Those failures were nothing compared with the betrayal of her greatest asset. When he came to her years ago, she knew she finally had a way to take back the Deantan.

She was so close to the one thing she wanted above all else, that which would elevate her above all, make her a ruler of worlds...

And now, without him, she had nothing. The girl had the stone and the Cait Sídhe would surely tell her the location of the Silver Bough.

Niamh was in the dark, with no way to find them, unable to access the manor.

"Stop," she said.

The men stilled and took their hands off of her. She rose to her knees and scrutinized them, settling on the one who was massaging her head.

"Tie him up," she said, and the other two moved to do her bidding. All three of them were visibly excited. She licked her lips, anxious to forget her troubles, to enjoy a bit of distraction.

A sharp knock rapped on the door.

"Whoever that is, kill him," she ordered, her eyes still on the naked man restrained on the bed before her.

"Mistress, wait," came a muffled voice from the other side of the door. "It's *him*. He's returned."

Niamh whipped around. She climbed swiftly off the bed and slammed her chamber door open. Not bothering to clothe herself, she marched down the hallway, guards at her heels.

When she entered the large counsel room, she sat upon her throne-like chair and crossed her legs.

"Let him enter."

Two guards ushered him in. He shuffled forward, his hands tied behind his back, with his eyes downcast until they brought him fully into the room. Then he lifted his gaze to hers and smiled.

Niamh sat up with a hiss and the guards forced him to his knees, one pulling his head back by the hair and the other pushing a knife to his throat.

"See how they are poised, traitor? Ready to end you? I would do it myself, but I was in the middle of something I'd rather not get dirty for."

"I can see that," he said with another wicked grin and the guard to his right forced his head back farther.

"What could have you so brazen before me?"

"I've come back for your forgiveness, my Mistress."

"And why would I give you my forgiveness? You betrayed me. You left me."

"Please," he said, still staring at the ceiling. "I have a peace offering. Something you want very much."

"A desperate man will say anything to escape his own execution."

"Why would I come here and risk getting executed at all, unless I knew I had something that would guarantee my absolution?"

Curiosity won over her fury. She nodded to the guards. They released him and stepped back, but not far.

"You have ten seconds."

"I'll take five. Ever since the girl activated it, I can sense the stone."

Niamh inhaled sharply. "You tell the truth?"

"I do," he said, rising to his feet. "I sense it now. I can take you to it. To them."

"What about the bough?"

He hesitated. "I did feel it, but... I'm not sure..." He shook his head. "It's no matter. We will find it. The stone calls to me."

"Where is it?"

"Where do you think? At the estate. And I can take you there."

Niamh sat back. His psychic abilities had always proven true before. His arrival to her had been a miracle, a sign to her that she was destined to carry out her goal when all others had failed. Him leaving... perhaps it had been a temporary setback. If he could indeed sense the location of the stone, they had won already.

"Why did you leave?" she demanded.

"It is my greatest regret. It will not happen again." Any hint of shame on his face evaporated. He lifted his chin and looked her in the eyes. "We serve the same master. My doubt was a weakness I have cut out like a festering tumor. Let me worship you, my Mistress. Let me show you how... sorry I am."

Her skin flushed and craving flooded her.

"Leave us," she ordered the guards. One cut the traitor's hands free and then left the room with the others.

They were alone.

He approached slowly, his eyes dark with hunger. Niamh uncrossed her bare legs and spread them wide, propping a foot on the arm of her throne.

"Yes," she said as he knelt before her. "Show your Mistress the depth of your regret."

He met her gaze one last time before her eyes rolled back in her head as he proved his remorse to her.

21

The discoveries of modern science add validity to the existence of magic in both its creative and destructive forms.

Seamus Dannan, *Lore: The True History of the Celts*

After they ate and freshened up, Kian brought Saoirse down to the shabby kitchen. She stood frozen on the threshold. Blood still stained the concrete floor.

Kian stopped short and looked at her.

"It's where they tortured Hawking."

Kian put his arm around her.

Her grief was overshadowed by the sudden physical contact. He had finally donned a shirt and her head was pressed against the soft material over his hard chest. She caught a whiff of what must be Hawking's deodorant or cologne, which was quite nice...

"Okay," she said, her voice muffled in his right pectoral. "Thank you."

He released her. "Are you okay?"

"Yes, let's—" She motioned helplessly forward to where he had been taking her.

He gave her another concerned look but continued on, leading the way to a short hallway off the kitchen. Inside was a small room containing an electrical panel with breakers for different parts of the house. Kian flipped them off and on, seemingly at random.

The entire electrical panel popped open. Amused, Saoirse followed Kian through the false door.

Light revealed a long, concrete staircase. This ended in another door, metal and heavy, with a keypad on the wall next to it. Kian punched numbers in, gave Saoirse a swift grin, and opened the door.

All she could do was stare.

The room was a bright, clean laboratory full of beautiful plants. Some surfaces contained vials and beakers of bright green liquid, microscopes of varying sizes, and other gadgets she didn't recognize. To the right was an enclosed greenhouse.

Saoirse walked around in wonder. So, this explained why they'd found not a hint of Melinda's life's work. It was contained here, underneath the house.

"These here on the tables were grown by hydroponics," Kian explained, motioning to trays holding myriad shrubs and herbs. When she gave him a questioning look, he added, "It means without soil."

Indeed, there was no soil to be found; each plant sat inside its own slit in a white tray. She moved to the greenhouse and peered through the glass. Humid and moist, vibrant flowers splashed color throughout the green.

"Why did she never show us this?"

"She conducted sensitive experiments in this lab and in the one beyond. Hardly a place for small children."

"The one beyond?"

"I'll show it to you in a moment. But it's important to understand this part first. Botany is where it all started for Melinda."

"With plants?"

He nodded. The stark contrast of his dark hair and brows against the white light of the room made him all the more handsome.

"Strange, almost intelligent, plant behaviors have been well-documented. There are plants that can smell and have scent preferences, plants that are carnivorous, plants that recognize threats and prepare to inoculate themselves. Some plants track the sunlight and move accordingly to get the best exposure. Others recognize which surrounding plants belong to their immediate 'family' and only share resources with those of their own kind.

"But it was one particular behavior that changed Melinda's life."

Saoirse looked at him quizzically. "What was it?"

"Their growth response to auditory stimulation. Music and human voices." Kian gently touched the leaf of a large flowering shrub. "Many experiments conducted over the years show plants responding to diverse auditory stimuli. Various types of music, positive versus negative human speech. Scientists have even tried to isolate the vibrational sounds of insects."

"I'm sorry," Saoirse interrupted. "When you say the plants *responded*—"

"They grew better," he replied. "Healthier. Faster. Yielded more seedlings. Some stimuli got better results than others; some yielded no results at all. But it's always been a controversial subject, more anecdotal from farmers and gardeners than scientific.

"Melinda, however, went to painstaking efforts to isolate other variables and was able to prove, time and time again, positive growth response to one type of auditory stimulation in particular."

"Which was?"

"Nurturing human speech."

"You mean, talking nicely to plants?" Saoirse grinned in spite of herself. It was endearing, the idea that plants liked to be spoken to.

"Essentially," Kian said and moved to a door the end of the long room. "This idea took hold of your grandmother, consumed her...and led her eventually to the field of quantum physics."

She saw another concrete staircase and door. Kian worked the keypad and opened it.

"Holy shit."

The botany lab was nothing compared to this.

The room was a vast, concrete cavern, bigger than any room or warehouse she'd ever seen. Indeed, it was larger than the ceremony room underneath Niamh's mansion.

Gargantuan machines filled the space.

At the end, built into the wall, was a massive, round machine with a gaping hole. A long metallic tube curved around half the lab and appeared to continue through the walls. One hung from a concrete overhang and looked like a science fiction chandelier, all winding and twisting gold coils. To her bewilderment, she also spotted what appeared to be a tuning fork.

"What is this?"

"One of the best-kept secrets in the world. Over the years Melinda worked with the top physicists across continents to develop this lab, using her and Seamus's personal resources, which were considerable. These scientists swore secrecy in exchange for Melinda freely sharing her data and giving them access to this place. She hadn't pursued recognition since the cult discovered Seamus from his book, and her colleagues were all too happy to take credit for her findings."

Her grandmother—who had played dress up with her and slipped her candy whenever her parents weren't looking—had run a top-secret scientific laboratory?

"But what—" Saoirse stood close to the long, disappearing tube. "What do all these things *do*?"

"That's a particle accelerator," he said. "Normally they're enormous, miles and miles long, but Melinda used plasma technology to build a smaller one..."

Kian trailed off at her look of bewilderment. He motioned for her to join him at a large desk surrounded by multiple computers, whiteboards with mathematical equations, and thick volumes. Saoirse noticed with a jolt a familiar quote written on the nearest whiteboard:

If you want to understand the secrets of the universe, think in terms of energy, frequency, and vibration.

Nikola Tesla

Saoirse smiled at this, understanding at once where her father had gotten the quote, and turned back to Kian. He leaned forward with the air of someone about to explain something very simply.

"All of these machines were made to detect and study

the most fundamental building blocks of nature. Atoms, subatomic particles, energy fields."

"Look, I don't remember a thing I ever learned in a science class, and even if I did, I hardly understood anything I was taught."

"That's alright. Basically, we're dealing with the things of space and time. The fabric of reality. The behaviors of the most essential aspects of living things. These behaviors have confounded scientists for centuries, but to one who understands the existence of Cruthu, they suddenly make sense."

Saoirse frowned. "How? What does Cruthu have to do with this?"

"You know how I said Melinda had confirmed the effect of talking to plants? As if plant-life has some kind of sentience, preference, *emotion* even? When Melinda got into the world of quantum mechanics, she discovered similarities."

"Such as?"

"Electrons exist in an *undefined* state until they're measured by a person. Atoms can exist in two places at the same time." Kian sprung from his chair, his eyes shining. "The universe, which should be collapsing inward due to gravity, is actually expanding rapidly due to some mysterious energy scientists can't find. A single photon has proven to follow two pathways at the same time when scientists expected it to follow a single sequence of order. Some particles, once entangled, are separated by vast distances and will *still* mirror each other's actions."

"Okay..." While she found his excitement endearing, she understood him even less now.

"Scientists have all of these hypotheses about these behaviors that they can't *prove*," he continued, walking around the chamber. His tall, muscular body looked even sexier with clothes on somehow. "They can't measure dark energy to know that it truly exists. They can't validate String Theory because they can't measure anything as small as a trillionth the size of an atomic nucleus."

"But what does this all *mean*?" Saoirse asked, exasperated.

To her shock, he knelt at her feet.

"Melinda realized that modern science's understanding of how things work is so elementary, even infantile, that it would be thousands of years before anyone would begin to grasp it," he said as he looked up at her. "What I'm showing you here is how that gap is bridged by the knowledge that these properties of reality have *intelligence*." He lifted a hand and lightly touched her temple.

"Intelligence?" she said weakly.

"Cognizance. Choice."

"But how? I mean, a—" she grappled for one of the terms he had used and he took his hand away. "A photon doesn't have a *brain*."

"That's the sort of thinking that has people stuck. The assumption that 'things can only be intelligent if they have a brain' prevents us from exploring what else might be possible."

"Well, my brain hurts. I thought we came here to give me answers, to help me understand how this all works."

He shook his head, still kneeling in front of her. "I'm showing you how little we know and understand because of a crucial but missing concept. Something that comes as naturally to humankind as breathing, an idea dismissed as fantastical.

"Seamus attempted to understand Cruthu through legends and lore. Melinda did it through science."

"What idea? What did she learn?"

"Particles—these fundamental building blocks—hover in a state of *decision*. When scientists measure them, they hunker down in one position of perceived concrete reality, but truly they are waiting."

"For what?

"To be directed."

He gazed at her so intently that she leaned away. "What—by me?"

"By you."

Saoirse sat for a while, trying to put it all together. So, what Kian was saying was that there was some scientific evidence of this intelligence he spoke of. Scientists couldn't figure out why phenomena happened, but they never looked to the possibility that it was because of a connection. A natural link between humanity and what everything is made of. Her frustration and confusion gave way to curiosity.

"Why? Why do they want to do what we tell them to do?" she asked.

"It's like... a partnership. A collaboration. They *want* to be used to create. It's their purpose."

"And the way I communicate with them is..."

"Telepathic. Sort of." He half-smiled.

"Sort of?"

"I learned some about Cruthu from Ciar, but I've pieced together more over all these years. To my understanding—"

"Hold on—to your understanding? Have you ever actually used Cruthu?"

Kian hesitated. "A little."

"A *little*?" Saoirse exclaimed, her voice echoing through the lab. "I thought you were like, some kind of Cruthu master."

"Well, compared to every other person alive right now, I am."

Saoirse cursed under her breath and rubbed her forehead.

"I understand the theory and I have limited experience with it," he said. "That's enough; I know it is. You *ask*—you state the intention of what you want, but you also imagine it. Ciar told me that while she didn't know exactly how it would all work, she would try her best to picture the changes happening and at some point, her imagining would be taken over by images and a sense of what actually *was*. Like they were filling in the gaps for her, allowing her to participate."

His bright green eyes filled with yearning. Regret wrenched inside her. Kian was passionate about Cruthu, not only because it was the key to stopping Niamh, but because he longed to use it. And because of her, he never would.

"I'm sorry," she said before she could stop herself.

"What for?" he asked, still kneeling in front of her.

"You sacrificed it for me. To save my life."

He stared at her intensely before he spoke. "I would do it again."

She flushed.

"Our participation in Cruthu *changes the rules*," he said, and she was grateful he was back on the subject. "Think of a Rubik's cube. You know what that is?"

"Yeah, but I've never solved one."

"I haven't either," he grinned.

She laughed.

He reached out and took her hands in his. She tried to hide her sharp inhale at his touch.

"If I scramble up a Rubik's cube," he mimed doing this with their hands, "no matter how I do it, it will still be solvable. My actions upon it work within its system, according to its rules."

Saoirse nodded, trying to focus on his words instead of how good his warm hands felt on hers.

"But if I break the cube apart," he again mimed this with their hands, "and put it back together incorrectly, the system is broken. The property of the Rubik's cube changes from solvable to unsolvable. I then exist as an outside force. I change the rules."

He took his hands away, leaving hers to hover in the air.

"This is what the elements are waiting for, Saoirse. Humans are the key to changing the rules, the system."

"We are the outside force," Saoirse said, staring at her hands.

"Exactly. A human is a human and a cat is a cat but when Ciar used Cruthu, she broke apart the Rubik's cube. She didn't do something wrong or unnatural—the elements cooperated—she simply showed what else is possible."

"What *is* possible?" she asked.

Kian pondered this, a slight smile playing on his lips.

"I would guess there are infinite possibilities. Cruthu can do everything that exists outside the paradoxical."

"What does that mean?"

"Just because we can conceive of a concept doesn't mean it's possible. I can't give you a vial of blue ink that is red. It's either blue or it's red. An all-powerful God can't create a rock that is too heavy for Him to carry. It's a contradiction. A paradox."

Saoirse exhaled. Kian was right; showing her these labs, explaining the otherwise unexplainable but observed phenomena, it was helping. Instead of defeated, she was curious; even excited.

Then a sad thought occurred to her. "All this and my grandparents still couldn't use it because of their *pride*?"

"A failsafe. This was all arranged to prevent us from using the infinite powers of creation for evil. Your grandparents weren't *evil*, but human beings tend to become corrupted by power. And people who already crave accolades and praise are even more susceptible to corruption. If I had realized this while they were alive, maybe they could have worked on changing that about themselves, but perhaps not."

Saoirse thought back to some of the comments her father had made about his own parents. Obviously, he'd had his biases and she understood them now, but perhaps there had been some truth to the way he talked about their overlarge egos.

Then something he had said caught her curiosity.

"Who arranged the failsafe?"

"Danu," he said with a sad smile. "The goddess who created us. She's long gone, though."

This final piece of information—that the world had been created by a goddess—was a bit too much for her. She rubbed her forehead again.

"They loved you, though," Kian said. "Your grandparents. They quite literally sacrificed their own lives for you. Never forget that human beings are complex. No one is all bad or all good."

"But *I'm* good enough for nature to trust me?"

"Yes, Saoirse. They don't require perfection. You are good enough."

Why did he think he knew her? And well enough to decide things about her that she didn't believe about herself? It warmed her in a way she'd never felt before.

"So, are you ready to try again?"

And this time, Saoirse smiled.

Hours later, her good mood had quite dissipated.

A lone pencil sat on the desk before her.

It's possible, she told herself in a mantra. *It's possible, I can do this, I'm not corrupted by power. It's a natural connection between us. They want to be directed. They want to work together. What makes up this pencil and the air around it and gravity and electromagnetism* (a term Kian had taught her) *and all mass and energy wants to listen to me.*

She stared at the pencil hard enough to pop blood vessels in her eyes.

Motherfucking move!

Kian yawned. She raised an eyebrow at him.

"I'm sorry, that was distracting," he said as another yawn overcame him.

"You're exhausted."

"No," he said, rubbing his eyes. "I swear, I'm fine—"

She stood up. "Don't be ridiculous. You didn't sleep at all last night. Your human body needs rest."

He tried to protest but was overtaken by another loud yawn as Saoirse jerked her head for him to follow her back upstairs.

"Actually," Kian said once recovered, "Melinda had living quarters down here for when she didn't want to leave an experiment."

He staggered to his feet and Saoirse followed him down the giant room and through a plain door in the concrete wall. He flipped on the lights.

The room appeared to be a bunker, albeit cozier. The bed was simple but had a large, fluffy comforter and plush pillows. A door to a bathroom stood ajar and on the opposite side of the bed was a kitchenette.

Kian climbed into the bed at once and turned her, raised on one elbow.

"You should sleep, too."

"Right," she said, glad to get a break from the pencil, even though she knew time must be running out before the cult came back. She turned to walk out of the room.

"No, sleep here." His eyes were clear, his expression neutral. "It's safer. That is, if you're comfortable," he added.

She hesitated, her heart pounding. He had moved next to the wall so there was space for her to join.

"We have slept together before." He grinned.

She laughed in spite of herself, even as her face warmed. "I hoped you wouldn't acknowledge that."

"It was nice," he shrugged. "I didn't get much physical contact as a cat."

"You mean my grandparents never pet you?"

He wrinkled his nose. "Absolutely not."

"Well... alright," Saoirse said. She turned off the light and climbed into the soft bed. A small glow from the kitchenette prevented them from being in complete darkness.

The bed was not large. There were only inches between their bodies. Saoirse shivered.

"Are you cold?" He reached his arm across her and rubbed her bare arm.

Not anymore, she thought as heat flooded her body. She thought back to the hug in the kitchen and the painfully intimate experience at the top of the hill. He touched her a lot. What did it mean to him? Was he simply comfortable with contact now that he was human again? Was it because she was the only woman around? What if he... wanted more? Like a man who'd been in prison for years and can finally be with a woman again. He was the most attractive man she had ever met. Would she take the chance to sleep with him if he wanted to?

Something about that thought made her cold again. She'd been in that position before—slept with a guy for fun, *his* fun, when he hadn't loved her or even liked her. She had never been as lonely as she was after an act like that; lonelier than she'd ever been when she was alone.

"Is this okay?" he asked.

"It—yes, but I'm fine now. Thank you," she replied tersely.

He withdrew his arm. "I never want to disrespect you, Saoirse."

She turned to him in surprise. Through the soft glow of the small light she could see the concern in his face.

"What do you mean?"

"I know how men treat women. I've watched people over all these years. It isn't right and I never want you to experience that from me."

It was like he'd read her thoughts. She would be intimidated by this if he hadn't looked so nervous and vulnerable.

"I grew up in two worlds," he continued. "One was evil and one was good but they had something in common: neither was a patriarchy. Women were never second-class. They were equals in one, revered in the other."

"What worlds?" she asked.

He hesitated. "I was raised Fomorian, Saoirse. Niamh is my cousin."

Her mouth fell open.

"But I hated it—I refused to participate in their rituals and..." He swallowed hard. "I only survived because my father was one of the leaders and he protected me as much as he could. My mother was killed when I was a child. I never knew why until I met her sister, my aunt. She had left the Fomorians to join the Tuatha dé Danann—your ancestors."

He gazed past her, his face drawn with pain. Saoirse again fought the urge to touch him.

"My mother tried to join them, too, but she was caught and executed. My aunt contacted me when I was a teenager. It was she who taught me about Cruthu. And when I was older and the other elders, including Niamh, realized the traitor I was and my own execution was imminent, it was she who saved me. She had the cat hair that contained the DNA I needed. She tried and tried but it was so complex. Only when I was moments from dying was she able to pull it off."

When he'd said his aunt had changed him into a cat, she'd assumed it was as some sort of experiment. She had no idea she'd done it to save his life.

"How were they going to kill you?"

"You saw it, in the cult's ceremony room," he said. "They were going to burn that poor boy's parents alive inside of it. The wicker man."

Nausea swept over her as she remembered the towering structure.

"As a cat, I was able to slip through the wood and run away. My aunt kept a bit of my own human hair; she was going to change me back as soon as I was safe. My mind didn't work well as a cat. But I had enough awareness to run back to her hiding place. When I got there she was already dead.

"I didn't know where the Tuatha dé Danann were and wandered for a long time. I almost lost myself in my new form. My thoughts were stunted and muddled. My senses were different; my desires had become cravings and my decisions instinctive impulses. By the time I finally got hold of myself, wars had been waged. Your ancestors had gone into hiding. And when I found them, Cruthu had already been lost."

"Why? Why was it lost?"

"War," he said. "There's nothing more damaging to the human spirit than the atrocities of war. Generations have been destroyed by it. Your people were so broken and psychically damaged that they couldn't access Cruthu anymore. And eventually, it was forgotten."

Saoirse thought about his words for a long time, a deep heaviness pulling her down. The tragedy and horror Kian had endured. The fall of such a great people—*her* people. Niamh and her victories. Now she wanted revenge not only for her family, but for her ancestors. For Kian. And it all came back to one person.

"What do you want, Saoirse?" Kian said, jarring her from her thoughts.

"To kill that bitch, Niamh."

He laughed. "No, I mean... I never want to disrespect you," he repeated, his eyes bright, "but I enjoy... touching you."

Heat rose to her cheeks again. The statement was so naked and bold.

"Because I'm the first woman you've been around in thousands of years?" she blurted.

"No. That's not why."

While she gazed at him, wanting to know what he meant but too afraid to ask, his eyes drifted shut, his breathing deep and slow.

You've got to be kidding me.

Saoirse rolled onto her back, her heart hammering.

I enjoy touching you.

He wanted to touch her. He'd opened up about his childhood, about his worst memories. She thought about everything he told her. He'd grown up in the same circumstances as Niamh but was nothing like her.

Kian, Saoirse decided, was the bravest person she had ever met. And possibly one of the best.

She turned and drank in the sight of him as he slept until she did, too.

Saoirse awoke with a start. She didn't recognize where she was, whose arm was curled around her waist, whose hard, warm body was pressed against her back...

Then she came to herself. Kian breathed deeply into her hair. His arm was mere inches below her breasts. Her rear was nestled very close to his—

How had they ended up *spooning*?

She blinked in the dark, sensing every place where his body touched hers. She wanted to nudge closer to him, to turn toward him. Would he respond? When he'd said he enjoyed touching her, did he mean in a friendly affection-way or in the way she yearned to feel him?

And then a fear greater than potential rejection rose inside of her, something she refused to think of, the reason she'd shut herself off to these kinds of feelings long ago.

Inching away from him, she let his arm fall from her as she slinked from the bed to the ground. After using the bathroom, which didn't have a mirror for her to obsess about her appearance in, Saoirse crept back into the main room. A small clock said it was five in the morning but she was wide awake. Wanting to let Kian get more rest (and to keep herself from sliding back under the sheets with him and potentially making a huge mistake), she left the room.

The laboratory was as vast as she remembered it; a temple built to worship the unknown. Admiration filled her, for her grandmother's genius and passion, for the power of these computers and machines. Her intelligence didn't come close to her grandmother's, nor her father's, but their blood still ran through her veins. All the way back to the ancient people who had lived and created hand in hand with reality itself. She was of these people. Their descendent.

This was *her* temple. After all, she owned it now. Her birthright.

Just like Cruthu.

They are waiting to be directed.

Wandering nonchalantly over to the desk, Saoirse glanced at the pencil. So, the particles in this pencil and in the air around it were waiting for her, were they? Waiting for her to take apart the Rubik's cube, to break the rules.

She raised her hand and flicked her fingers.

Move.

The pencil twitched, rolled several inches across the table, and stopped.

Saoirse glanced around for a draft that could have caused it, but the air was still.

Stepping closer, she watched the pencil. She raised her hand again, moved her fingers in a circular motion, imagining it happening.

The pencil spun.

A smile spread across her face. She could feel it. The connection.

She raised her hand and the pencil rose with it, hovering in the air in front of her.

"That's it," she whispered. She made it move through the

air, back and forth, twirled it again. Then she raised both hands and moved them apart. The pencil broke in half.

Breathless, she watched the two halves of the pencil linger in the air. Once more she imagined it, saw it happening, as she moved her hands back together.

The two halves knitted back together.

She stumbled back in shock and the pencil clattered onto the table. Trembling, she picked it up and looked at it from every angle, feeling it between her fingers.

It was whole, as if it had never broken.

Tears pricked at her eyes. It was real. Cruthu was real and she could use it.

Sprinting back to the bunker, she found Kian was still asleep, his face buried into his pillow.

The sight made her smile. He would be so thrilled when she told him, but she could wait and let him rest.

Her stomach was painfully empty. She would make them breakfast, another surprise for when he awoke. Feeling as though walking on air, she made her way back to the main house. Since she didn't know the codes, she propped the doors open behind her.

I'm doing it, Hawking, she thought when she reached the blood stains on the basement floor. *I'm doing it, and I'll make sure that you didn't die in vain.*

Everything looked different now as she walked through the house. She was capable of almost anything. Immense power lay at her fingertips—

"There you are," a male voice said.

Her blood drained from her.

In the sitting room stood five men dressed in black.

22

The psychically vulnerable who come in contact with Scrios magic are at risk of becoming more unstable in response to its destructive nature.

Seamus Dannan, *Lore: The True History of the Celts*

Eoghan stumbled through the woods, thinking about Michael.

Michael was his patient with dissociative identity disorder—multiple personalities, to the layman. The patient he'd approached with a caring, yet clinical eye—whilst remaining blind to the similarities between the man and himself.

His entire body shook.

Psychogenic tremors. Don't let panic overtake—

"I know, I know." His own voice sounded foreign to him, a pitiful whimper. He thought of Hawking and Saoirse, he had to get to them, he had to find his way back—

Pain gripped his brain in an unrelenting fist.

"What is wrong with me," he panted, "what the hell is wrong with me—"

Psychalgia. Pain with no pathophysiological cause. Stemming from extreme stress and emotional anguish.

"No," he moaned. How could he ever face them, how could they ever love him if they knew how sick, how twisted—

Catastrophic thinking. Mind-reading. Use thought-stopping technique.

Eoghan gripped his head and screamed.

Catharsis.

What if he was like Michael? What if he was split, what if he was these two men? One viciously violent, one his rational self? How could he ever integrate—

"*No*," he howled and fell to his knees. He began pounding on the ground with his fists like a tantruming child.

Eoghan wished he *was* a child again. Not for most of it, but for the times he was at the manor, running through the grounds with Hawking and Linnaeus and little Saoirse, sitting at Seamus's feet near the fire while he told stories, Melinda allowing him to help harvest fresh herbs in her garden. It was a safe place. And he'd felt that safety again, so briefly, when they had all reunited.

When his parents died, he was not sad. He hadn't told his cousins that part. They wouldn't understand. No one understood him.

It was why he'd lived alone all these years. Comfortable in a quiet apartment, spending most of his time treating patients, keeping people at a distance. He knew he could never be understood. And if anyone ever came close enough to try, they would run.

They should run.

He was still now, sunken to the ground with the weight of desolation. Desolate. That's what he was.

Depressive state. Use dialectical behavior skills for emotion regulation. Opposite action. Sit up. Smile. Use an upbeat tone of voice.

He didn't.

"I have to get back," he spoke into the lonely forest. "Get back. Get back to them... get back..."

Pain shot through him again. He raged against it, ripped chunks of his hair out as he wrestled with it, tried to excise it.

But that was impossible. It always had been.

Eoghan inhaled, his eyes now unseeing, his whole body submerged in pain. Until he quit being so pathetic.

The clinical voice was an exercise he had learned in school. To speak to himself as he would a patient, with compassion and guidance.

It was gone now.

Eoghan did not need it. All he needed now was to move, to act.

To go forward.

23

A mastery of Cruthu magic can be accomplished only when the wielders accept the connection between themselves and all that surrounds them.

Seamus Dannan, *Lore: The True History of the Celts*

Saoirse turned and sprinted back to the stairs.

"Shit, shit, shit," she hissed. Down the stairs she tore. They were closing in. She threw herself through the false door in the electrical panel, trying not to let fright overcome her. Down the stairs, through the botany lab, down the second flight—

"*Kian!*" she screamed into the physics lab, which seemed miles long. Kian stumbled out of the bunker.

"Kian, they're coming—"

"Follow me," he shouted, sprinting toward the far corner of the cavernous lab. She pumped her legs and arms, willing her body to go faster.

The men were in the lab now, and she knew they were stronger and faster than she—

Saoirse reached Kian as he threw open a door in the corner. He waited for her to pass and then followed, slamming the door behind them and engaging several locks, including one on another keypad next to it.

"Can they get through it?" she asked in a high and frightened voice she'd never heard from herself before.

"No," he panted.

They were in a tunnel, eerily similar to the one she'd passed through in the cult's mansion, except it was made of concrete instead of black granite. Industrial bulbs in wire cases lit their way.

Sounds of pounding and shouting on the other side of the door made Saoirse jump. Kian beckoned her forward.

"How long is this tunnel?"

"Long," Kian said. "But they have no idea where it leads and that door is made to withstand a nuclear bomb."

With everything else the extraordinary lab contained, she wasn't sure if he was exaggerating or telling the truth.

"We knew they would come back for the Deantan," he said, sounding downtrodden. "It's too bad, I would have liked more time in the lab to help you—"

"Kian," she said, grinning in spite of the terror she'd just experienced.

"What?"

"I did it. I moved the pencil."

His face brightened, and she knew in that moment that causing him this amount of happiness was something she wanted.

"Tell me everything."

And so she did, standing in the dim concrete tunnel,

ignoring the muffled attempts of the men to get through. When she finished telling him how she'd made the pencil whole again after breaking it, she stammered to a stop.

Kian had crossed the distance between them and took her face in his hands. His green eyes were intense as he looked at her.

"I knew you could do it."

And then he pressed his lips to hers.

The kiss was soft and sweet, his mouth tender against hers as he stroked her hair. A thrill of warmth ran through her as she kissed him back.

Then it changed.

The kiss became hungry. He pushed her against the tunnel wall. She grabbed his thick, soft hair and arched her body against his. They kissed frantically. He slid his tongue into her mouth and she didn't know if he or she moaned or if it was both of them. She pushed her aching breasts against him. Nothing existed, nothing but this—

"Saoirse," he muttered against her lips.

"Kian," she sighed, trailing her hand down toward his hip.

"Saoirse," he said again, and pulled his mouth from hers. She gasped for air, staring up at him. Kian's eyes were penetrating. His chest rose and fell rapidly. Bringing a hand to her face again, he stroked her temple and tucked a piece of hair behind her ear.

"We should keep going."

"What?" Her brain was muddled. The sounds of shouting and movement on the other side of the door came back to her, and she remembered where they were.

"Oh—yeah," she said, and he withdrew, leaving her trembling against the wall. He took her hand and they continued down the tunnel. Her legs were quite unsteady. She glanced at him and he smiled.

"Amazing," he said.

"Yeah," she breathed. She had never experienced anything like it. Any physical encounter she'd had with a guy had been fraught with self-consciousness and hesitation. Never had she been so *in* an experience, so consumed by passion...

"How did you do it?"

She frowned at him, confused, and then realized what he was talking about.

"Oh!" Right. The pencil. *That* magic. Not the magic of their kiss. "While you were asleep, it clicked. I don't know, I got it. I don't know how to explain it."

"It's alright. You don't have to."

Was that sadness in his voice? she wondered with another pang of guilt. If it hadn't been for her, he would get to feel that thrill, that rush.

Then she thought of what he'd said earlier when she apologized for being the reason he couldn't use Cruthu.

I would do it again.

"Well," he said, squeezing her hand. "You were incredible."

She gazed back at him, the same old doubt creeping in and ruining a good moment. Had he only kissed her because he was impressed with what she'd done? What if she couldn't do it anymore?

"Where does this tunnel lead?"

"To the woods. This is how Melinda smuggled in all those scientists and engineers without anyone knowing, including her own children. It had to be kept top secret—governments tend to be uptight about citizens messing around with atoms without their oversight."

"I bet."

He ran his thumb over the back of her hand. She felt another flood of warmth.

"Not far now," he said.

The tunnel angled upward and turned the journey into much harder work. She swore this incline went on for another mile before abruptly transitioning to a flight of concrete steps leading to a metal hatch. Kian pushed it open.

The morning was overcast and the air chilly. An overnight frost had changed the forest; the leaves were now more yellow than green. A path cut from the hatch and wound through the trees.

"This leads to the main road," Kian said, shaking his black hair out of his eyes. He let the hatch close and re-spread the dirt and brush that had fallen off of it. "We're safe here—for now. They'll come looking for us, but the forest is large and we're quite deep into it. We've bought ourselves time for you to practice."

"So that I can confront Niamh," she said fiercely.

"She'll never know what's coming," Kian smiled. "There's a stream nearby. Come."

He reached his hand out once more for hers. His hand was warm around hers, his skin somehow rough and soft at the same time. As dubious as she was about his feelings for her, he certainly didn't hide his desire to touch her. He played no games. She had never encountered this from a man before, especially not a stupidly handsome one. Her experience with stupidly handsome men was that they were lazy in love—so used to women throwing themselves at them that they hardly put in any effort.

Then again, Kian was no ordinary man.

They approached the stream. Water flowed over shimmering rocks. Her mouth was parched.

Kian found a spot nearby where he dug up the grass until he had made a decent-sized patch of dirt. Then placed large rocks around the patch in a circle.

"What are you doing?"

His black hair fell into his forehead, his brow slick with sweat. "Making a fire."

"It's not too cold yet."

He grinned. "It's to purify the water so it's safe to drink... unless *you* want to do it?"

"I don't know how to purify water."

"Cruthu does."

Ah. "That sounds a bit advanced right now."

"Suit yourself," Kian said as he bent to gather sticks and twigs. He laid them in the clearing of dirt and covered them with dry leaves. Spinning a smooth stick atop a hunk of bark, Kian created a wisp of smoke that grew to spark the leaves.

"You're a regular boy scout," Saoirse said, impressed.

"You have no idea," Kian said, and he blew on the leaves until the fire spread. "This is when I could really use your help."

They went to the stream. He reached into the clear water and pulled out a large, flat rock.

"I need something to hold the water while it boils. But rocks don't tend to form in a cup or bowl shape."

Her jaw dropped.

"You want me to—what, turn this into a bowl?"

The grin on his face was so endearing that she ached to kiss him again.

"Saoirse, you mended a broken pencil without touching it. I think this is well within your wheelhouse."

Doubt curled inside her, but something else was there, too. Excitement. A longing to try more things.

What else can I do?

She sat down and let her eyes relax and her vision blur. Holding the rock with one hand, she swept her other across it, moving back and forth.

"You don't have to use your hands, you know."

Her eyes flew open.

"It helps," she snapped.

"Okay, okay, I'm sorry," he said, backing away.

"And you can stop staring at me while I try to do this."

Kian grinned and walked a few paces away. She closed her eyes again.

I am the outside force. I break the rules.

Like those who came before me.

Bringing her hand down to touch the rock, she swept her fingertips along it, willing it to change shape.

Not with desperation. With expectation.

Instead of jarring, the sensation of its transformation against her hands felt natural and right. Like molding clay.

She opened her eyes. She held a large, deep bowl of stone.

"I did it."

"You did," Kian said. "I've never seen anything so beautiful, Saoirse. This is you. This is yours."

This is me. This is mine.

Kian took the bowl from her and scooped the cool, running water into it. Then he nestled it in the fire, careful not to burn himself.

They sat and watched as the water boiled. Kian waited several minutes, then stripped his shirt off. He twisted his shirt around the bowl and lifted it off the fire and onto the ground. It was several more minutes of watching steam rise from the water in the dim morning light before it was cool enough to drink.

After drinking their fill, Kian gathered more water in the bowl to purify. After settling the bowl back in the fire, Kian turned toward her.

He gave his handsome half-smile and came close, locked on hers. Her heart pounded.

"Do you know what I want, Saoirse?" he asked, his voice husky.

She shook her head, unable to speak.

He stepped closer. "What I want... right now... is food."

She blinked and then hit him as hard as she could on the arm.

"Ow," he laughed.

"Men." Maybe he wasn't so unique after all. It took several breaths for her to calm down, from being turned on or pissed off, she wasn't sure.

Kian picked tart wild berries and they ate these while taking sips of warm water from the newly purified batch.

"The mac n' cheese was better," he said and Saoirse laughed hard enough to fall onto her back on the forest floor.

At once, he was over her, his black hair falling into his eyes. The berries had stained his lips red. "May I—"

"You don't need to ask," she murmured and arched up to meet his mouth. He lowered his body on top of hers and it was the most delicious feeling to have his hard weight on her. She wrapped her arms and legs around him as they kissed and he groaned into her mouth. Throwing caution to the wind, she grabbed his glorious backside and pushed him more firmly against her as she lifted her hips into his.

"Saoirse," he moaned. He moved his mouth to her neck and she gasped as he kissed and licked along her jaw. His right hand stroked down her side and then pushed up sharply against her breast. Desire throbbed in her painfully.

"Ah, I can't," he sighed against her skin. "I can't..."

"Can't what?" she panted as she kissed his hair.

"I can't do this," he said, pulling himself away from her.

"What?" Disappointment washed over her like it had in the tunnel.

"Not yet." He sat with his head in his hands, trying to catch his breath.

Keenly aware of the absence of his body on hers, she laid on the forest floor and waited for him to speak.

"These acts carry a lot of weight," he said. "I have respect for you, for what our joining together would mean."

Her mind was becoming sharper and less muddled by arousal but she didn't understand quite what he meant. She waited for him to explain more.

"I want it to symbolize something. The timing... I don't want to do it just because I want you in the moment, I want it to accompany a certain..."

He struggled for words.

"I'm not experienced with love."

A thrill went through her. She thought they were talking about sex but he was talking about *love?*

Did he love her? Did she love him? Aside from wild and consuming physical attraction, she admired him. His goodness, his intelligence, the gentleness of his character. She wanted to make him smile, wanted to comfort him when he was sad. She was incredibly fond of him.

What more was love than this?

"I'm not experienced with it, either," she said. "I've never had a real relationship."

"I know."

She frowned. "How?"

He looked suddenly young, like a boy caught in something. "Seamus and Melinda asked me to check on all of you at times and I found myself checking on you a bit more often."

"Why?"

He rolled his eyes. "Why do you think?"

"Oh."

"I know it makes me sound like a stalker. I promise I never spied on you naked or anything."

She laughed, amazed at what she was hearing.

"But I did watch you. I wanted to know you. To know about your life."

So, this wasn't just about physical attraction. He had watched her for years, wanting to know her, to be close to her.

Then shame, sharp and cold, cut through her pleasure. This meant he'd seen...

"Did you like what you saw?" she asked.

"I did," he said, gazing at her. Maybe he had missed *that* part. She didn't ask; she didn't want to know. If he had been around for that portion of her life, he had the sense not to bring it up.

"This isn't fair—you know so much about me and I know nothing about you."

"There's not much to tell," Kian said with a humorless laugh. "I've been a cat for thousands of years."

"You never had a relationship before you transformed?"

He shook his head.

"Not even... did you ever..." Why was she having such a hard time articulating it?

"No, I never had sex. I was supposed to." Suddenly, he looked almost frighteningly angry—a wild, hard side of him she hadn't seen before. "The Fomorians have a virginity ritual called The Taking. It was a repulsive rite of passage to mark when we came of age."

"What was it?"

"The elders would kidnap someone from another tribe and in the ceremony, we were supposed to..." He trailed off.

"Rape them?" Saoirse asked in abhorrence.

He nodded. "The girls, too. They would give the kidnapped boys something that made them—able to be raped." He took a deep breath. "I refused. My father was angry but there was nothing he could do. I had to *take* from another person and he couldn't force me to."

Disgust washed over her. "And others would?"

"Oh, yes. It was highly anticipated."

She shook her head, her respect for him growing impossibly larger.

"Why were you so different?"

"My mother," he said, smiling. "My father loved her, he must have, but even he couldn't let her live after realizing how she was raising me."

"I'm sorry." He'd been through so much—lifetimes of pain.

"It was a very long time ago," he said. "And I'm proud of my mother. She was one of the bravest people I've ever met."

"Now I see where you get it from."

He glanced at her, a smile brightening his face. Yes, she loved making him smile.

But then that old enemy, doubt, hit her stomach with a pang of uncertainty.

"Kian?"

"Yes?"

"Why are you into me? You're thousands of years old. I'm a baby compared to you."

He was silent for a while. When he spoke, he sounded thoughtful, like he was considering the reason himself.

"I understand what you mean. And it's true that I have lived for a long time, but not as a man. Sure, I've had millennia to learn and observe, but it's different when you can't *live* it. It's all in my head—intellectual knowledge. But my development as a man was arrested that entire time. I've been on the outside, watching humans, but not human."

She let the weight of his words settle. She could never understand what his odd life had been like for him, but she could understand at least that he wasn't truly thousands of years old in every way.

"There's no one alive that's like you, Kian."

"There's no one quite like you either, Saoirse."

"You don't know that. You've just become a man again. Don't you want to date around?"

His eyes twinkled. "No, I don't. I've at least acquired enough wisdom to know that."

She looked at him quizzically, but before she could ask what he meant, thunder rumbled around them. While they talked, the overcast sky had turned to dark rain clouds above the canopy of trees.

Kian sprang to his feet. He marched to a tall, skinny tree that was leaning quite a bit. He grabbed hold of it and jerked it down with all his strength until it leaned nearly parallel to the ground.

Saoirse watched, bemused, as he then broke off branches of other trees and stacked them close together on either side of the leaning trunk. When he gathered clumps of dirt, moss, and leaves from the ground to pile upon the improvised shelter, she got up to help.

"You're amazing," she said when they were finished. It looked like a wooden tent made out of green moss. Kian placed the warm bowl of water inside as the first drops of rain fell.

"Just in time," he said, grinning. "Shall—"

But the rest of his words died in his throat.

A large figure stepped out from a shadow of trees.

24

In addition to accepting their connection with the reality around them, the wielders are required to ultimately accept themselves.

Seamus Dannan, *Lore: The True History of the Celts*

Kian shielded her. It was a man—dark skinned and barely clothed. He had pure white, glowing eyes.

"Run," Kian said.

She turned and sprinted through the trees, Kian close behind her. She tried to think but her mind was like mud, all she could do was run—

A shout and a thud made her stumble to a stop. The figure had caught Kian and tossed him aside like he was a child. Then he lunged at Saoirse and seized her around the throat.

Choking and spluttering, she scrabbled uselessly at his hands as rain poured down on them.

Do something, she screamed at herself. She tried, but her mind was flooded with panic. Making a pencil float around and turning a flat rock concave was nothing. What could help her now?

He shoved her against a tree, still squeezing her throat. She glanced down. Despite his eyes, everything else about him appeared humanoid. Hopefully that meant he had balls, too.

Bringing her leg up sharply, she kicked him as hard as she could between his legs.

The male grunted and let go. She slid from between him and the tree as he doubled over. She sprinted a few feet, coughing. Pain suddenly exploded at the back of her head and she was yanked backward.

The male had caught her by the hair. He dragged her back and threw her to the soaked forest floor.

Do something, do something!

The male stood over her and to her horror, he knelt down and tugged at her pants—

"No." She struggled to get away, but he was so strong. She was weak, useless—

A hand came from nowhere, burying something deep into the male's shoulder. He roared and lurched away as Kian jerked the thing out of his shoulder and leapt backward. Blood poured from the wound.

Saoirse scrambled away, tugging her pants back up.

Kian stood feet away, holding a sharp rock covered in blood.

"How many more of you are there?" Kian demanded.

The male laughed. The words that came out of his mouth were not what Saoirse heard inside her head.

"Just me," he said, grinning. "For now."

"Good," Kian said, and he attacked.

The male was larger but Kian was fast. He dodged the male's blows and lashed out with the stone blade, slicing him here and there.

Help him, she told herself.

But she couldn't.

The male was furious now, and he fought ferociously, forcing Kian backward until his back hit a tree.

No.

The male leered and to her shock, Kian smiled back. As the male lunged closer, Kian struck in a flash and buried the rock into the male's chest.

The male staggered back and collapsed.

Kian stood for a moment, panting, and then dashed to Saoirse's side.

"Are you alright?"

She let him help her to a sitting position in a daze. Rain poured down.

"Is he dead?"

"Yes."

"How can you fight like that?"

"All Fomorians are trained in combat," he said, scanning her and then glancing around them. "I don't know who or what he was. Or when more will come, but I believed him when he said it was just him." He looked at her. "Why didn't you fight?"

"I did, I kicked him in the—"

"No, I mean why didn't you use Cruthu?"

She turned away, hiding her face behind her drenched sheet of hair. "I couldn't."

"Why not?"

"I don't know, I couldn't." She squeezed her eyes shut.

"Saoirse—"

She gritted her teeth at the way he said her name. Pity. Disappointment. She wanted to defend herself, but there was no defense.

"I did *nothing*."

"Saoirse, look at me. It's okay, you're new to it," he said. "You panicked—"

"It's not just *panic*," she screamed and flew to her feet. "You think you know me but you don't. Obviously when you were hiding around watching me you missed the most important parts. I give up, Kian. It's what I do. I give up on *everything*. I'm a fucking *loser*."

He stood as well. "Saoirse, you only give up on *yourself*—"

"Exactly. Like you said. I'm fucked up in here." She pointed at her head.

"No, I never said you were—"

"Why wouldn't I give up on myself? I'm a piece of shit. I've proved it time and time again." She laughed without mirth. "It's the one thing I'm consistent at."

"*No*," Kian barked and she jumped. "Stop. You are *not*. You just don't trust yourself. So then you don't act. You don't do what you're capable of. It's a vicious cycle. Just *stop*."

Her face crumpled and tears spilled from her eyes. She felt humiliated, pathetic—naked in the worst way.

He didn't comfort her. He let her cry.

"Why," she sobbed. "Why do you believe in me?"

He stepped closer, rain dripping from his black hair. "I have good reasons, but they don't matter, Saoirse. Every person on the planet could believe in you and it wouldn't matter. There's only one person you need to believe in you. You."

"But I don't because I'm fucked—"

"You're not fucked up," he said as he touched her arm.

His words and the voice in her heads were so at odds that she couldn't take it anymore. She snapped.

"Shut up!" she screamed and shoved him away. He stumbled back and was quiet for a moment.

"I didn't deserve that," he said. "Please don't do that again. If you want me to be quiet, if you don't want me to touch you, just say so."

She almost wished he'd hit her. This was far more humiliating. She looked down in shame.

"I'm sorry."

"Thank you."

"I guess you don't want me anymore, now that I've screwed up so much," she said, almost against her own will.

"Of course, I still want you," he said and her eyes snapped up. He looked at her earnestly. "You think screwing up sometimes means—what? You don't deserve love?"

She stared at him, wanting to believe but not daring to—

"You think I don't screw up, Saoirse?" He stepped closer again.

"Not that I've witnessed."

"Stick around." His eyes were bright green in the darkness of the storm. He was very close now. "Am I allowed to screw up, Saoirse?"

She gazed at him and nodded.

"So are you."

And this time, he didn't ask and he wasn't gentle. He grabbed her roughly to him. She felt his pounding heart.

"I want you, Saoirse. I have for a long time. And yes, I've seen it all. I've seen you, I know you, and I want you." He paused, his mouth inches from hers. "I always have."

He pressed his mouth to hers and it was molten. She wrapped her arms around his neck and he grabbed her

True Lore

behind, hitching her legs up around his waist. He carried her, and she didn't know how he could tell where to go as she kept her mouth glued to his. When they stopped, he lowered her down at the shelter he'd made for them. She scrambled inside and as soon as he joined her, she seized him to herself, touching him everywhere, even as they shivered.

"It's s-so cold." His teeth chattered and they both laughed at the absurdity of it, soaked and freezing as they were.

She took in his face and naked chest and her throat tightened at the sight of him. It was more than his handsomeness. It was him. She knew at that moment that he could have been far less good-looking and he still would have been beautiful to her.

She knelt in front of him and stripped off her shirt with a complete absence of self-consciousness. Kian didn't care if she was perfectly skinny, or toned, or curvy. He wanted her. She unhooked her bra and let it fall.

His eyes were mossy as he stared. The hollows under his cheekbones were darker, his chest heaving as his eyes found hers again. Kian reached for her and his grasp was rough and strong like it had been in the rain as he crushed her body to his. He lowered her down onto ground. As he laid his body on top of hers, his hardness pressed against her. She reached her hand down and touched him, stroking him through his pants. A moan rumbled through him. He grabbed her hand and pulled it above her head. He kissed and licked down her throat and she bucked her hips against him, wanting to feel him there. He pressed her down firmly.

"You're driving me wild," he said, his hair falling in his face. "But I want to drive you wild."

She moaned and tried to hold still as he continued down

with his mouth, kissing the hollow of her throat. His hand traced down her stomach, stroking her skin, and stopping at her hip, which he held tightly. His mouth explored her skin, but not quite where she was dying for it. Her nipples ached as he trailed around the curve of her breast with his lips, kissing her ribs.

"You—you missed a part—"

He lifted his head and smiled in a way she'd never seen before. Naughty. Wicked.

"Did I?"

And then his tongue flicked her nipple, hard.

Saoirse cried out, arching her back, heat throbbing between her legs. He consumed her breast, licking and kissing and nibbling, as her hips strained against him.

"Please."

Kian moved his hand from her hip and cupped it firmly between her legs. She moaned again, moving against his hand as he pressed the heel of his palm against the most sensitive part of her.

"More," she begged.

He grabbed the waist of her pants and jerked them down, and it was nothing like the violation she had almost endured earlier. She wanted this with her whole soul. She was free and on fire all at once. He ripped her panties off— she heard the fabric tear—and then one of his strong fingers plunged inside of her and she gasped. His thumb slid and flicked against her clitoris as his finger thrusted in and out, as his tongue continued to caress her breast, and the tension rose and rose... she had never experienced this with a man, never once like this.

"Kiss me," she panted as the tension made her body quake, and he lifted his head and kissed her as he slid a second finger inside. She grabbed his back and rode his hand until it was too much and she fell over the edge with a scream against his lips as sharp throbs of pleasure pounded through her body.

She trembled in his arms, holding him close to her, and kissed him deeply.

"That was..." she breathed against his lips after a while. "How did you know how to do all that?"

"I've been studying it for centuries."

She grinned.

"Are you tired?" he asked, stroking her hair.

"Not one bit."

And she pushed him over.

Every part of her was alive with pleasure and anticipation. She tugged his pants off and Kian raised himself on his elbows, watching her. Her eyes devoured him. This was male beauty as she had never seen it; in fact, in all the rushing awkwardness of her other sexual encounters, she had never properly looked. She wanted to touch and feel every part of his body, but she knew where he needed her to go, and fast.

Dragging her hands down his chest and stomach, she settled herself between his legs. Kian breathed hard and fast as he stared at her. She grasped his silken hardness, ran her hand up and down the shaft. Then she lowered her mouth to him.

Kian's head fell back against the ground, his hands covering his face as he moaned. His hips moved as she ran her tongue up and down and then took him into her mouth.

"Saoirse," he groaned.

When his breathing came even faster and harder, she let him slide past her lips as she pulled herself up. She trailed him down her throat, between her breasts, and down her stomach as she rose to straddle him. He watched. She pressed him between her legs, to the area that was wet and aching to be filled, and moved her hips up and down as she slid him against herself. Then she rose on her knees, angled him at her entrance, and sharply lowered down upon him.

"Yes," Kian moaned, an expression on his face like he was in pain, but she knew it wasn't pain he felt. It was need. He grabbed her hips. She rose and fell, over and over, savoring the deliciousness of him filling her. His hands were on her breasts, pressed hard against them. Then she slowed her movements, gazing at him, waiting.

His face was set, his eyes burning with hunger. He reached up and curved his arm around her, flipping them over so he was on top of her. He thrusted into her and she moaned, too. He gazed into her eyes, his black hair slick with rain and sweat as he moved. She raised her head and flicked her tongue over his lips.

"Saoirse, I can't hold on much longer," he said in a rough voice.

"Come on, then," she whispered.

Another groan rumbled through him, and he slammed his hips against her. She held his backside, urging him faster. Wrapping her arms and legs around him, she held him tightly as he pounded into her, deep and hard. She grabbed a fistful of his hair as he slammed to the hilt while he came.

Then they held each other, slick with sweat, no longer cold, their hearts and breathing slowing. Rain lashed against their shelter but the clumps of dirt and moss kept them dry. Kian shifted to his back and pulled Saoirse against him, stroking her hair.

She took it in. She didn't let doubt ruin the moment this time.

Doubt wasn't real. This was.

"Whatever happens," Kian said, "we'll make it through. Together."

"Together," she said.

25

While the philosophy behind Cruthu magic is one of partnership and co-creation, the credence of Scrios hinges upon the forceful submission of the natural elements.

Seamus Dannan, *Lore: The True History of the Celts*

Kipp could have gotten them there much faster than Hawking, but she hadn't moved from her fetal position. The stars and bright moon illuminated his way.

He glanced at her as they neared the shore. Her blonde hair glowed white in the moonlight. All of the Changed were like family to her, but then she'd come face to face with her *actual* family, her brother, and had to kill him. His own grief over Linnaeus gave him an idea of her pain.

And he realized that while her hope was to *un*change all of her people, Ris was probably the one person she wanted to help most. And now he was gone.

A large, dark shadow shimmering with an odd glow told Hawking they were nearing land. As he paddled nearer, he saw that it was a tropical beach sparkling with light. The water, the leaves on the palm-like trees—all shone brightly.

A sloping beach made it easy for him to dock the tender. When the boat bumped the soft sand, he sloshed around in the shimmering water to lift Kipp out. He carried her (no easy feat, she was so tall and muscular) up the beach and under the vibrant tree line. He lied Kipp down as gently as he could onto the ground. She did not stir. He felt for her pulse. It beat strong.

Heaving a deep sight, Hawking turned back to the beach to see if the sea water was drinkable; perhaps he could get her some. Then, she spoke.

"You did well."

She sat up, hugging her knees to herself and staring past him at the water. Hawking sat down next to her. Their clothes were still wet and although the air was pleasant, they both shivered. He raised his arm and put it around her.

Kipp stiffened and he dropped his arm. Then she waved her hand half-heartedly and Hawking's clothes were instantly warm and dry. She did the same to herself. The bough laid on the sand next to him.

"They must be attracted to it," she said, motioning to the white branch. "Somehow they sense its presence. It's the only explanation."

Hot shame slashed through Hawking. He had been so naïve to come to Tír na nÓg expecting help, and all he'd done was bring them more trouble than they already had. He was a fool.

Kipp's eyes no longer looked agonized. They were blank. He knew well the tempest inside that made a person look like that.

"The person I'm trying to stop on Earth," he said. "Her name is Niamh. She killed my family. First my parents, and then my sister. I heard about my parents' death while I was away. But Niamh slaughtered my sister in front of me."

Hawking stared at the sand, pain heavy inside him, but he could see in his periphery that Kipp was looking at him.

"You're not the bad guy, Kipp. You didn't kill him, not really. It was whatever Changed him that's to blame. Maybe Niamh is to blame for it all; I don't know. But it isn't you. You were put in an impossible situation. As was I."

She didn't reply but continued to look at him.

"I know your grief. It's a nightmare you can't wake up from. And it isn't fair."

They sat in silence for a while longer. Then Kipp lifted her hand in the direction of the incandescent water in front of them. An orb of liquid rose from the gently lapping waves. It drifted toward him until it hovered in front of his face.

"I've removed the brine," she said. "You can drink it."

Hawking leaned forward and let the cool water spill into his mouth. It was such an odd sensation that he coughed, and then drank more. When he was finished, she spoke.

"I need to rest a little more and then we'll keep going. We don't have much time and they'll be coming for us again."

"What about you?" he asked, but Kipp had already lied down in the same fetal position, turned away from him. "Kipp, you need to drink."

She didn't respond.

Hawking gazed back out at the water, glowing under the sky. It was even more beautiful than the Sea of Stars in the Maldives. He was falling in love with this place. Not only with the exquisiteness of the land and with the astonishing power of Cruthu, but the society that Kipp had described. In his world, everything was about competition and creating a spectacle for others to admire. But here, he imagined there was no competition. Everyone was a team, a family. He'd felt that, back at the manor with Linnaeus and his cousins. It was the first time he'd felt that way in a long time.

Another pang hit him at the thought of Linnaeus. She would have loved Kipp. He glanced back at the blonde-haired, dark-skinned form lying on the sand. Then he got up.

Hawking walked down the beach, the sand like velvet between his toes. The tender rocked serenely in the small waves. He stopped where the luminous water met the sand. In spite of the mysterious glow, his own reflection was clear.

He looked like a different man.

His hair was overgrown and wild. His face scruffy from not being shaved, as was his chest. His spray tan had faded and the skin on his neck and shoulders had splotches of sunburn. His muscles looked diminished; his pants dirty and tattered.

In that moment, he realized it was all bullshit. The ways he'd embellished himself were the ways he'd hidden himself. Like a mask or face paint. This man reflected in the water wasn't someone else. *This* was him. He wasn't put-together. He wasn't an alpha. Not fearless or dominant or charismatic. Maybe sometimes he could act those ways. But it was just acting, wasn't it?

"You are beautiful, Earth-born."

Hawking jumped. He hadn't noticed her approach him. She stood on the soft sand, gazing at him.

"I was thinking the opposite."

"Why?"

"I guess because right now, I don't fit what's attractive on Earth."

"Do I fit what's attractive on Earth?"

He hesitated.

"Come on," she said, and the corner of her mouth twitched. "You can't hurt me."

"No," he said truthfully. "Maybe to some, but..."

"Not to you?"

Hawking opened his mouth and closed it. The truth was, his heart raced at the sight of her. He wanted to keep looking at her, to touch her. An uncomfortable thought occurred to him. Kipp wasn't anything like the women he was usually attracted to, and yet he *was* attracted to her. Had he been brainwashed to think a woman like this couldn't be beautiful?

"How odd," she said, stepping closer to him, "that you Earth-borns judge each other's desirability by your physical looks."

"How do you do it here?"

"Well, take you for example, Earth-born. I desire you."

She was inches away.

"Why?" he mumbled. Something didn't make sense here, but his mind was losing its capacity to think.

"You're brave and determined," she replied, "but that's not really it."

"What is it then?" he asked, his stomach leaping when she placed a hand against his naked chest.

"It is because you are kind," she whispered, and pressed her mouth against his.

Hawking kissed her back without restraint. He plunged his hands into her thick hair, something he finally acknowledged he'd wanted to do since he met her. She immediately slid her hand down to his groin.

"Whoa," he gasped and stepped back.

Kipp frowned at him.

"What is it? I know you desire me as well; I've known it perhaps longer than you have."

Brain focused now, he felt exposed. It was raw and painful and he wondered if this, right here, was what he'd been avoiding with women all these years. And what he'd been doing to them.

"Why do you want this, Kipp?"

She blinked.

"I mean, you just had to kill your own brother."

Her jaw clenched, her eyes growing cold.

Hawking took a deep breath. "I get it, I do. And you're right, I desire you. I want to comfort you, but... not like this."

Was he insane? Was he actually saying this? Who cared if she wanted to use him; had he ever turned down getting laid by a beautiful woman before? He almost took it back, but then her face transformed in front of him. Her eyes filled with despair again and her mouth trembled. All anger and desire left her, replaced by sadness.

"That was wise of you, Hawking."

He crossed the distance between them and took her into his arms. She stayed grounded where she stood; she didn't lean against him, but she returned his embrace. Her strong body pressed against his and her arms held him as tightly as he held her. They didn't speak. He had no idea how much time passed as they stood that way. But he relaxed in a way he never had before. It was as though he'd had a couple of drinks: he was profoundly calm, almost drunk with contentment. He molded to her, and she to him. He drew in her scent with each breath and soon they breathed together. Maybe their hearts even beat together.

He didn't know who broke the embrace first, but Kipp smiled up at him as they let go.

"You know more about intimacy than I thought."

"I think I'm finally learning." He'd been with a hundred women, had done all sorts of things to and with them naked, but he had never felt close to a woman like he did now.

She took his hand. "Come."

He followed her back toward the colorful, glow-in-the-dark palms. She stopped and faced him.

"We have quite the hike in front of us. I can change some of the—" she said a word he didn't understand.

He shook his head.

"The physical properties of our bodies, the way they metabolize energy. Anyway," she said, looking at him with warmth and openness that made her even more beautiful, "it will enable our bodies to make this journey very quickly. You'll experience an intense rush of energy. Go with it, use it. If you try to stop or slow down, it won't feel good," she warned. "And then when we're close, if I've estimated the distance right, we'll suddenly be depleted. I'll need to restore our bodies to full functioning. It won't take long but I want you to be prepared. It's quite jarring."

"You've done this before?" Hawking asked, trying not to sound nervous.

"Once," she grinned. "Are you ready?"

He picked up the Silver Bough, tucked it into his pants, and nodded.

Kipp stared at him and he watched her vivid eyes blur until she was no longer focusing on him.

Then he felt it.

First, a tingling that spread up from his toes to his scalp. Sweat broke out on his skin. His senses were suddenly acute

—his eyes took in all sights, his ears all sounds. His heart rate felt out of control, his muscles flexing involuntarily.

"Holy fuck," he said.

He looked at Kipp and instantly grew hard. He didn't know who seized who first but they were locked in a furious embrace, his hands and mouth were everywhere....

"Oh my," Kipp gasped, pressing her hips hard against his. "Yes.... but—no." She pulled away and he heard himself make a sound he'd never made before, an animalistic expression of displeasure. "That's not what this is for. Well, it could be..." She was quite breathless and he reached for her again. "*No.*"

She slapped him. This brought him back to himself a little.

"Go. We need to go." She shoved him toward the jungle of trees. "Go, you dumb idiot, go!"

Energy pumped painfully through his body and he had to do *something*; if they weren't going to fuck he needed to release it some other way. Kipp took off—*yes*, he wanted to *run*. He sprinted after her, taking in instant information from his surroundings. He knew exactly where to leap and dodge. He ran impossibly fast, and it was exhilarating, like every part of him was made for this, right now. His skin tingled and his breath came fast and hard, his heart threatening to burst from his chest. He pushed faster.

They ran through hills and valleys of verdant tropical forest. Whenever the trees broke, the dark sky smattered with stars spread above them. Hawking pumped his legs and his arms, wild and unleashed. The land ascended steadily and he relished the challenge.

Then, their surroundings changed.

The jungle darkened, the colors became more muted. As he ran, Hawking noticed the plants looked rotted. The ground on which they ran was brittle and ashy. The trees were so decayed that no leaves obscured the sky, which was no longer clear. Dark storm clouds swirled overhead and sparks of deadly light flashed through them.

They were close.

It grew so dark that Kipp flung out a hand and cast one of the glowing orbs ahead of them. They raced on, the incline brutal now, and Hawking wondered how much longer he had in him when he collapsed.

He fell face first into an ashy mound of leaves. This was more than exhaustion... his body had never hurt like this and at the same time he was weighed down with such heaviness that he might sink down into the core of the planet. He coughed, helpless, his head throbbing with agony, his throat desiccated. His heart beat feebly...

Through heavy lids and stinging eyes, he saw Kipp nearby. She was lying on her back with her eyes closed, completely still—he couldn't even see whether she was breathing. Did she overdo it? he thought with panic. Did she underestimate what her body could handle, could she be—

She sat up, halting his terrified thoughts, and scrambled over to him.

"You're okay, Hawking," she said as she took his face in her hands. "You're going to be fine."

Everything went black.

Moments or years or lifetimes later, Hawking sat up, as Kipp had, abruptly awake and lucid. His body no longer hurt. He felt rested and hydrated.

"That was intense," was all he could say.

Kipp laughed, but the mirth died away as she glanced around.

"Can you feel it?"

He could. It reminded him of being a kid, exploring the

large sewer drain opening near his house with his friends, and catching the scent of dead animal. Wrongness. Death.

That's what this place was.

As he gazed at the skeletal tree structures and that lethal coruscation illuminating the sky, he noticed an area further away where a dim but cold light source pulsed...

They got up and approached. They followed the glow around a jagged peak to find the gaping mouth of a cave, the cold light pulsating within.

"Briosun," Kipp said grimly.

Hawking realized at once that this entire idea was stupid. What was the plan here? What weapon did they have against whatever the hell this was? Kipp's mastery of Cruthu would have to be enough; he was worthless.

"Shall we?" Kipp said.

He grasped her hand, looking into her eyes with earnest. "I wish I could protect you."

She frowned. "Is that an Earth thing? Males protecting females?"

"It is."

She smiled—not in a mocking way, but tenderly. "Thank you for wanting to." And she squared her shoulders and walked toward the entrance of the cave.

But you're right, you can't, is what she hadn't said, and with a lurch of unease, Hawking followed.

The iciness of the glow inside chilled his skin as they stepped into the cave. A high-pitched whine issued from deeper inside, reminding Hawking again of something electric gone wrong. The light came from around a bend in the cave, and Hawking's foreboding increased the closer they got to it.

When they turned the corner, Kipp stepped back into him and Hawking stopped breathing.

Surrounded by the black rock of the cave was a large structure that looked transparent like ice but rough, like stone. And encased within was...

"Evil," Kipp whispered.

There was no other way to describe the feeling that came from it. A churning, dead brightness. It sparked like the unnatural lightning above in a throbbing rhythm, like a heartbeat.

A jagged line cut down the front of the enclosure and the vile light seeped out of it...

"No—Kipp, *run*—" Hawking shouted, but it was too late.

The light reached them.

He collapsed and everything went black again. This time, however, he wasn't unconscious. He was ... somewhere. Or nowhere. It didn't feel or look like anything. Silence. Nothingness.

And then he saw.

A vision flashed before him like a film. A young boy, just entering his teenage years, crept through the mouth of the cave. His face shone with anticipation as he approached the light, which was a calm glow. The boy's eyes—a dark, warm brown, like his skin—reflected the glimmering within the clear stone enclosure. He advanced in awe and pressed his hands and face against it, trying to get nearer to the brightness.

He raised a hand. Hawking screamed at the boy, but he couldn't hear him. The boy used his power to cause a crack in what held the glow inside. Cruel light misted through, reaching his eyes and turning them white.

Hawking saw the light spread over the land, causing it to die and rot. He saw the boy go back to his people and slay them in madness and rage. He saw the unnatural glow touch the people, saw them turn just as the boy had...

And then, a familiar tree and another boy, this one terribly familiar to Hawking, seizing on the forest floor with lips stained red from blood—

Hawking wrenched himself away from the dark, semiconscious place and opened his eyes to blinding, grotesque light. He scrambled to his feet. Kipp—

She was there, standing before him, her face hard with fury, her eyes fading from their beautiful turquoise, becoming fainter and fainter.

"Kipp. Kipp, *no*," Hawking shouted, and he reached for her—

She slammed him back against the cave wall without touching him. But no invisible restraints followed, no suffocation of his breath although he could tell she was trying.

Her power was gone. She was Changing before his eyes; Cruthu had given up on her already. With an animal sound of rage, she reached for the bough at his waist. Her eyes were only the faintest blue now.

Hawking knocked her hand away and grasped her arms, pinning them to her sides as he wrapped himself around her. She struggled and fought but he held her with all of his might, backing her against the opposite wall of the cave. The icy light in the prison sparked rapidly now, in a frenzy of dead energy, and the high-pitched whine grew deafening. Hawking held tight to Kipp, breathing deeply, willing her heart to beat with his as it had before, all the while whispering in her ear.

"Stay, stay with me, stay."

Her struggling weakened and her snarling turned to a sob. He did not know what to say but the words poured out anyway.

"Remember your people and your world. Remember Una and Alasdar. You came to stop this, not become it. Stay.

Stay for your people. Save them. Save your world. Come on, Kipp. Stay."

The whine reached a crescendo and Kipp screamed with it as the light exploded within the prison.

"You can do it, Kipp, I'm here, I'm right here with you!" Hawking shouted into her ear as she screamed until she fell silent and limp in his arms.

He picked her up and carried her away from the frenzied light, out of the cave, down the slope and as far as he could from the wrongness, the false radiance that was truly darkness. He didn't stop, he couldn't stop, not until the land around him lived again and the sky above was clear of the dead storm.

He laid her down in the soft grass. Her eyes were closed. He felt her chest; she was still breathing.

"Kipp, Kipp, sweetheart, please. Please, wake up—"

Her eyes fluttered open. Turquoise.

"Sweetheart?"

Hawking wept, pulling her close to him. She held him back.

"You saved me," she said.

"You saved yourself. I could feel you fighting it."

She pulled away. Tears streaked down her cheeks.

"I couldn't have done it without you."

"Well," Hawking sniffed, wiping a tear away from her face. "One could argue you wouldn't have even been in that situation if it wasn't for me."

"What was it?"

"It gave me a vision," he said and described what he had seen. When he got to the last part, the part with the convulsing boy, he halted. Was that *the* oak tree? Was the boy—

"The curiosity of a stupid youth," Kipp said. "That's why this all happened."

"Kipp, we have to seal that prison. Can you do it? Can you use Cruthu?"

"I don't dare go near it again."

Hawking shook his head in frustration. "What if we got Una, what if we found others—"

"If she's even alive, Hawking," Kipp said in despair. "And I don't know anyone else who hasn't Changed or been killed by the Changed. Even if I did, I doubt we would be powerful enough."

"Powerful enough," he murmured to himself. It was right there, an answer—

He looked into Kipp's clear eyes.

"I know something that's powerful enough."

He stood. Kipp followed, looking bewildered.

"We have to get back to Earth as fast as we can."

26

A psychically vulnerable person who comes in contact with Scrios magic is in greatest danger of becoming a medium for its most dominating and vicious aspects.

Seamus Dannan, *Lore: The True History of the Celts*

Saoirse opened her eyes and gazed around the makeshift tent. If they survived all of this, she would immortalize this place.

They had made love a few more times, Kian showing her more of what he had studied all these years, until exhaustion had claimed them. They'd then tangled together and slept.

Saoirse stretched against Kian, who took a deep breath and continued to slumber. She stroked his high cheekbone, his jaw, his lips. With all the tragedy and loss she'd known, she could never have imaged waking up this happy, this *alive*. It was Kian, it was Cruthu. If Kian wanted her and nature itself trusted her, perhaps she was worth something. Maybe it was time to stop doubting herself.

She went back through everything in her mind. Their sensual adventures in this wooden shelter...their fight in the rain... and then before that. They'd taken a little time between lovemaking to wonder who—or what—the male with glowing eyes was. Although he couldn't make sense of the different language he'd spoken, nor how it was translated in their minds, Kian thought he was a new creation of Niamh's. He was certain that she had access to some sort of magic beyond Spellbreaker.

Saoirse bit her lip. The male was brutal. That'd he'd intended to rape her... she clenched her jaw. No more freezing up if she found herself in another situation like that. Today would be about training and preparing.

Anxious to start, she put her hand on a part of Kian's body that was sure to rouse him from sleep.

He groaned and opened his eyes.

"Hi," she said.

"Hi." He glanced down to where her hand moved. "I don't know if I can do that right now. I'm sore."

"Me too," she said and it was true—the area between her legs was quite tender. It had been a long time since she'd had sex, and whenever she had it was never so many times back to back.

"You look beautiful."

"You, too." She kissed him. "Actually, I wanted to wake you so we could start practicing."

He sighed. "Yes, I guess we should."

She put on her slightly damp clothes save for the torn panties. The sight of them made her blush.

Kian only donned his pants.

She kicked him playfully. "I think you know how good you look without a shirt."

"Maybe I'm enjoying it a little."

Saoirse chuckled as she climbed out of the shelter. The sun's warmth hit her, sharp and unfiltered after the rain. She barely took in the forest around her when she saw him.

"Eoghan," she gasped.

He stood at the edge of the clearing, pale and trembling.

"Saoirse," he called.

"*Eoghan!*" They ran to each other. She threw her arms around him and buried her face in his shoulder. "You're alive," she cried.

He shook in her arms.

"Eoghan, are you okay?" Kian asked nearby. "What happened to you?"

Eoghan took in a shuddering breath and then something strange happened. An odd blow to her back, a cold, numb sensation. Her cousin shoved her aside as he spun away from her.

As she fell, he shoved a knife into Kian's stomach.

Kian staggered toward her. Eoghan grabbed his shoulder and drove the knife in again. As Kian collapsed, Eoghan knelt on the ground next to Saoirse and brought the blade down on her body again.

Her shock faded enough that pain finally overtook her, pain as she had never felt. She couldn't scream. Blood covered her, covered Kian. His face was so pale. He stared at her, wide-eyed.

Eoghan turned to Kian and Saoirse put her hand out to stop him from hurting him again. But Eoghan rummaged through Kian's pockets until he pulled out something gold and grinned.

The necklace. The Tanist Stone.

Eoghan stood, the Stone in one hand, his knife in the other. He glanced at Kian.

"So. The King of Cats is human once again. Too bad you didn't get to enjoy it for long."

There was no trace of the tremulous man she first saw in the woods. His voice sounded different than she'd ever heard him. Cold. Cunning.

He held up the Stone and grinned again. Then something changed. His entire body slumped forward, his eyes haunted. He spoke in a whisper.

"She'll be so happy with me. She *is* happy. I can feel her."

Then he straightened up and spoke in that same cold voice as before.

"You didn't really know me as a child, Saoirse. Neither of you did. I kept it hidden, what my mother was like. Cruel. Hateful. I think she regretted every moment of my existence."

He smirked, and Saoirse thought she saw a flicker of disturbance in his gaze.

"But not *her*. My life changed when Seamus and Melinda performed the immortality ritual. I was chosen as the conduit. When I had my fit, that was her, entering my mind, giving me a new purpose."

Saoirse twitched on the ground. She reached out for Kian and he grasped her hand with his own, slippery with blood.

"Touching," Eoghan said. "You two have formed a bond; use it for mutual comfort. Allow yourselves to be distracted by my words. It will make it easier."

His words sounded helpful, but his voice was cruel and mocking.

"She guided me for years and brought me to the Cult of

Balor when I was older," he continued. "They had been waiting, you see. Waiting for me to be... ready. I knew of her plan for our families. And I relished my assignment."

He fixed an unyielding stare on Saoirse.

"I killed them."

A different pain hit her. No. It couldn't be.

"I contacted Seamus and Melinda, asked if I could visit. They invited me. They had no idea what I really was."

Saoirse couldn't speak.

"Before moving on, I meant to search for the Deantan and then use Spellbreaker on each of you to break the protective enchantment. But then I found the letters he wrote for us. I decided to wait, to spare you, and when we were all together, use our combined memories to find them.

"I went to my mother next, and my father who never once came to my aid against her. Then, Hawking and Linnaeus's parents... then yours."

Here, he hesitated. His face blanched. When he spoke next, it was in a small voice.

"I..." He shook himself.

Saoirse didn't know what to make of his changing behavior and she didn't care. He killed Patrick and Janey. Rage burned underneath her almost consuming pain.

"When I slaughtered Seamus and Melinda and the rest and became an heir to the estate, it was most pleasing to *her* that I could now lead the Cult of Balor to the grounds. Finally, I could be of true service."

He frowned. "You confused me, though. You, Linnaeus, Hawking. You got in my head, made me... you made me betray her. I fought against my own people, killed them, for you. One of the men you knocked out woke up, saw me... saw me do those things to their bodies..." He shuddered. "Sometimes I get carried away...."

Pleasure and pain flashed across his pale face.

"That man went back to the Cult of Balor and told of my treachery. Niamh was angry. I could sense the Tanist Stone through the connection from the moment it was activated. But I... I betrayed her... I hid from her... though I could never truly hide..."

He dropped the stone and the knife and hunched over, grasping his head like he was in excruciating pain. He grunted for a few moments and then straightened up, his face clear again. He picked up the knife and the stone.

"See, you—" he glared at Saoirse. "You confused me again. But she set me right. She always sets me right." He bared his teeth. "Goodbye, cousin. You fought well, but you're no match for her. It was over before it even started." His eyes roved over their bloody bodies. "It won't be long now."

And then he was gone.

Kian squeezed her hand weakly. His eyelids were heavy, each blink longer than the last.

She couldn't speak.

No, Kian. Don't go.

Kian coughed and blood sprayed his lips. A tear fell from his eye onto the dirt.

His eyes closed and didn't open again.

Kian, no, no, no...

She shook his hand using all her strength, but it was cold and limp in hers.

Don't leave me...

Her head fell back and she gazed up at a sky obscured by branches and yellowing leaves shimmering in a wind she couldn't feel. Her mind struggled to put together cohesive thoughts. Eoghan, alive. Eoghan, the killer. He took the Tanist Stone. He would give it to Niamh. It was over.

She looked again at Kian's still body.

It was all over.

Her body sank into the ground, becoming as cold as the earth beneath her. She closed her eyes.

Somewhere in the distance, a wolf howled.

PART IV

As a fully integrated being, the magician is able to access the most vital and fundamental powers of creation within herself.

The writings of Seamus Dannan

27

While many interpret Danu to have been a goddess, she was in actuality a being who had advanced in the principles of Cruthu to the point of becoming godlike in creative power. Whether there is a first and supreme creator, we do not know.

Seamus Dannan, *Lore: The True History of the Celts*

Ragged huffing filled Saoirse's ears. Hot breath blasted her face. She opened her eyes.

"No," she whispered.

An enormous wolf with piercing yellow eyes stared down at her. Her blood must have drawn it. She squeezed her eyes shut.

Just die. Just die before it starts.

She laid there, willing her body to let her go, when a small whine made her open her eyes again.

The wolf sat nearby on its haunches. It wasn't alone. Five or so others had joined it. They all sat, watching her, until the wolf nearest her whined again and pawed the ground. Then he sank down, lying his huge head on his paws. The others followed suit.

Was she hallucinating? Movement above the wolves caught her attention: she glanced at the trees overhead. Was she imagining it, or were the branches leaning toward her? She moved her head as much as she could to look around. Trees bent in her direction from all sides.

Her eyes found stubborn blades of grass shooting through the dry leaves on the ground. They leaned toward her, too. Tears pricked her eyes.

They've been waiting. They want to be directed. It is their purpose.

All was not lost. There was an answer.

The wolf nearest whimpered again. He couldn't tell her what to do; unlike Kian, he was only a wolf. Yes, she had to figure this out for herself. But she was not alone.

There were only minutes. Gazing at the sky above, she let her eyes lose focus. Kian's voice came into her head again, talking about his aunt's experience with Cruthu.

Ciar tried her best to picture it... her imagining was taken over by images and feelings of what was actually happening. As if they were filling it the gaps for her, allowing her to participate.

How it was possible, she did not know. But she imagined that it was.

Her wounds knit together in her mind, just as the pencil had. Her bleeding stopped. But she'd lost so much blood...

Fear jolted her at this thought. How was it possible to replenish one's own blood without a transfusion?

Kian's words about the extent of Cruthu's power rose to the surface... *Everything that exists outside the paradoxical.* She didn't understand how her blood could be replenished without a transfusion... but that was the limit of human understanding. Just because she didn't know how didn't mean it was a paradox... that it was impossible...

Heal me, she commanded. *Heal me. Restore me to full health.*

She saw the blood she did have multiply, imagined the cells replicating and increasing. She saw whatever it was in her body that created blood in the first place working rapidly, and whatever resources her body needed were there...

Images nudged their way through and she let them. She didn't recognize what she saw, didn't even have words to describe them, she and wondered if she was seeing things happen on a much smaller level than she had ever conceived.

As she watched these things she didn't feel outside of them. She was there, too, contributing in an ineffable way. Part of her mind wanted to fear and fight against it, but she kept it at bay.

This was real. Let it happen.

Warmth spread through her. Her lungs drew in air. She felt strong and calm. The visions disappeared, replaced with the sky and vibrant leaves above her. She felt the wind.

Saoirse sat up. The wounds were gone. The wolves were gone as well.

Kian.

She rushed to him. His eyes were closed, his skin unnervingly pale.

"Please." Her voice broke and tears streaked down her face as she felt for his pulse and stared at his chest.

He was just barely alive.

"Okay, you know what to do," she said and put her shaking hands on him. No longer afraid of falling unconscious, she closed her eyes.

This time, she went straight to those images she'd seen. She didn't let fear touch her, didn't allow herself to think about how little time Kian had. She stayed with the visions and added whatever she could to their rapid work—her desire, her trust, her hope. She sank so far into a place of certainty that she was unsurprised when Kian's body tensed under her hands. He took a great, gasping breath.

His bright green eyes were wide. Color had returned to his skin. For a moment they only looked at each other.

Then he smiled. He sat up and took her face in his hands.

"I knew. I knew you could do it. I always knew."

She leaned her forehead against his and tears came again.

"Eoghan," she said through gritted teeth, that hot rage now twisting inside her. "That fucking liar. Murderer."

"I don't know that he's a liar," Kian said.

"What?" Saoirse snapped.

"You saw him. It was like he was someone else. And then he would change as if he was possessed or something."

"He admitted to killing my family."

"I know," Kian said quickly. "I just wonder... it's like Niamh has some kind of hold on him. He was always the most fragile one. He wasn't lying when he said his mother was cruel. She beat him, brutally. And his father let it happen."

Saoirse didn't care. Eoghan was behind all of this. He took everything from her.

"He has the Tanist Stone," Saoirse said.

"Cruthu is more powerful than the Tanist Stone."

Saoirse nodded, swallowing hard. "We have to go after him. Not only because I want revenge," she added. "We need to get the stone before he gives it to Niamh."

"You'll have to fight him. And potentially the stone itself."

She stood. Power thrummed through her.

"I'd say the floodgates are open for you," Kian said.

Saoirse knew what he meant. Cruthu was hers now.

It was time. Time to see what she could do.

28

The power of the Silver Bough is an imitation of the Tuatha dé Danann's ability to travel between dimensions.

Seamus Dannan, *Lore: The True History of the Celts*

The forest was a new world to Saoirse. She didn't see trees and dirt and sky, separate from each other, separate from her, all abiding by their own rules. The spaces dividing her and them no longer existed. Neither did the rules.

This is me. This is mine.

Kian gaped at the trees overhead.

"It's you," Kian breathed as they walked through a tunnel of trees reaching for them, trying to touch them. "They serve you."

"It wasn't like this when you practiced Cruthu with your aunt?"

"No. It wasn't. I've never seen anything like this."

They walked with purpose through the forest. They figured by now Eoghan was at least back at the mansion, if not already en route to the cult's headquarters.

"Why is it different for me?" she asked.

When he continued to smile at her, she grew annoyed.

"Why do you look at me like that, like you know something I don't know?"

"Because, I do," he said.

They held hands as they walked, their other hands gripping daggers Saoirse had made out of rock before they left. She relished the memory of holding the shapeless pieces in her hands and asking them to curve and bend and change. Feeling them move in her hands was like how it felt with the bowl, but creating the daggers was much more complex.

"What is it? What is this thing you know that I don't?"

"You haven't been able to see yourself clearly before in your life," he said, not for the first time. "It happens. We have this filter of belief that clouds us from really seeing our accomplishments, our character, our value. Some have a filter that does the opposite and keeps them from admitting their own flaws and mistakes. It's self-deception in both forms. But I watched you from the outside, so I could see it."

"You haven't answered what *it* is?"

"You're close to figuring it out yourself," he said, his face conveying something like pride.

Saoirse rolled her eyes.

"So," she said, changing the subject as their feet crunched through leaves, "what if Eoghan has already left the estate?"

"The Tanist Stone helped you locate me when I was held captive, right?"

She nodded.

"And then took you to me when you commanded it?"

"Yeah, and it almost killed me," she said darkly.

"That's Scrios magic. Cruthu can do anything Scrios magic can, remember? Or rather, Scrios was made to do what Cruthu does."

Kian stopped suddenly. He let go of her hand and raised his dagger.

"Get ready, Saoirse."

Several figures in black stood in the trees, tattoos of a giant eye stark against their pale skin.

The cult.

"What are they doing in here?" she whispered.

"Not searching for us. Eoghan thinks we're dead."

"Don't move," one man in black shouted, stepping from behind a large tree. He held a gun in front of him. "Give us the Silver Bough and we won't hurt you."

"Bullshit," Saoirse murmured as Kian said, "The bough?"

After a small hesitation, Kian shouted back, "We don't have it."

"Then tell us where it is, Cait Sídhe," the man sneered. "We know you know where it is."

Saoirse finally caught on. They wanted the Silver Bough? Why? They had the Tanist Stone. Whatever reason Niamh wanted the bough even though she had the stone surely wasn't good.

"*Do* you know where it is?" Saoirse whispered to Kian.

He gave a small nod.

"Then we need to get it before they do." Saoirse studied the gun. Just as she practiced before they left, she gave the command in her mind, envisioning the process.

"I'm going to count to three," the man shouted. "If you don't tell me where the bough is, I shoot. One—"

Saoirse's hands hung at her sides.

"Two—"

Without raising her hand, she twitched her fingers.

"Three."

The gun exploded in the man's hand.

He collapsed.

At least a dozen men moved forward. All carried their own firearms and stood in solid stances, ready to fire.

She made quick work of their weapons, jamming them as she had with the first. Another explosion confirmed to her that it worked.

"Don't shoot. Drop them," another man shouted.

The men obeyed but immediately changed tactics. Chaos ensued as they dropped their guns, pulled out long blades, and sprinted at her.

Saoirse knew a moment of panic. Then one of the knife-wielding men gained on Kian and her mind cleared. Instinctively, she pushed out and slammed the man away from her with invisible force. He flew back several feet and hit a tree.

Two knives sailed through the air, one at her and one at Kian. She pushed out at them the same way and they changed directions, imbedding themselves in trees.

"Move behind me," she ordered. Kian did as he was told.

One man rushed at her.

She froze him in his tracks. He stood, unable to move, reminding her of the people she'd immobilized at the cult's headquarters. But she didn't feel weak now. If anything, she felt stronger.

Awed by her own power, she extended her hand. The remaining men froze as well.

"I don't know how long this will hold," she said, turning to Kian. "But—

Her words faltered.

One of them had snuck around behind them. He held

Kian, a sharp blade pressed against his throat. Blood beaded there. Kian stared at her with his green eyes, his face set, his chest heaving.

"Move even a fucking millimeter and I'll kill him."

She stopped in place, not daring to move.

"Release my men," the man continued, "and take us to the branch. Now."

Her eyes darted between the man's face and Kian's. Kian hissed as the man pushed the knife deeper into his neck. Blood trickled down his throat.

Saoirse blinked.

The knife fell from the man's hand. He crumpled to the ground.

Kian leapt back, a hand at his bleeding neck.

"What did you do to him?" he asked in shock.

"I stopped his heart."

She hadn't realized that her hold on the men had lifted until the whole lot of them turned and ran.

Saoirse watched them go. Rage still coursed through her body. She stepped forward and spat on the dead man on the ground.

Kian stared at her.

"What?" she said. "He was going to kill you."

Kian gathered her to him and they held each other until both stopped trembling from the adrenaline of the fight.

"Where's the branch?" Saoirse said, pulling away.

Kian actually smiled. "I'm surprised you haven't put that together yet. You've seen it."

Saoirse looked at him curiously as she followed, giving one quick glance back to the dead man on the ground. They walked for a while, alert for others, but they heard no one.

"Ah," Saoirse said when she spotted a large and striking tree peeking through the branches as they neared.

The oak. And now she did remember: sitting in this tree with Linnaeus, Linnaeus picking up a smooth white branch, Kian in cat form snatching it from her protectively.

"Not a bad place to hide it," she said.

"Thanks, it was my idea," Kian said as he climbed. In spite of everything that happened, she appreciated how his muscular body looked as he scaled the beautiful tree.

"I've never understood why they wanted it," Saoirse mused out loud. "I remember Hawking saying he read in Seamus's book that it created a passage between our world and Tír na nÓg."

"That's right," Kian said from higher up. "Seamus and Melinda didn't dare use it because they knew there would be a price."

"What's the price of using the bough?"

"Time. It moves much slower in Tír na nÓg, which means minutes there could be years here for all we know. They didn't dare risk it." Kian paused at the top of the trunk. "Shit."

"Don't tell me it's not there."

"It's not here."

Her stomach sank.

"Who could have taken it?" Kian said as he frantically searched through the leaves gathered there. "We know Niamh doesn't have it because her henchmen were sent to look for it. Unless they searched in groups and one group found it and hadn't communicated with the others when we fought them—what?" he asked in alarm.

For Saoirse had stopped listening. She stared, motionless with shock.

A circle of light hovered in front of her, expanding with each passing second. As it grew she could see indistinct images within.

"Get away," Kian snapped, scrambling back down the oak.

Saoirse backed up just in time. Three human forms leapt through—

The next several seconds were a blur.

One of the people was a dark-skinned blonde woman being attacked by a man with long hair and white eyes—

"Kipp," someone shouted and Saoirse gasped as she saw the third person—

Hawking

"Kipp, fight!" he shouted at the blonde woman.

"I can't, it's not working," she cried as the man mounted her with his hands over her throat.

Saoirse watched, still frozen, as Hawking launched himself at the white-eyed man. The man jerked his elbow back with such force that when it connected with Hawking's face, he flew backwards—

Saoirse pushed outward and threw the man from the blonde woman. He scrambled to his feet, snarling, and set his haunting white eyes on Saoirse.

She closed outstretched fingers in a tight fist.

The man staggered, clawing at his throat. She watched as he collapsed, twitching and flailing, trying to breathe air that was no longer there.

He stopped moving. There was a second's pause, and then—

"*Saoirse?*" Hawking exclaimed.

A sob escaped her as her cousin scrambled to his feet and they met in a tight embrace.

"You're alive. I thought you were dead," she wept.

"You—how did you do that?" Hawking asked, pulling away. "The stone?"

"No," the woman spoke, and both Saoirse and Hawking turned to her, releasing each other. "That was Cruthu."

The woman's mouth moved with different words but Saoirse heard her voice clearly in her mind, just like with the white-eyed man who had attacked them.

Hawking's eyes widened. "You can use Cruthu?"

Saoirse opened her mouth to explain when she noticed the bough in Hawking's hand and her eyes snapped back up at him. "You went to Tír na nÓg? Is that where she—"

"Yes," Hawking said, moving close to the woman and putting his arm around her.

Saoirse raised her eyebrows.

"This is Kipp. Kipp, this is my cousin Saoirse, and—" He tilted his head at Kian in confusion.

"Hawk, this is *Kian*," she said as Kian came to stand next to her.

Hawking's mouth fell open. "Kian? How did you—"

"I used the stone to transform him."

"I was a cat," Kian explained to the woman named Kipp, who frowned in bewilderment.

"Saoirse, where is the Tanist Stone? How much time has passed? We need—"

"Hawking, Eoghan took it. He's bad, he tried to kill us. He was the one who killed our families, he works for Niamh—"

"No," Hawking groaned, stumbling against Kipp, who held him up. "Eoghan..."

"I know," Saoirse said. "He was against us all along, it's how the cult got into the property in the first place."

Comprehension dawned on Hawking's face. "After you disappeared, he went insane. He fought like..." He turned to Kipp. "Honestly, he was like the Changed. Crazed with blood thirst."

"The Changed?" Kian asked.

Hawking jerked his head toward the body of the man who'd attacked Kipp, which was now motionless.

"Most of the people of Tír na nÓg have become possessed. Kipp is one of the last people who hasn't been."

Kipp gazed at the dead man, her beautiful face distressed.

"Who is possessing them?" Kian asked.

"This... thing," Hawking said, his face pale. "Something evil. Maybe evil itself..." He swallowed. "Kipp can use Cruthu but she was no match for it. We came to get the stone. This thing is trapped but a fissure in the prison is causing it to be able to possess people. We need to fix the fissure and reinforce the prison."

"This is all connected, right?" Saoirse said. "It has to be. Somehow... Could Niamh be possessed?"

"Her eyes aren't white. And she doesn't seem insane. Evil, definitely, but more rational." Hawking paused. "Why did you come here?"

"We were coming after Eoghan," Saoirse explained. "But we got held up—Niamh still has people searching for the bough, so we came here to find it first."

"Surely she doesn't still want the bough?" Hawking said.

"Oh, I do," a deadly female voice spoke. "I definitely do."

29

While Spellbreaker demands the blood of an innocent child to grant extended youth, the true price of the dagger is that its use in acts of violence guarantees the wielder will never be worthy of Cruthu magic.

Seamus Dannan, *Lore: The True History of the Celts*

Saoirse saw a flash of black behind the enormous trunk of the oak dash behind Hawking—

Blood spurted from his mouth as he pitched forward.

"*No,*" Kipp screamed.

Hawking fell facedown, revealing Niamh.

A wicked grin spread across her face, the image of an eye on her forehead partially obscured by her dark hair. She held Spellbreaker, red with Hawking's blood. She bent down and snatched the Silver Bough.

In her rage, Saoirse sent a blast of power, greater and more destructive than she'd used so far. Niamh flew backwards through the air, disappearing into the thicket.

Rushing to Hawking, she knelt at his body and heaved him onto his back. His chest rose and fell in sharp gasps.

He's still alive.

She closed her eyes and went deep into her connection with the magic, seeing and repairing the damage Niamh had done. It happened quickly this time, much faster than with herself and Kian.

Hawking opened his eyes, his wound gone. Kipp fell into his arms.

"Cruthu doesn't work for me here, I don't know why," Kipp sobbed.

"It's okay," Hawking murmured into her hair.

"I couldn't save you," she continued, her body shaking.

"That's alright. It was getting to be a bit emasculating to be saved by a girl all the time."

"I know the feeling," Kian said.

A rasping cry sounded nearby.

Saoirse twisted around. Rage, greater than she'd felt after Niamh stabbed Hawking, burned sudden and bright inside of her.

Eoghan.

She drew back her hand, ready to blast him into oblivion, when Kian caught her arm.

"Wait. Look."

"Are you fucking kidding—"

"Saoirse, I mean it," Kian said urgently. "Look at him."

The man who murdered her family crouched on the ground, heaving. Tears streamed down his face.

"What's wrong with him?" Hawking asked.

"*Help me,*" Eoghan moaned. "*Help...*"

And then he transformed before Saoirse's eyes. He sat back on his knees, his face clearing, a haughty smile playing on his lips. He rose off the ground—

Then he slumped forward, heaving again. This time when he raised his face—

"Holy shit," Hawking said.

Eoghan's eyes were crazed, his teeth bared. He beat on the ground in a frenzy, making strange sounds like an animal—

"*No,*" he suddenly screamed, rolling over onto his back. He closed his eyes. Then he muttered to himself.

"Deconstruct. Integrate. Re-unify. Deconstruct. Integrate. Re-unify. Deconstruct. Integrate. Re—"

"Eoghan?" Hawking said.

Eoghan sat up, his eyes full of sorrow.

"Hawking? Saoirse?" he gasped. "You're alive?"

He cried like a baby.

Saoirse's fury gone, she turned to Kian. "What is this? What's happening?"

"He's splitting," Kian said. "Between identities. These are all parts of him, fighting for control."

A scream rent the air around them.

They all turned from Eoghan to the direction Niamh had flown.

"You destroyed the bough, you fucking cunt!" she shrieked. "It's nothing but ash—"

Niamh dragged herself into full view. Her black clothes were singed, her face bloody and cut, but wrath flashed in her eyes as she wielded Spellbreaker at Saoirse.

Saoirse raised a hand.

The dagger wrenched away from Niamh's. The woman

stared in shock. Saoirse raised her other hand and Niamh rose in the air. Moving her hand in a twisting motion, Saoirse caused invisible cords to bind Niamh's arms to her sides.

Niamh struggled, hovering in the air above them like a dark specter. "Where is the Tanist Stone?"

Saoirse glanced at Eoghan, who was still weeping on the forest floor. He hadn't told Niamh he had it?

"I don't know why that concerns you now, seeing as you're about to die."

Niamh lifted her chin. "Go ahead and kill me. Then you'll never find out how to stop her."

Saoirse froze. "Her?"

Niamh's smile widened, her teeth covered in blood.

"You don't know? She does." Niamh motioned to Kipp. "She's imprisoned in her world."

Kipp stared back in horror.

"You wondered why I wanted the Silver Bough? Why I desired access to Tír na nÓg? My ambition for thousands of years. The reason behind all of this." She smiled triumphantly. "To free Carmun."

Hawking took in a sharp breath.

"I've always liked that one," Niamh said with a leer.

"What we saw in that prison was not a woman," Hawking said.

"You saw her?" Niamh hissed.

"Wait—Carmun, like the Song of Carmun?" Saoirse asked.

"Carmun, the creator of the Deantan," Niamh said, her eyes flashing again. "Objects made from her own brand of magic that she created to fight against Cruthu and to destroy Danu. Objects she gave to those loyal to her. We Fomorians follow Balor, but we have always worshipped our true master."

Niamh's face darkened, the eye on her forehead smeared with dirt.

"Carmun destroyed Danu, but your ancestors, the Tuatha dé Danann, managed to steal three of the Deantan from us after imprisoning Carmun in Tír na nÓg. Only Spellbreaker remained with us to keep us young and strong through blood sacrifice...

"And only Spellbreaker can free Carmun from her prison."

"Well, the bough is destroyed, so I'd say your plan is fucked," Saoirse said.

"There is always the stone of all power. An unsavory but necessary backup."

Saoirse again glanced at Eoghan's weeping form. Did he still have it?

"The Coire is of no use to us," Niamh continued, clearly stalling. "But we'll always be grateful for it. You see, if your grandparents hadn't used it to protect the four of you, Carmun would never have been able to forge a connection."

"What connection?" Kian asked.

"Between Carmun and Eoghan, of course," Niamh said. "Spellbreaker never went dormant. But the other Deantan were kept hidden from us, unused, for millennia. When your grandparents used the Song of Carmun to activate the Coire, Carmun was able to forge a connection through a break in her prison to the person who last drank from it, the person who completed the spell. Useless as he is right now, Eoghan was once my greatest asset."

Saoirse now understood what Eoghan was talking about after he stabbed them. He said he was chosen as a conduit... she'd assumed he meant by Niamh, but it was never Niamh.

It was Carmun, the creator of Scrios magic.

"Carmun could sense the locations of her activated Deantan through Eoghan. He felt the presence of the stone, here. Where is it? What have you done with it?"

Kian turned to Saoirse. "You know what we need to do, right?"

"Kill this bitch and go to Tír na nÓg?"

"Exactly."

"How?" Hawking asked. "You sort of demolished the bough."

"She can do it," Kipp said, staring at Saoirse with wide turquoise eyes.

"But," Saoirse said, flattered by Kipp's confidence in her, "what if Cruthu doesn't work for me there like it doesn't work for you here?"

"You're different," Kipp said, "I can feel it. You may not even need my help to fix the prison."

"Fix it?" Saoirse said, turning back to Niamh. "We're not going to fix the prison and keep Carmun contained."

Niamh stared back, her eyes burning.

"We're going to destroy her."

Niamh glared at Saoirse, truly distressed now, but then her expression changed.

The woods were eerily quiet. Eoghan had stopped crying.

Suddenly, Niamh dropped to the ground and stood, a vicious grin on her face.

Reaching out with her hand, Saoirse tried to restrain Niamh again.

And couldn't.

Something was wrong. Her power was still there, but it stopped short of something that pressed in on her, like a barrier—

Remember me, Saoirse? a familiar, ageless voice spoke in her mind.

She whipped around. The blood drained from her body.

Eoghan knelt with the Tanist Stone held to his lips, rapidly whispering to it even as sweat broke out on his pale face.

"Eoghan, no," Saoirse moaned, trying and failing again to reach out with her power.

Kian and Hawking and Kipp were thrown together, back to back, bound to one another. Niamh snatched Spellbreaker and stalked over to Eoghan, who was panting on the ground.

"You had it?"

A smile broke over Eoghan's face—the cunning, callous one Saoirse had seen when he tried to kill her. There was no kindness in his face, no warmth in his eyes.

Saoirse urged herself to fight. She asked, she commanded, she tried to visualize what force held her prisoner and blocked her power—

You really believe what the others say, the stone spoke into her mind again. *You really believe there is something special about you...*

"I took it from them," Eoghan replied.

"When? Why didn't you give it to me?" Niamh snapped.

"I was... confused."

You are not special. I knew the first time we spoke. I can see all of you, Saoirse. You're no match for her.

Saoirse pushed harder but panic now hammered inside her. She glanced at Kian and his green eyes reflected her own terror.

"You will be punished," Niamh said, her black eyes full of fury.

"I look forward to it," Eoghan replied sensually.

"Give it to me."

Eoghan reached out to hand her the stone.

Then his gaze flickered to Saoirse. Eoghan's eyes were not cold and merciless. They were sorrowful.

Niamh's hand closed around the stone.

At the same moment, Eoghan tore Spellbreaker from her other hand. He lunged at Niamh with the blade. Saoirse knew a moment of hope—

The dagger stopped an inch from Niamh's chest. Then it twisted around in Eoghan's hand.

Spellbreaker tore through the air, imbedding itself in Eoghan's chest.

He gasped and fell to the ground.

He was just as weak as you are.

Eoghan gazed at Saoirse, his face contorted in pain.

"She fears you," he whispered.

"Eoghan," Saoirse cried.

"I'm sorry..."

And he went still.

Niamh stumbled, more haggard than before. Her breath came in shallow gasps as she clutched the stone.

"It's time," she panted.

"You'll die!" Saoirse screamed.

"And she will raise me again." She held the stone in the air, her arms trembling. "Free Carmun from her prison."

Saoirse's scream rent the air as Niamh's body disappeared in a billow of ash.

The invisible cell around her disappeared. Kian and the others rushed toward her, now free from their bonds.

"Maybe it didn't work—" Kian gasped.

A fierce wind ripped through the forest, which was dimming under rapidly gathering storm clouds. Saoirse tried to think, tried to come up with a plan—

You are not special.

With the towering oak in the background, lightning flashed and illuminated a great shadow before them.

The four held on to each other in terror.

The dark outline took solid form before their eyes.

A woman. Sparks of electric light took place of her eyes.

Saoirse gave desperate commands. *Take her air. Stop her heart.*

The figure only grew larger, looming over them, her hands like claws.

Fire, Saoirse thought, and she held her hand in front of her, palm up.

A wall of flame appeared, bright and hot. She sent it at the shadow woman, willed it to engulf her.

Come on, Saoirse urged the flames. *Come on. Destroy her.*

Lightning cracked through the dark sky. Saoirse watched as the shadow whipped this way and that. The fire spread out among the blackness and then—

Went out.

No.

The dark, jagged fingers, each as long as a person, reached out—

"No, *no*," she screamed, for those fingers had wrapped around the bodies of Kian and Hawking and Kipp.

Fight it, fight it, fight it—

Saoirse tried to block and freeze and combat those shadows but nothing worked, her friends slid out of her hands...

"Saoirse!" Kipp screamed over the howling wind.

Saoirse looked into her bright blue eyes.

"*Choose the right sacrifice,*" Kipp said.

The three were dragged across the ground away from her.

"No, no, *Kian*," Saoirse howled.

"I love you," he mouthed.

They were taken into the bosom of the darkness, and were gone.

30

The truth that lies at the core of the relationship between science and magic is that they are synonymous terms for the same power.

Seamus Dannan, *Lore: The True History of the Celts*

Saoirse dropped to the forest floor.

She wept into the dirt, despair rolling through her in excruciating waves. She grasped toward the place where the darkness had been, trying to get them back. The storm left with Carmun. Sunshine poured down into the clearing.

Gone. Like Linnaeus. Like her parents. Like Patrick and Janey. Brilliant lights that should have burned forever, flickered out in an instant.

Saoirse screamed as she seized handfuls of dirt and dry leaves. She couldn't save any of them. And now they were gone and she was alone. No wolves sitting in a circle around her, no blades of grass leaning toward her. Nature wasn't here to remind her of what she could do because there wasn't anything she could do. It was over. She failed.

Her body twisted in agony until she lied on her back, weeping with an arm over her eyes to block the sunlight. It had all been for nothing. Everything she'd done, from rescuing Kian, to Kian sacrificing his access to magic to save her, Hawking's journey to Tír na nÓg and back, Eoghan's last attempt to fight the evil possessing him. She twisted her head toward her cousin's fallen body and wept harder at the memory of his last words, a whispered apology for all the horrors he had committed.

Carmun won. And now there was nothing for her anymore. Saoirse wanted to die.

The attempts to kill herself before came to her mind. The magic summoned by the cup always blocked her path, but there was no protection now.

She put her other hand over her heart. She could extinguish her own light with the tap of a finger. Use Cruthu one last time, not to create, but to destroy.

Taking a deep breath, her tears gone now, she took her arm away from her face. She gazed around at the deep blue sky above, framed by shimmering yellow and orange leaves. What would happen to Earth and Tír na nÓg now that Carmun was free and there was no one to fight her? Saoirse truly had been the last chance.

She laughed, low and mirthless, as apathy spread through her. Her hand still laid on her chest. They were doomed from the start. The stone was right.

You are not special.

It was odd, now that nothing mattered, to note that the stone seemed to be some kind of projection of Carmun. It made sense, since Carmun had created it. For her followers, like Niamh said. Items imbued with Scrios magic to mimic Cruthu.

Her face threatened to crumple again as she thought of Kian telling her she was stronger than the stone. She didn't doubt Cruthu's ability, but it was her as the wielder of it that was the problem.

"Why, Kian? Why did you believe there was something more to me?" she whispered. Deep down she had been waiting to see it, daring to hope that maybe he was right. But what she'd always known about herself was true. She fucked everything up. And it didn't matter if her dad and Kian said it was her lack of belief in herself was the problem; ultimately, it was still *her*. She couldn't think and believe in the right way.

With her hand resting over her heart and her index finger raised, she thought of her dad. His empty room and empty office and the empty stages he would never speak on. She wished she could speak to him so much it ached. What would he say to her if she could?

For some reason, she thought of the quote, which she now knew he had gotten from his mother. The one she had read so many times she had it memorized.

If you want to understand the secrets of the universe, think in terms of energy, frequency, and vibration.

Something deep in her brain nudged at her, breaking through the fog of grief. What had that quote ever meant? Why had he and Melinda loved it so much? These suddenly felt like crucial questions.

Energy, frequency, vibration. The words had always

meant nothing to her. But in this moment... the secrets of the universe... Cruthu and how it worked, the subatomic level, the way she'd healed herself and Kian and Hawking just like she'd put the pencil back together. Something that appeared impossible but wasn't impossible; she simply hadn't realized it until she did it.

Saoirse took her hand off her chest and sat up.

Carmun could have obliterated her. Why leave her alive?

She fears you, Eoghan had said. Even more reason to kill her. Indeed, she could have killed them all, could have annihilated her and Kian and Hawking and Kipp with a mere thought and yet, she hadn't killed them... she'd *taken* them...

And now Kipp's last words came to her. *Choose the right sacrifice.*

Sacrifice... what had the stone told her about sacrifice? It was when she's asked it what would happen if Scrios and Cruthu magic fought with equal power... it said it would trigger the Law of Opposing Magic.

An exchange of sacrifice. The greater sacrifice wins.

Saoirse, equal to Carmun in power? It was laughable. And yet...

She fears you.

Choose the right sacrifice.

If Carmun hadn't killed them, if she'd taken them somewhere, was Saoirse meant to follow?

Where? How?

That nudge was back. Energy, frequency, vibration... the way Cruthu worked... The Deantan were created to *imitate* Cruthu. The Coire granted immortality. The dagger Spellbreaker undid magic and granted youth. The Tanist Stone had all power, though no one could live long enough to wield it. And the Silver Bough...

Could travel through dimensions.

Saoirse stood, her heart thundering. Kipp had said it herself, when Saoirse accidentally destroyed the branch. She said it didn't matter, that Saoirse would be able to travel to Tír na nÓg anyway.

She gazed around. The air was electric, like everything in the forest around her had paused in anticipation.

It needed to happen this way. No open support from her natural surroundings, no clues or hints, because she had to figure it out herself, she had to *decide*...

And now she knew what her father would say if he were here.

Dig the deepest you've ever dug. There is a way. And Carmun knows it.

Saoirse faced the area in front of the oak. Her palms were slick with sweat. Her heart that she had been planning to stop was now pumping with life.

She didn't need to understand how to do it. She only needed to know that she could—Cruthu's power and her belief, together.

She took off in a run toward the great tree, reminded of when she tried to run off the edge of the cliff. This was a different leap and one into life, not away from it. When she reached the spot where Carmun's black form had disappeared, she jumped, thrust her hands in front of her, then ripped them apart, leaping through the portal she created into another world.

31

In the Law of Opposing magic, two divergent forces meet in a battle between the greatest desires that lie in the hearts of their wielders.

Seamus Dannan, *Lore: The True History of the Celts*

It was dark but not dark. Hints of light, hints of life... of form and shape... Saoirse breathed fast, almost hyperventilating as her mind tried to make sense of where she was. Something was different about her body. Her hands and arms were covered in something that crackled and hummed.

"*Oh, shit. Okay,*" she muttered. She drifted in the air, in the vagueness... there was no up or down. She felt cold—was that even the word to describe it?

Calm down, she ordered herself. Her mind was trying to put names and labels to what she was feeling and experiencing. But it couldn't.

"I'm here, wherever this is," she said out loud, hearing the sound of her voice (or was she feeling it?). Then something made sense. Pieces of things not put together. A canvas with raw materials.

A world before it was a world.

She took a deep breath. *Focus.* Carmun was here somewhere. Where?

Composed now, she sensed the connection. Cruthu had gotten her here. Cruthu had put some kind of forcefield on her skin to protect her body in this place. She put a hand to her solar plexus and extended it out. A thread of bright gold stretched from her body into the distance. She could not see where it ended, but she knew it would do what she'd intended.

Lead her to Carmun.

She made to pull on the thread to propel her body forward and found herself sliding along.

The urge to panic was still there, but she breathed it down. She had no plan, no support, no ideas, no certainty except one thing.

If Carmun believed she was a threat, then she was a threat.

Saoirse exhaled.

And then she was somewhere else.

Instead of darkness, light. It blinded her eyes. She sat upon something soft and wet. The air was warm—

She blinked rapidly until her eyes adjusted. She was on a beach. No substance glistened on her skin besides the sparkles of sand on her arms. No thread extended from her. She faced the ocean—

"*Shit.*"

The water receded from the sand, slinking and rolling

back. Far in the distance, darkness built; it rose in the sky. Gargantuan. Annihilating.

A wall of water miles high raced toward her. She sprang to her feet, looking around in a panic, but she could not outrun this.

It blocked out the sun and roared. She wouldn't drown when it came down; she would be crushed, torn into pieces and swept away forever...

"Fuck that."

Saoirse brought her arms up and put her hands together. She bowed her head and waited for the wave to crash.

She moved her hands apart. A tunnel of light and air formed above her. She inhaled and stared into the sun as the water plummeted around her.

At a blink, she was somewhere else.

This was true darkness, where nothing winked or flickered. Her body laid on cold metal.

She made to sit up—

Her head hit something so hard that she gasped in pain and fell back. She reached out with her hands.

Less than a foot from her body was more metal.

She felt all around her.

"No. No, no, no..."

She twisted her body, kicking out and feeling everywhere—

She was trapped.

Then she felt the metal prison around her move.

"Help," she screamed. The sides were closing in, slowly but surely. They would crush her—

Wait.

"Not real," she breathed.

The tsunami was not real. This was not real either.

Carmun was doing this, trying to stop her, to get in her head—

But what if it is real?

Her panic rallied itself, along with despair.

No, Saoirse. She could have killed you already. It's just an obstacle, a test.

She fears you.

And then it came to her. Stop playing the game. Break the Rubik's Cube. Break the rules.

Saoirse took a deep breath, stopped fighting against the collapsing metal walls, and lie still. The metal touched her on all sides—

She was somewhere else. It was bright again.

So bright.

Instead of sand or metal was grass. Instead of an ocean or prison was wooden fencing. A play structure to her left. It had two slides and two swings, perfect for two young children.

"No."

Saoirse bowed her head and squeezed her eyes tight. For she knew what lie ahead in the soft grass.

Beautiful little bodies lied sprawled together, their tiny hands almost touching.

Covered in blood.

Forcing her eyes open, that inhuman sound came out of her again.

The children.

Their births weren't a mid-life surprise for her parents. That was the story they told, that they planned to tell for Patrick and Janey's entire lives.

They were born, not out of years of hope, but out of carelessness. Born to a girl too young and unreliable to be their mother.

Patrick and Janey weren't Saoirse's siblings.

They were hers.

She crawled toward them, her hands slipping in blood.

My babies. My babies. I'm sorry.

She remembered how they had felt inside her. Rolls and bumps and quick jabs that sometimes stole her breath away. How her round stomach was so soft and she would run her hands over it, as if she were touching them.

Patrick came first, and shortly after Janey. She remembered how she wanted to hold them, really hold them, like a mother would.

But she was not a mother.

When the doctor handed her children to her own parents instead of her, she shut down. She would not love them like that. They did not belong to her. She wasn't good enough.

Her parents wanted this for her, wanted her not to be burdened with responsibility she wasn't ready for. They wanted her to live freely, where children could come when the time was right.

But Saoirse didn't live. Her life halted in its tracks, refusing to go forward. To move past this one, greatest failure.

She touched their little feet. Her fault. It was all her fault. She had recklessly brought them here. She wasn't a mother to them. She couldn't even protect them.

Through the blur of tears, she saw something black glinting in the grass next to their bodies. Her father's gun.

"Oh, fuck you," she moaned into the grass. "I know what you're doing."

This was no Rubik's cube. This couldn't be broken apart like a crushing wave or a collapsing tomb. Magic couldn't conquer this threat.

Because the threat was her.

Dig deeper than you've ever dug.

"I'm trying!" she screamed.

How could she ever conquer *this*? Her longing for oblivion, to be nothing. A life where she knew what she was and what she had done was not worth living.

She stretched a hand toward the gun, her other still touching her children's feet. It would work now if she tried. The Coire's protection hadn't given her a chance, but Carmun was.

She could end it now.

A chance, a decision. A choice.

With her face pressed against the grass, she realized that there were more choices than the one that lie here.

Just like with Cruthu. The choice to believe one thing or another. A decision of what a thing meant. She had been assigning one meaning to her actions and thoughts and feelings for a long time.

Yes, this was a chance. But a different kind.

Something had always prevented her. A truth she had denied for so long, a truth that hurt worse than anything else.

Was she ready? Could she face it at last?

Saoirse turned back to the bodies of her children. She pulled herself up to her hands and knees and crawled over them. Their pale faces were smattered with blood but she could see their beauty easily. Patrick's playfulness. Janey's curiosity. The lives they could have had. The people they could have been.

She gathered them into her arms, an ache in her so deep that she might tear apart. Their bodies were still warm, as if they were only sleeping.

And then she admitted it. The truth.

"I wanted you. I wanted to be enough for you. I wanted to try." She rocked them as the truth broke free, pummeling her with pain at each admission. "I wanted you to be mine and I wanted to be yours. I didn't do what I wanted. I ran from it. From you. I abandoned you.

"I abandoned me."

And then the choice came. Her mind wanted to fight it as it always had, wanted to sink into the despair of believing that she was worth abandoning.

She gazed down at the children in her arms, and swore an oath.

Not to them.

To herself.

"Never again."

And then they were gone.

Saoirse found herself once again in the unformed void that could one day become a world. Her body crackled and hummed and the thread of gold light extended from her.

It was time, she knew. No more obstacles. No more tests.

She let herself be led along, past the forms that drifted by, both dark and bright.

It wasn't far until those forms and substances were out of view. Ahead of her was pure space. Silent. Peaceful. Stars flickered light years away.

And in the distance, a dark thing that blotted them out.

She was afraid but something was different now. Her head was clear and inquisitive. She studied Carmun as she came nearer, a formless darkness that sparked with poisonous radiance. It shifted and churned, vibrating with power. Carmun no longer bothered to look human, because she was no longer human.

This was her true form. Beautiful and terrible. Real and formidable and unnatural.

Words came into Saoirse's mind, the same ageless voice as the Tanist Stone.

I brought you here to see what Danu's last threat to me could be.

"That was risky," Saoirse replied softly.

Not really.

"Why didn't you kill me before? Why make me go through... all that?" Saoirse asked the darkness. "Because you knew I would make it here. You aren't surprised. You expected it."

She sensed Carmun's presence in her mind, like a mocking smile.

You remind me of Danu. She, too, passed my tests. She grew stronger as she conquered them. You are powerful, young one.

Why would she test Danu if doing so made her enemy more powerful?

I will benefit greatly from destroying you

The answer came to her. Destroying Danu had made Carmun more potent. She'd imbibed her opponent's strength somehow.

Those obstacles hadn't been to stop Saoirse. Carmun knew she would survive them, wanted her to conquer them. They were meant to strengthen her.

She was being fattened up for the kill.

Clever. You persevered for once. You overcame a great weakness in yourself. I thank you for it.

A disturbance in the air alerted her to the oncoming attack. As the force of Carmun's fury came down, Saoirse roared and threw her own energy to meet it.

The power of creation was a coin with two sides. Create, destroy. Break apart, put back together.

Carmun's power was something else.

While creative power made and unmade, Carmun's

power consumed and fed.

Where the two forces met, a battle of terrible beauty ensued. Saoirse kept pushing with all her might. It was nuclear, no—beyond that. Energy that existed in the in-between of time and space. It held everything together; it forced everything apart. Death, life, potential. The quantum level of gravity and light. The elemental beginnings and ends of the largest black hole.

Power met power; worlds were created and destroyed in the intensity of their meeting. Saoirse summoned it all.

They were hurtling toward the inevitable.

That's right, Carmun's voice whispered in her mind even as their forces collided. *Look upon your loved ones.*

Kian, Hawking, and Kipp came into view, their bodies hovering in space.

They were alive, watching her from a prison that was almost invisible except that it shimmered in the brightness of the battle before them.

Choose the right sacrifice.

This was why Carmun kept them alive.

Because they would be her sacrifice.

It made sense, didn't it? Sacrificing the people she loved in order to win the war.

Pain clenched her chest and throat. Could she do it? To save the world?

She had to. There was no other choice.

So why did Carmun still think she would win? What could Carmun choose that would overpower Saoirse's own sacrifice?

Ready yourself, the voice whispered. *The time swiftly comes.*

Carmun had lured her here because she *knew* her sacrifice would win. Why? Niamh was already dead. Niamh...

True Lore

Carmun never intended to raise Niamh from the dead and reward her. She was prepared to sacrifice every single one of her followers in order for herself to live. What Carmun had for her followers wasn't love; Carmun couldn't love. But satisfying the law wasn't about love.

It was about *cost*.

Saoirse and Kian, while in love, had just barely met. She and Hawking had known each other as kids but only just reunited. Carmun's followers had dedicated their lives to her for thousands of years. Maybe that *would* be the greater cost.

She knew Kian and Hawking and Kipp would sacrifice themselves to save the two worlds from Carmun. It wasn't really a sacrifice because it's what they would choose.

It would mean a life for her without them.

A life...

What was the one thing Carmun *wouldn't* sacrifice?

The devouring power surged against hers, and she threw herself back at it with cataclysmic force as her mind made the connection.

It was *she* who was meant to die.

Her life that she finally wanted to live had to end.

Her love for her friends was real, but the love she at last had for herself... Carmun wanted to live and exist as much as Saoirse did, maybe more, but she knew Carmun would never, ever sacrifice her own self.

As tears spilled down her face, Saoirse chuckled at the irony. Her whole goal, ever since her parents and her children were murdered, was to kill herself. If she was honest, she had longed for death even before that. Now that she finally wanted to live, the only way to win was to die.

But this wasn't abandoning herself. Her oath kept true.

This was her choice.

The moment came. The apex of battle, when force

opposed force in an uncompromising, immovable conclusion. Equal. Opposite.

It's me. I choose me.

Saoirse let down her arms and stopped fighting.

When her power vanished, Carmun's engulfed her in a wave of cold light. Not meant to only destroy her body, but her soul. And since nothing could truly be destroyed, she was to be scattered, dispersed, uncreated, never to be returned whole again.

Saoirse closed her eyes and let out her last breath.

And then gasped as the cold left her.

It roiled away toward the darkness with its frenzy of sparks.

She was left unscathed, vibrantly whole and alive.

I won.

The presence raged, tried to flee, tried to fight its own annihilating power. Violent vibrations rent the air, Carmun screaming into the cosmos, as consuming force met its master in an implosion of power. Saoirse saw it collapsing inward, readying to rip itself apart forever.

She had to act quickly. She flew to the glistening prison that kept Kian and Hawking and Kipp trapped. Reaching through its field, she enveloped her friends in the same protective forcefield she wore around her own body. Then she broke the prison's bonds.

"Hold onto me."

No longer needing a thread of light to guide her, Saoirse steered them back through the uncreated world. When she reached the place she'd entered, Saoirse mentally opened the door just as the dead power burst in an explosion that warped time and space. The final obliteration of Carmun.

Saoirse gave her command.

"Take us home."

32

While Carmun created Scrios for her followers to protect her whilst unable to match her in power, Danu gave Cruthu as a gift for the peoples of Earth and Tír na nÓg to aid them in their development and as their inherent birthright.

Seamus Dannan, *Lore: The True History of the Celts*

The sky above the clearing was vivid blue, like no time had passed. A gentle wind caressed her.

"Saoirse," Kian's voice broke as he scrambled over to her. Before she could react, she was in his arms. She squeezed her eyes shut as the others joined the embrace. The group rocked her tenderly as they held her.

"We saw it," Kian said, his voice full of emotion. "We saw it all."

Saoirse looked up at him. Hawking and Kipp's faces were near. "You mean—"

"All of it," Hawking said with tears in his eyes.

"You did it, Saoirse," Kipp's words came into her mind. "You chose the right sacrifice. You were ready."

Saoirse knew what Kipp meant, but something occurred to her.

"If Carmun hadn't given me those obstacles—that last one—I wouldn't have—"

"You're right," Kian said with a smile. "In her greed to defeat you at your most powerful, she gave you what you needed to win. Your forgiveness and commitment to yourself. It made your life worth living. Something you could truly sacrifice."

Saoirse relaxed in his arms, exhausted and drained. She didn't know what to say. Maybe she didn't need to say anything.

Through the gaps in their bodies she glimpsed something that made her start. She disentangled herself and stood, pointing.

Hawking swore in astonishment. "Is that—"

"The Tanist Stone," she said, for in the dirt before her lie a mottled, shattered version of the Deantan, decayed and useless.

"And there," Hawking said, pointing to an object near it.

Spellbreaker, which was now nothing more than a cracked and rusted dagger.

"The Deantan were destroyed with her," Kipp said.

Something occurred to Saoirse, something that filled her with happiness. She looked at Kian with fresh tears.

"That means—"

And with a grin that lit up his face, Kian bowed his head. A bit of green twisted its way out of the dirt. Tendrils sprouted from the root. Kian stepped back as his creation grew, rising in a tall plant with feathered leaves. At the height bloomed beautiful, pure white flowers.

"See," he said. "You don't need to use your hands."

"Show off," Saoirse muttered, wiping her eyes.

Hawking whistled. "You guys have to teach me how to do that."

"Deal," Saoirse said. Linking arms with Kian, she led the group back through the forest to the house.

PROLOGUE

Three months later

The sidewalk was cracked, the fence around the small house made of chain link. A large *Beware of Dog* sign adorned the gate.

Houses with dogs never get broken into, the owner of this house once told her. *But I don't actually have one. Allergic.*

Saoirse smiled and pushed open the gate.

A wave of dizziness hit her, and with it, nausea. She paused, a hand on her still-flat stomach. She knew she could make the sensation go away but she never did.

She welcomed it. Every minute of it.

The yard was well-maintained, even though winter had iced over the plants and shrubs. Warm light glowed inside the house where the sounds of a family drifted toward her.

Saoirse thought of her own family. Kipp's access to Cruthu had returned soon after they came back through the portal, the unhelpful lag accounted for by the distance between dimensions. Saoirse had taught her how to create a portal back to Tír na nÓg so that Kipp could return and rebuild her world, her people now free from Carmun's influence.

Hawking, of course, went with her.

"I'll see you soon, King of the Land of Colors," Saoirse had said as she'd hugged her cousin.

"I'll only be king if the queen accepts me," Hawking said. Saoirse had been amazed at the change she saw before her. The swaggering, preening man with his obnoxiously huge truck and constant bragging was gone. Here was the real Hawking: vulnerable yet strong, generous and determined. It looked good on him.

"I think she will," Saoirse had said with a wink.

After Hawking and Kipp had gone, Saoirse asked Kian the question that had been bothering her.

"How did you know I was special?"

Kian grinned. "Everyone is special. Or then, no one is."

"What?"

He kissed her. "It's a choice you make, and I knew you would make it."

After that, Saoirse had known what she needed to do next. What she would do now for her entire life.

And whom she needed to start with.

Saoirse braced herself for what she knew was coming, and knocked on the door.

It opened almost immediately.

"What the *FUCK*—"

And then Saoirse was pulled into a crushing hug as Betsy sobbed onto her shoulder.

"You—you never called me back, you never came home, I didn't know what the fuck happened to you—"

Saoirse mumbled apologies into Betsy's large bosom. Her friend pulled away, wiping eyeliner tears from her face.

"Where have you been?" she demanded. "What have you been doing?"

Saoirse smiled. "Let me in and I'll show you."

The End

ACKNOWLEDGMENTS

If it takes a village to raise a child, then this novel was my child and it's time to thank my village.

First and foremost, my editor Nicole Van Den Eng. To carry the metaphor further and into awkward territory, you were my partner in conceiving and birthing *True Lore*. Your advice and coaching made my dream of becoming a writer possible. Your editing was absolute genius. Thank you for the incredible work you and your sister, Rebecca Zornow, are doing at Conquer Books.

Lindsay Manly at LadyManlyReads, you believed in me and my story. Your encouragement and advice has made all the difference. We've come a long way since reading *Twilight* in your car instead of working. (Or have we?)

Next, I want to thank my dear friends who were willing to read my first novel. Dayne Ngakuru, I can't thank you enough for your feedback and proof-reading. Riley Moore, expert on steam and spice, it was an honor to have your approval. Keri Deschenes, thank you for reading it in the midst of incomprehensible life challenges. You and your family are warriors. Rachel Williams, I'm sorry for the darkness and violence and child deaths. Charlotte Andrews, you're a brilliant writer and having your eyes on my work was a true gift. Lauryn Howell, your feedback made me cry (in a good way).

To my media team at IKA Social, you guys are the best in the world. Mikey, Jenna, Tori, Taylor, and Bryan: thank you for making me look good and getting my face out there for people to see, even though I never wanted to watch a single video of myself.

Mom, the most voracious reader I know and the woman who taught me to love fiction, thank you for loving my book. I'm not entirely sold than it's not just because I'm your daughter, but I'll take it.

Dad, I remember you working on creative writing projects when I was a kid (specifically, a children's book and a screenplay) and I know that had something to do with this. Thank you for the example and sorry about the sex scene.

Calvin, Samantha, and Skye, you can't read this book until you're all 18. Thank you for being good sports while Mommy was shut inside her room writing. I adore you guys.

And finally, Kyle, who most certainly inspired Kian's character. I'll never forget our second date when you asked me what I'd really love to do with my life. When I told you shyly that I'd always wanted to be a writer, your whole face lit up and you said, "You should do it." You've supported me in every way since. You're the love of my life.

ABOUT THE AUTHOR

Siobhan Moore is devoted to giving her readers thrilling stories with intricate plots and unforgettable characters. Her debut novel *True Lore* comes after years of studying the craft of great storytelling. Siobhan lives near the mountains with her husband and three young children. Learn about her future projects and sign up for her mailing list at www.SiobhanMoore.com.

Made in United States
Orlando, FL
20 April 2023